CRITICIS

MW00936605

"I'm still reeling after finishing Susan Wingate's latest, STORM SEASON. Brilliantly written, here is a tale that grips you by the throat from the opening prologue to the gut-punch of an ending. Both tender and brutal, intelligent and visceral, each page carries a reader further down a harrowing path to a conclusion both inevitable yet also shocking. This novel will leave an indelible mark on your soul. Don't miss it."
—James Rollins, *New York Times* bestseller of *The Demon Crown*

"In STORM SEASON, bestselling author Susan Wingate delivers a spellbinding page-turner. Harrowing and heartbreaking, this is the story of a grief-stricken mother's tenacity in her efforts to bring to justice the monsters responsible for her daughter's drug overdose. Meg Storm is a heroine you can really root for. Once you pick up this riveting thriller, you won't want to put it down." —Kevin O'Brien, *New York Times* Bestselling Author

"Meg Storm is intimate with grief, and with guilt. And if Storm is, so must Susan Wingate be, author of this heartbreaking thriller. Both emotions are palpable in STORM SEASON, from the first to the final page. With a fine eye for detail, and an exquisitely tuned empathy for her character's agony, Wingate leads the reader from worst to worse as Storm allows no stone to go unturned in her pursuit of the carrion eaters responsible for her daughter's death. A visceral, personal, unflinching look at the insidious plague decimating this country, STORM SEASON will have you double-checking the locks every night and holding your loved ones a little bit tighter." —Randall Silvis's writing fellowships from the National Endowment for the Arts, the prestigious Drue Heinz Literature Prize, a Fulbright Senior Scholar Research Award, six fellowships for his fiction, drama, and screenwriting from the Pennsylvania Council On the Arts, and an honorary Doctor of Letters degree awarded for distinguished literary achievement.

"The author writes with a shrewd, confident style; the characters' experiences are often perceptible to readers. For example, Meg endures an emotional reaction as physical anguish: "This new pain was like a shot to the chest, radiating down and dark, through the soles of her feet." Violence is stark but fleeting, as the profound tale is more about loss than revenge. A bleak but undeniably affecting family tale." —Kirkus Reviews, August 2, 2018

"Susan Wingate is guilty. She caused me to lose a full night's sleep. That's how engrossing her newest novel, STORM SEASON, is. Like an onion, the layers keep peeling away revealing new twists and turns that keep you glued to the page. Her writing is impeccable and the world she creates, while at times as tragic as a car wreck, is both haunting and impossible to ignore." — New York Times and USA Today Thriller Award winning author, Vincent Zandri.

"Grief, guilt, and punishment for crimes walk closely together in an evolving story which brings both Meg and her readers on the brink of disaster as reconciliation and recovery remain elusive goals for many of the characters. The result is a riveting, action-packed inspection of one woman's life gone awry as she sets out to rescue others only to come full-circle to discover her own strength and ability to survive." — D. Donovan, Senior Book Reviewer, Midwest Book Review

"When the book starts out with the death of her daughter, you'd think things couldn't get much worse for Meg—but they do. More deaths, manipulation, revenge, and redemption all play important roles in Susan Wingate's fast-paced masterpiece STORM SEASON. Susan's deftly controlled writing style has the reader feeling everything the character goes through—which is exhausting and wonderful." — Terry Persun, Award Winning & Amazon Bestselling Novelist

"In the tradition of GONE GIRL, Susan Wingate's STORM SEASON is both layered and nuanced. Like a striptease. the story unwinds itself, building one fear above the other. She has created a world both surreal and REAL, where regrets don't just swallow you whole… They KILL you." –JCarson Black, NY Times Bestseller, www.jcarsonblack.com

"STORM SEASON… ranging from the book's dense prose to its format, Wingate demands readers' close attention from the very first sentence to the last. But does it pay off? Absolutely. Prepare to be haunted long after turning the final page." –*BestThrillers.com*

BOOKS BY SUSAN WINGATE

The Last Maharajan

The Deer Effect

Way of the Wild Wood

Troubled in Paradise

The Bobby's Diner Series
Sacrifice at Sea
Hotter than Helen
Bobby's Diner

Of the Law

SUSAN WINGATE

STORM SEASON
A MEG STORM THRILLER

ROBERTS PRESS, AN IMPRINT OF FALSE BAY BOOKS

For information contact : Roberts Press

http://robertspress.wordpress.com

Book design by Book Covers by Authors
Book cover by Warren Design

First Edition: September 2018
10 9 8 7 6 5 4 3 2 1

Wingate, Susan

STORM SEASON, A Meg Storm Thriller by Susan Wingate

1.Psychological thriller/Women's fiction-fiction, 2. family drama-
fiction, female protagonist
3. History—Mexican drug cartel lord Ismael « El Mayo » Zambada,
4. Heroin addiction-fiction, 5. Crime-fiction, 6. San Juan Island-
fiction 7. Opioid crisis 8. Vigilante justice

ISBN: 978-1795519199

STORM SEASON

For Sarah

"You will never know exactly what another person is going through or what their whole story is. When you believe you do, realize that your assumptions about their life are in direct relation to your limited perspective." -M&A Hack

THE ROAD BEFORE

Life changes in a blink. Say, when, on a dusky evening, a deer leaps from the woods at the exact moment you're passing the spot in your car. Say, you're driving home from an interview—say, a high-level legal interview and your mind is wrapped up in detail. Boom, it happens. Deer appears. Sudden. Deadly. A coin flipping in the air, end over end, up, up, up, then back down flipping, flipping until it lands on cold, black tar jittering to a stop, until it struggles no longer.

Tails not heads. A broken back. Gasping for breath. A pin-prick. An overdose.

Change comes swiftly, like a snapping branch shorn off under the weight of heavy snow. A pelt shred on a bumper. Blood curdling on pavement.

Your car stalls. Your hand covers your mouth. You may cry inside the car for the deer lying dead on the street but, in the end, you drive off. Because, why would you stay? So, you leave the thing on the side of the road. Maybe you pump your taillights. They flash red as your nerves jump, your foot pumps tentative against the brake pedal. You expect more deer to emerge now, so, you're skittish as you drive along the wooded way.

It's only a few minutes later, when you ease up on the taillights and pull away. You try to wipe the scene from your mind and resume your speed hoping for a future when the memory of the dead deer isn't a haunting. You race forward hoping for life to move along, of course, with one less deer.

Two turns toward home and the scene is no longer visible in the rearview mirror. Just then, a fawn tracks over the doe's steps, out of the woods. It stops at her dead body on the side of the road, sniffs one leg, and bleats like a lamb might right before the slaughter. The small deer curls up in the lowest spot of the ditch near the doe, off the road but near. And it will starve to death there because it knows nothing other than its mother. With the doe, all survival instincts will die for the fawn.

PART ONE
MEG STORM

Spring 2017

1

You don't suddenly awaken as a wailing, angry, distant woman. She was once a child, Meg Storm was—a child riding a tricycle, once a teen hoping to make the cheerleading squad, once a young woman working toward a degree in accounting then bagging that idea when, suddenly, she was once a mother and a wife. Not in that order.

She'd once played with Barbie dolls. Her Tootsie Roll brown curls swishing against her plump pink cheeks as she played with baby dolls, ones with miniature diapers, ones that cried "Maa maa," while weeping real tap-water tears. A baby doll she carried around by the foot in one hand as she ran home to her mother who called her in for a grilled cheese sandwich, orange slices, and to watch Jot—the dot cartoon—on TV.

Becoming an angry, middle-aged, upper-middle class woman rang trite, rang average to Meg. Like something of the 1970's and valium, of self-medicating, of complaints about getting a raw deal on life, being dealt a crappy hand. She longed for her dolls.

The change in her personality came on in shades of blacks marbling with whites. Then she realized one day who she was, like someone snapped their fingers—one moment she was happy. The next? Meg had fallen despondent.

Her battery was dying. And yet, there she sat gazing at Lil's message.

With her right index finger on the cell, she scrolled back up to the beginning of the IM. How many times had she read these same words? Nearing thirty times, was it?

Each time, starting with the first sentence: My name is Lily.

Each time, ending with: See you on the flip-flop.

Each word was the same, in the same place, each time she'd read them before. To Meg, each word seemed methodically placed. But how methodical can the fuzzy mind of a heroin addict be?

The battery showed only twenty-seven percent juice available. She pushed the power button on the side of the phone with one fingernail and watched the digital display prompt her, asking if it was okay to power down. She swiped the "OK" option and closed the phone's pink leather case with a snap. Lily had bought the case for her. She often got small gifts—plies trying to get back into Meg's good graces. But these gifts came with a price and she wondered how Lily had earned the money. Was it on her back? Selling drugs? How? She didn't want Lil's god-blessed gifts. She wanted her daughter clean again. Rephrase: she had wanted her clean... all these years.

It's funny how time runs out on people. You only get so many tries. Then sayonara, bitch. Time's up.

The morning held a cloying heaviness in the air, mustiness dripping from every molecule. The sky was in a slow burn from a coming rainy-day sunrise. Meg noticed she'd been holding her breath. When she finally let go, when she finally breathed out, she realized the mustiness wasn't outside her body but within her own lungs, in her heart, in her mind, and not in the kitchen where she sat now, where she often sat early mornings thinking about how her world had spun upside-down, upended, and landed on its noggin.

She tipped her head left then right in two, hard snaps. Her neck popping in each direction sent a twinge of relief that circulated across each shoulder and down into her spine.

The house was quiet now. She liked this time of day when her thoughts were all you could hear in the absence of all other sound, your thoughts, those, and the yellow climbing rosebush clinging to the window trim with its leaves and thorns gently grating the glass in rhythm with the wind.

She laid the phone onto the table. Lily sent the original message in December. This one was edited May 9th. The auto-initiate feature had resent it months before from an updated publishing of the original post, one she'd first read nearly a year ago.

Lily's posts were a curse and a blessing. A curse because the latest posts showed Lily's desperation. A blessing because the posts made Meg feel as though her daughter were still alive—as though Lily was whispering to her from somewhere inside the house, from a different room, perhaps the attic, or through a vent in the ceiling.

The house was warm, yet Meg shivered and tightened her cat insignia sweater close across her chest. If she'd simply thought to put on socks, she might not feel so chilly. At least she'd had sense enough to pull on a pair of sweatpants, her "gray, boring sweatpants," as Jay would've said.

Her bare toes glimmered under the soft morning light in a nail-paint sparkling with flecks of silver over a lighter pink hue. It had been a whimsical choice by the pedicurist, which now seemed stupid, childish. Her knee-jerk reaction was to refuse applying the sparkly topcoat but the pedicurist, Winnie, insisted. Said it would make Meg smile when she glanced down at her feet. It never did. Meg wasn't a whimsy-sort-of-gal. Never had been. As a young woman she was all about black slacks and tight hair, little make-up, the least accessory—diamond posts and a thin gold crucifix.

Her father once told her she was "as angry as an aneurism, and twice as deadly." He'd said it after one particularly bitter argument. No matter now. The old man couldn't hurt her anymore.

She tried to keep her thoughts from the old man and spoke little to him these days because, honestly, what would she say? Screw you. Die. Go to hell. What she had wanted to say to her father but couldn't, maybe shouldn't because her father was an invalid, incapable of walking on his own or feeding himself but who was able to communicate through the miracle of technology. Oh goody. By moving his eyes in a sequence, he could tell a computer what to type. Meg would rather he couldn't communicate at all. At least then he might appear to be pathetic, and perhaps, lovable.

He lived with his youngest sister, Emma, who cared for him a few hours during the week, but he also paid a flood of nurses around the clock to wash his scrawny body and to wipe his bony ass. His other sister, Blythe, lived across the country in New Hampshire and "wouldn't be bothered until he kicks off," she'd said.

Her dad had sent the message via email which Meg had opened on her phone. He was letting her have it. He was "sick to death" of her complaining. His version of "tough love." Because what did she have to complain about? "No one is wiping your butt or spoon-feeding gruel into your feeding bag or rolling your body over to change the bedsheets." He finished the note by telling her that she had "become a wailing, bitter, angry woman."

And that's when she thought, "Screw you, old man. Die and go to hell."

In the bathroom, the window was letting in fits and starts of sunshine due to a craggy system of clouds sweeping through the morning sky. The room held a tinge of rose oil mixed with lavender, of cleaning solution from when she disinfected the toilet, and of glass cleaner from polishing the mirror. Her face wore the age of sadness. No eye cream, no matter what the stated clinical tests promised, could ever reduce the puffiness in those eyelids. At least the extra ten pounds she'd gained from overeating after Lily died were gone. Grief is its own special diet plan.

She flexed her left arm and pressed her fingertips onto her bicep. Not bad. She'd seen flabbier. Meg sighed and shred her eyes away from the mirror. Every emotion felt strained. Every thought, exhausting.

She opened a lower-tier drawer in the vanity, pulled out a sleeve of cotton squares, and sandwiched two squares together. Next, she got out some nail polish remover and began to scrub clean her stupid toenails.

Note to self: never take advice from a pedicurist.

Meg had fallen headlong into a series of clichés…

Bad things happen to good people.

This too shall pass.

You'll look back on this and laugh.

No. No she wouldn't. She would never, and she envisioned the future as a place where there existed zero laughter.

And it's funny how a memory will try to turn your opinion. Because right then she remembered laughing with Jay. They were watching Lily dance for them. "Do the ballerina pose," he'd say, and Lily would lift her arms overhead, each fingertip touching lightly, and she'd spin. Her little tutu edging up higher with each turn until she could no longer balance herself and end up off-kilter, teetering to the point of tipping over. Lily was five then and wore a little pink ballerina costume. Five held so much promise. A sweet girl who said funny things like, "Lily no poo-poo," when

Jay and Meg would smell something sour emanating from her diapers. "Oh, yes, Lily did poo-poo," they'd say in unison.

And her mind turned again to a time when she was laughing as a girl, playing with locust skins. Each delicate shedding reminded her of scorched egg whites, scrapings off the bottom of an overcooked frying pan. She always found the skins in a backyard tree preferring the bark of the old bottle-brush tree to slough away their previous life. Each molting was the spitting image of a locust. The shells remained intact. She wondered how they escaped their own skin and the little-girl-Meg acting out make-believe scenes on the kitchen table after which her mother would toss each locust shell into the garbage when Meg abandoned the game, with each shell ending up a throw-away.

How was it locusts were able to shed one life for another? How was it that they were able to remake their existence? And do we all become cast-offs?

But that was then.

This is now. With now offering nothing but grief for Meg.

TODAY

2

"One thing led to another. It wasn't like I planned it," Meg Storm told the man sitting across the table from her. Her stomach cinched into a knot and she dropped her gaze from his face to an issue of *Serial Murder: Pathways for Investigations*.

The man typed something into his laptop, scrolled down the page, typed again, then said, "You don't have many options at this point. It's either, or..." He glanced down briefly to the screen. When he pulled his eyes up, he held them on hers, without blinking, waiting for an answer.

The hour was still early in the morning. Officers had showed up right after the owl broke through the window and killed the bat—after the face appeared through the broken glass. That was around four a.m.

Meg shifted in her seat and glanced down at her wrist at a watch that wasn't there. She rubbed the bare spot on her arm. A light bristling of fuzz grew peach-like and so blonde you could hardly see the hair. Her skin there felt cooler under the skin on the palm of her hand. But what part of her body was she really sensing—her hand or her arm? A sudden wave of heat cloistered her. Maybe she had a fever. But, of course, she knew she didn't. A full-on bout of nerves consumed her. She grabbed *Serial Murder* off the table and fanned herself with the magazine. She glanced off his face, past his right ear, and out the window behind him. The sun was crawling up the backs of three restoration homes across the street, with the sky turning a shade of orange she'd only seen in ice cream shops, with the orange melting into a popsicle blue horizon.

A jet stream from a faraway plane underlined a soft cloud that looked as though it had strayed from its cloud-family. A light breeze rocked a stand of poplars that lined the street. Their leaves cascading beneath them creating skirts of yellow on the concrete sidewalk, spilling off into the gutter, and speckling the pavement—waiting for cars to swirl them around with each passing tire.

They sat off from the kitchen in an old clapboard house she'd passed by often while driving home down Argyle from town. A rental sign faced the road. It was buried in front of the mailbox, but she had never seen the place rented. Now, she knew why. Authorities, not headquartered on the island, used the place as a false front.

Meg dragged her attention back. Her words felt like a prayer but held and emptiness as dark as the morning outside when she said, "It came on sudden, you know, the urge." She paused, then said, "But given my faith, my understanding of right and wrong, I tried to suppress it." She continued, "You may have heard: thoughts lead to words and words lead to action?" Her eyes dropped, and she confessed, "It was a lapse in faith."

Finally, their eyes connected. He was squinting at her as if trying to understand but not.

She added, "Easy as dropping your keys."

"That's when it happened?" He asked.

"Nah. I'm more of a planner than that."

"Sounds intentional."

"I planned around it, not the actual act. Good lord. Didn't you read the reports? There are pictures, right?" She paused again, to give herself a moment, to take on a less defensive tone. Then she said, "Psychologists call it intellectualizing—trying to understand what happened. Why it happened. Learning about something. Digging. You know?"

The man didn't answer. He was still squinting. Again, she shifted in her seat.

The sun was slow to light the sky. The assistant moved away from the kitchen counter and began to pull down mini-blinds over the windows, Meg supposed to prevent anyone from seeing inside. The assistant was a smallish sort of guy, different from the one questioning Meg. No, the man talking with her was tall—probably six-four by her estimation. But like the tall man, the smaller guy wore similar slacks and a pressed shirt. Both donned standard, authoritarian haircuts sheared close around the napes of their necks and ears, shaved in back, cut short on the sides and crown. Both had dark hair, the smaller guy's tinged with orange hues as if each spike were taking on the color of the morning sky. If it weren't for their size differential, they might be clones. They both wore shoulder holsters strapped to the left side of their chests. Each holster housed a black handgun. But the man sitting with Meg wore thick black-framed glasses.

"Tell me about them," he said.

Meg's eyes dropped. "I didn't know them," she paused, expecting him to ask another question and, when he did not, she added, "Just about them."

He nodded. "That works. What exactly did you know about them?" He folded his arms and leaned back against the kitchen chair, waiting for her to respond.

"There were three," she said. Then she glanced away at nothing much, at the wall. She added, "They were petrified."

WESLEY

BEFORE
December 2016

3

"She's going to say something—something to the wrong person and we'll be screwed either by cops or Zambada. Either way, she's gotta go," Lee said.

Ribbons of pot smoke filled the dimly-lit room. Acrid plumes showed in stripes of light that filtered through the cracks of a set of vertical blinds. The thick plastic of the blinds swung and clacked at the window, blown around by an antique metal table fan.

Lee knelt on the floor. He picked something off his knee then wiped at his shin. None of the guys had cleaned in three weeks and bits of crap—soda crackers, and dried, shredded cheese, spit-out remnants of *Zig-Zag* rolling papers contrasted with the matted green carpet.

Lee leaned forward to hand Wesley the roach, its fiery torch pinched millimeters from his long black fingernails. After handing it off, Lee slumped back onto the heels of a clown-sized set of dingy tennis shoes he was wearing. Wesley took a short hit and

26

handed the roach back. Lee reached up for the joint, pinching it tight against Wesley's fingers. He took a drag then passed it over to Randy, who's stringy body was laying there, taking up the entire couch. His hair matched the noodle-white tone of his arms and legs but wasn't up in Randy's typical do, a man-bun.

Wesley liked coke better than pot. They were making a coke run later. Meeting a guy. Someone Lily had hooked them up with a while back. Joaquin. Someone new and un-vetted—a jumpy, Hispanic dude—straight from Sinaloa, she'd told them. "From a good family," she'd said, which meant good coke. He trusted Lily's taste and allowed her this one new coke connection. They'd bought from him once before and hadn't yet gotten stung. Newbies are either bold or nervous, at first, then they settle in. Joaquin was neither. He was all business. Older. And, yeah. The coke was excellent.

Wesley tried to listen to Lee but became distracted by the smudges of coal around his eyes and a new streak of pink dye in his black hair—a bright strand that people call fuchsia. The dye bled down from the part in his hair, curved around his ear, and stopped at the nape of his neck. Some of his hair was long and some shaved short. Like he couldn't figure out what length he liked best so went for both.

"What's with the hair?" Wes asked.

Lee lifted his shoulders. He wore a tight rainbow band around his upper arm, no shirt. Both ruddy nipples were strikingly small. And through the tender skin of each held a pinky-finger-sized, silver loop. Lee wore a pair of shorts made from something like tee-shirt material. The pants hung sloppy around his crotch. He had used the shorts as underwear and pajamas for the past three days. His pupils shone dilated in the dimness of the room and he spoke again.

"She has to," he said.

"Has to what?" The hit off the joint made it difficult for Wesley to remember what they'd been talking about. Smoke floated up from his nose and settled into his eye socket. Wesley pinched one eye to look at Lee. He was in charge…not this freak of nature. He went back to how or why they'd all hooked up in the first place and remembered, it was all the way back to high school, drumming in band. Wes wore his white dress shirt and black slacks and Lee wore a khaki jumpsuit. A jumpsuit? For band? How'd this idiot learn to dress? Apes?

"Great dialogue," Randy said, always the critic. "You're both stoned." His words slurred after lifting his head high enough to down a slug of the last dregs of the last can of beer in the house. Wes met Randy in Chem101. They were lab partners but "partner" wasn't quite the right word. Randy loved chemistry. Wes hated the class, so he let him do all the work, help him with the pop quizzes, and sit next to him during exams.

Randy lay his head back down on the couch, took another hit off the joint. He choked on the smoke.

"She's not doing anything," Wesley said after remembering Lee challenging him about Lily.

"'cept servicing you," Randy added.

Lee nodded furiously in agreement with him and grunted out something that was supposed to be a chuckle.

"Shut up, Ran. Shut your stupid face."

"I'm not the stupid one. Lee is the stupid one."

"Bite me," Lee said. He slapped a hand across Randy's shin as if brushing a fly off a breakfast plate.

"Wouldn't you enjoy that," Randy said. He made a bratty face like kids make at each other—he curled his top lip and grimaced and shook his head.

Wesley watched tension building between them and turned to go but stopped when Lee grabbed him by the wrist. He raised up on his knees in a praying position. "Wes, she's not right for you."

"Get off me, freak." Wesley yanked his arm free and Lee sat back on his haunches. He looked shocked, insulted, defeated. And was about to say something but stopped short.

"He loves you, Wes," Randy said, and laughed so hard, he choked.

"Shut up, Ran. You pig. That's disgusting," Lee said.

"Not to you, perv."

"Randy, I swear," Lee said.

"Shut up both of you," Wesley said. His tone ended their little tiff for a bit. "I'm going to the store. We're outta beer."

"Want me to come with?" Lee asked.

Randy mimicked him, "Want me to come with?"

"I swear, Ran."

"I swear, Ran," Randy mimicked again, making a girly gesture with his hand. The provocation was all

Lee needed. He lurched onto the couch and went at Randy. Randy held up his hands defensively, pushing Lee away. "Get off me!"

But Lee had straddled him and began clubbing him in the chest and arms with his fists.

Wesley's instincts kicked in. He leaned down to break them up but stopped short. He decided better of it and, instead, walked out of the smoky cabin, slamming the door, and leaving the two in their stupid brawl.

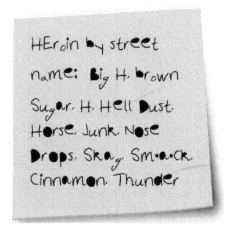

HEroin by street
name: Big H, brown
Sugar, H, Hell Dust,
Horse, Junk, Nose
Drops, Skag, Sm·a·ck,
Cinnamon, Thunder

LILY

OVERTURE UNO
December 19, 2016
(edited May 9, 2017)

4

My name is Lily Storm and I'm a drug addict. My drug of choice is heroin. And, like the sticker I made says, its street name can be anything from Big H to Thunder, Nose Drops to Brown Sugar. I prefer Cinnamon. I can send the boys to the store for Cinnamon (wink, wink) and no one's the wiser.

I started using about twelve years ago when I was eighteen. I've been through the gamut—alcohol, pot, pills, coke, meth (which I really liked but not as much as coke). Coke is a better high but doesn't last as long and is more expensive than meth. Smoking coke is the best, but it always scared me a little—I imagined myself running down the road, doing a Richard Pryor impersonation, my hair ablaze.

Anyway, I found my taste in heroin. It's not spooky like people want you to believe, like I originally thought it might be. It's the place where pleasure exists. It's chilling out on a beach and sipping margaritas with the most beautiful boy that God ever created, and this boy is all about pleasing you. He wants you to feel him, get in his head, and touch his love for you. He's yours. You're his. Total love. Total ecstasy. That's how heroin feels. Silky. Like you found the love of your life and all you can do is gaze into each other's eyes from now until the end of time.

And I never intend to let him go.

I decided to start this blog hoping to explain my drug usage to a few people. You know, my family— mom and dad, and close friends who don't understand, who are confused by my addiction. Or, those who are disappointed in me. To them I say, F-you. It's my issue. Deal with your own issues and get over me.

I've numbered these blog posts in Española. Don't ask me why. I'm just crazy that way. BTW, if anyone else can learn from these installments, or you happen to be going through something similar, maybe this blog can be a place of experiential union and healing. Feel free to leave a comment.

So, you know, I've written quite a few posts—thirteen to be exact—which I've already scheduled out to publish monthly from December 2016 to December 2017, over the next thirteen months. I've scheduled them out this way because I won't be around much longer. If you follow my blog, you will get auto-alerts of these pre-scheduled posts via email or via IM on your cell. Also, thanks for following. It's really cool. Maybe we can learn from each other. Did I say that already? LOL. Oh well.

Oh, yeah. About commenting. If you leave a comment, I will try to get back with you. But if I don't, I'm either in jail, in the hospital, or I'm dead. If I'm dead, well then guess I'll see you on the flip-flop.

ZAMBADA

May 2017
In Mexico

5

The girl, una criada, set a plate of chilequiles on the pink quartz counter in front of Ismael. Two other criadas followed in, bringing his daughter's and granddaughter's dishes—chilequiles for the daughter and crepes de fresa for the granddaughter. The niñas returned with refreshments—creamy horchata for the child and two papaya mimosas for the adults.

A vacant, mile-long strip of beach was speckled with men in white dress shirts. Each man wore shorts because of the heat that time of year. They wore sunglasses, binoculars slung around their necks, and running shoes. Each carried a 9mm Parabellum Micro Uzi, each weapon having a fire power of eighteen-hundred RPM—spraying over twenty-eight bullets per second.

A vessel loomed on lazy rolling waters off the coast of Mazatlán. Zambada chuckled to himself, thinking how someone had tried to disguise it as a leisure yacht, its name emblazoned on its side, "Gotcha!" The boat had dropped anchor three days before, the day after Ismael moved his just-widowed daughter and child into the condo. Well, nearly just-widowed. What she didn't know… and all that. Coincidentally, the yacht had anchored the same day Zambada had relayed the message telling his daughter that her husband had died from an apparent accident. An accident. Don't bother telling her about a bullet hole that'd leach blood out of him to the point of turning his skin blue, or singe marks the gun would make to each temple. Don't bother with the sliced electrical cord tying his arms, neck, and feet—hog-style. Don't bother.

The kitchen inhabited the third story of the condo and boasted a large bay window where Zambada kept a fat black Meade telescope. The telescope was powerful enough to spot a stray solar system in the night sky. The telescope's housing contrasted with the pink and white décor of the kitchen. Even the maids matched the kitchen, wearing white and pink uniforms. The cabinets, made from the finest ash, lent a rustic tone to the color scheme and sturdiness that harmonized with how the rest of the condo had been built.

Zambada's granddaughter shifted in her seat, rocking on one of the stools surrounding the kitchen island where the three ate. Sitting there with the high back of the stool as her background, the sable curls, white patent leather shoes, layered pinafore, and bib around her petite neck gave her a doll-like appearance.

Zambada smiled at Juaquita. "Esta muy bonita, mi amorita," he cooed.

Juaquita, named after her father, enjoyed the crepes she was stuffing into her mouth. She held her fork high in her left hand as she picked off strawberries with her right—one berry after the other out of a thick mountain of cream on top of the pancakes and eating the fruit first. Pink syrup covered her chin. She stopped eating briefly to smile at her abuelo, her grandfather. At five, Juaquita hadn't yet fully grasped that she would never again see her father return home from work, from his business travels in Los Etados Unidos.

Miriam's eyes bore the weight of her loss. Puffy and red, dull from tears shed before leaving her quarters that morning, she refused to cry for him in front of Juaquita. She needed to be strong for her daughter. Miriam didn't want to alarm her bebe. Mostly, she didn't want to have to explain why her papa was never coming back. Mostly, she didn't want to see Juaquita cry. Not yet. There was time for mourning in the coming days. Just not today. Por el amor de Dios.

Miriam sipped the mimosa twice before draining the entirety from the champagne glass.

"Mas, Pena," she demanded. Pena returned with a pitcher. "Tráeme un vaso más grande. Ahora."

Pena scuttled to the cabinet to retrieve a larger, thicker tumbler made of green-tinted, recycled glass. She rushed it over to Miriam and filled the vaso millimeters below the rim with the champagne-laced beverage. Miriam snatched the glass from Pena's hands, making juice slosh and dribble out onto the counter and onto both their hands. However, before anyone could reprimand her, Pena wiped up the spill with her apron. She grabbed Miriam's hands, one at a time, and wiped those too. But Miriam shook her off.

"Bastante! Enough," she chided the maid. "Papa? What will I do?" Miriam asked Ismael. Her voice had weakened, and her eyes went glassy.

"Pobrecita," he said, ", I'll handle it."

Miriam dabbed her eyes. Her jaw tightened. She couldn't give one damn about revenge. She wanted her husband back, but her father seemed to believe every action was either made for him or against him.

"Dios mio, papa!" she yelled, and lifted Juaquita, who had only eaten part of her breakfast. The little one began to wail. "Shush, bebe." She scowled at her father and stamped out of the room.

"Pena!" she hollered as she exited the kitchen, "Bring Juaquita's crepes! Ahora! And my, my juice, tambien!"

Again, Pena scuttled to the counter where the baby had been eating. She grabbed Juaquita's plate, the senora's mimosa, and took off after Miriam.

And there, Ismael sat, alone. Women confused him. He was only trying to be helpful. He'd gotten rid of two wives because they didn't "get him." He couldn't get rid of Miriam, his only daughter. He cherished her though he saw the same qualities he'd loathed in his first wife—quick to judge, mouthy. But he loved his daughter. Couldn't stand her stupid husband but loved her and the little one.

He gazed from the third-floor window at the thirty men below lining his beach. These men represented only one-tenth of his army—only one percent of three thousand he had amassed on his payroll, which didn't include any non-employees, like la policia and la militaria in Sinaloa. If he included the pay-for-hire governmental units in place, Ismael's army reached ten thousand bodies easily.

He glanced down at the counter. His cell phone vibrated and shimmied on the pink quartz. He knew it was Archevaldo. It had already gotten too late in the morning. He had to rush off before a shipment left. The shipment needed his special touch.

"Yes. I know," Zamabada said, then, "Ahora." He punched off the call.

Zambada knew the new recruit was doubling as a drug dealer. Ismael wanted to supervise the lad. He liked to handle infiltrators personally, with his own unique style. With precision.

First, el doctor removed their tongues so that they could no longer speak, so they couldn't scream. Then he would cut out one eye. Only one. The second eye Zambada wanted left so as to allow infiltrators to watch as Ismael cut off each finger, each thumb. So, they could watch him as he sliced into their stomachs to disembowel them. But today would be different. He was in a rush and had no time for niceties.

He called for his driver to meet him downstairs and, as he walked out of the kitchen, Ismael said a silent prayer.

LILY

OVERTURE DOS – Blog post
January 24, 2017

6

I thought about him often, my first heroin addict. Thought about how his head moved—rolled really, in a circle, his eyes closing as if reliving the sensation of smack hitting his brain. How he said he felt warm— the word warm cascading off his lips. The sweet nausea.

He didn't talk about certain things—the needle— the prick of it, its blunt entry as the needle's length filled his vein, or the vomiting. Instead, he spoke about the enjoyable moments spent mainlining. Unlashing the noose of rubber tubing from his bicep, sliding his body back onto a cool pillow, letting euphoria wash over him from his scalp to his toenails.

He'd said, his toenails.

But toenails have no feeling, I'd said.

They do. They do, He said back.

And at that moment, with nary a taste, I knew I was hooked.

When did you stop caring about me, mom? I keep going back over the years. Remember that trip to *Marineland*? I was eight then and I still remember how you would not let go of my hand. You were so freaked that someone might try to steal me. You made dad promise to hold me on his lap until you got back from the ladies' room and were furious when you saw us standing a couple of feet apart at the seal pool while we watched gulls steal smelt out of people's hands who weren't paying attention. I also remember you racing up to us, screaming at dad, and scaring off the gulls. That was hysterical. I suppose if anyone could, you could, ma. You were like that for a while and then there's this enormous gap of you caring. From the moment I entered high school to when things finally became obvious to you, when I became an embarrassment, that is. You were right though. There are people out there who will try to steal kids. Maybe not by kidnapping them but in different ways.

You let go of my hand, ma.

JAY

Late Spring 2017

7

"She wasn't wearing any clothes?" Jay's mind spun to a long-ago, black-and-white newspaper article reporting on Marilyn Monroe's death. She was lying naked on the bathroom floor, the article read. But the photos the newspaper chose to display were of Monroe with Jane Russell leaving their handprints on the sidewalk in front of *Grauman's Chinese Theater*. The two actresses had gotten their golden stars on the celebrated *Walk of Fame*.

A song filtered into Jay's subconscious but dissolved when Meg slipped from his side. She was needing to sit down, she'd said, and he guided her to the chair in front of the window, where her legs gave out. She plopped down and started to breathe heavily. How could they not expect this?

Jay set his view past Meg, out the window. The neighbors across the street had a FOR SALE sign posted. When had that happened? Why hadn't he noticed before?

He pulled his attention back when the two police officers—deputies, detectives, whatever—began to speak again. They still stood in the doorway.

Someone was burning a wood fire nearby. The toasted aroma was seeping into the house. Jay moved to close the door behind them but noticed inside the home now for sale, the neighbor boy was standing behind the drapes inside his home. He looked like a pressed flower against the glass. The boy sat riveted while the men in uniform spoke to the Storm's.

Typical. Police were magnets for looky-Loo's. For whatever reason, Jay left the door propped open. What was the point in trying to hide? They weren't going to see much. He wasn't about to crumble in front of the Sheriff and his deputy. That wasn't what a man does. He doesn't act weak even when he learns that his one and only daughter has just died. You stay strong. You just do.

Clouds pressed by in filthy cotton balls from east-southeast. The wind was bending the trees out front, making plum blossoms crush off, not in the dribs and drabs that calmer spring days allowed, but in droves. The delicate blossoms looked like fish scales covering the garden out front. Some lay mashed on the concrete walkway where the Sheriff and deputy had stepped. A concrete angel statue that sat at the edge of the porch had caught a pile of blossoms in its arms. But soon another strong wind swirled in and the blossoms skippered off. It wouldn't take long before the angel would be holding nothing.

Sheriff Joshua Peters introduced himself and Detective Lachlan Buchanan as if the three men had never met before. The formality irritated Jay but, honestly, what did his irritation matter right now anyway?

Peters had a man's man appeal about him. He was tall and clean-cut, muscular, and ruggedly good-looking, owning a square jaw, and pensive eyes. Buchanan was more of a pretty boy but tallish, and fit. To Jay, Lach always appeared to be flirting but that's how blue eyes were to Jay. They tugged at him in a magnetic, hypnotizing way. He stood only an inch or so shorter than Peters but had the same shoulder span, a narrower waistline, and was nearly ten years Peters' junior.

"Sorry," Jay said, and opened the door wider so the two men could enter.

"Mr. Storm, we just have a few questions to ask," Peters said.

"Come on, guys. We know each other. Call me Jay." Then, he led them near the couch, which was directly opposite from where Meg sat. Her face had gone pale. A blue vein in her forehead had enlarged. It ran vertical from her hairline down between her eyes, to the bridge of her nose. It bulged within her skin. Her eyes had grown thick with bags under, developing and looking pronounced, alerting Jay that she wanted to cry. But that she was trying to contain her emotions.

"Can I get you something? Water? Coffee?" Jay asked.

"Nothing. Thank you," the sheriff said.

Detective Buchanan shook his head in response then lifted his pen to write on a notepad he'd taken out of his left-hand chest pocket.

"Mr. Storm…"

He was going to ask the first question, but Jay interrupted him, "Please, Lach, you know me. Us." Jay gestured to his side, over to Meg.

"Okay. Jay, Meg," Buchanan responded, and continuing, he asked, "Where were you last night?"

Jay noticed in his peripheral vision, Meg lift her head. Her skull seemed to crawl out of her skin. In a flash, Meg had gone from morose to angry. But her anger seemed different this time, different from one he'd ever witnessed before. A strange voice emerged from her throat—a beast yawning from a long winter asleep, roaring awake, eyes flaring with wildness, and, like a trapped animal, she attacked.

"You think we had something to do with our own daughter's death?" Her voice pitched up and she stood but, as fast as she stood, she sat again. Her face went white. "Oh, my God. Oh, my God. Why are you asking that?" Her voice warbled and, what Jay knew to be the gates of her emotions, would break open— all the anguish she felt—the pain trapped inside her stomach, her heart feeling like a time-bomb. All that, came surging forth.

Jay hurried to her side. He bent down next to her, but Meg pushed him off.

THE SHERIFF & DEPUTY LACH BUCHANAN

8

Within fifteen minutes, Buchanan and Peters were standing outside the Storm's door. There, they tried to concentrate on the street, on the little boy in the window watching them, on the fallen blossoms skipping across the road and through the Storm's front yard. But all their efforts for distraction were futile. They were only able to concentrate on Meg crying and Jay trying to quiet her inside the house.

Lach slipped a regulation stretch-fit cap onto his head and pulled it lower than usual, down over his eyebrows. The county sheriff department logo was embroidered on the cap's brim with his name, BUCHANAN on the back under a U.S. flag insignia.

The air was wet. A marine layer of fog was rolling in. And after starting out earlier with a brilliant sunrise laced in a color that reminded Lach of a pink he'd only seen on steamed lobster. He wiped away some mist that had settled on his cheek and took the opportunity to covertly wipe under his eyes at the same time.

"Fog's coming in," he said.

Peters nodded in agreement.

"This can't get more screwed up," Buchanan added.

The two men had not moved from the porch.

"Outta control," Peters responded. He paused but then asked, "You knew the daughter, right?"

Lach turned his head west, down the street, away from Peters. He was thankful the sheriff hadn't referred to Lily as the deceased. "One date. Nothing happened." Then Buchanan changed the subject. "We need a detail on the lab."

"Can't. We're short. Kelley's on leave. Trent's gotta new baby. Wife's not doing well, I hear. Hard labor. They'll be taking her to the mainland."

Buchanan glanced over to Peters. He noticed the sheriff's jaw tighten. It must have sucked managing an under-funded, small town department. The sheriff had his eyes glued on some unseen monster across the street. Perhaps on the little boy in the window. Peters' gaze seemed to tighten when he squinted harder.

Buchanan looked away, toward their vehicle. The lights were spinning, sending off two silent but alternating fragments of light—white and red. "I'll do some drive-by's after work."

Peters lifted his chin, acknowledging his underling's commitment to arresting some people of interest. "Can't spook 'em," he said.

"They'll never know."

"Get pics of the cabin?"

Lach nodded and caught the side of Peters' face. He could tell when the sheriff was burning up inside, a smoldering mass of human flesh. The whole matter was gnawing at the Sheriff. "Drive-by images. Google Earth images too. The whole bunch o' bananas, Sheriff," he said.

Peters nodded his head, slipped on his sheriff cap, and took one step down off the porch. He turned slightly without looking at Lach and said, "There's a free steak at Vinny's later and a beer for unpaid help."

Lach smirked and followed him but stalled when he heard Meg again. She was trying to say something to Jay through her tears. He could only made out a couple of words, they were, why and my baby.

9

Later that day, Buchanan pulled his car off the pavement a gravel shoulder. He allowed his car to idle and was situated at a bend in the road pointing toward the Straits. He had driven off Cattle Point down the first stretch of False Bay.

He re-read the text. His sense of integrity was strong but maybe his sense of loyalty, stronger. Peters had been not just a boss but a friend for over six years. Up to now, he'd never had any cause to question the sheriff's judgment.

The interior of his car smelled like an ashtray. It was the second time in those six years he'd tried to quit smoking and doing great but after reading Peters' message, he pulled out a ready cigarette from his pocket and fired up.

Both eyes pinched when a thin plume of smoke hit one of his corneas. He rolled down the driver-side window and let the smoke siphon off into the air outside. He watched as a cloud tumbled away and dispersed into nothingness. A deer was eyeing him, standing across in the ditch near the woods. It was young, most likely a yearling. He didn't see any knots on its head or spotted sides and quickly judged it for a young doe. The deer was watching him watch her. Their eyes locked on each other's. Buchanan assumed, the fawn believed itself to be in danger, but he hoped the delicate creature wouldn't dart away. He didn't want to frighten her.

The deer on the island fascinated him. He admired them, admired their beauty. He hated deer season, especially doe season, hated having to down a deer when it got hit by a car, and never watched when he shot. He'd aim, hold steady, close his eyes, then fire— didn't want to look in its eyes.

His cell phone buzzed again. Peters was insistent.

When he glanced up again, the yearling was gone. He hoped further into the woods, away from the road. The message was another one from Peters, this time asking if he gotten the first message.

"Got it," he typed. "Not sure."

Peters response was fast. "Get sure," the message read.

He pressed the "thumbs-up" icon then clicked off his phone. Buchanan tipped his chin up and leaned the nape of his neck against the headrest, but he noticed a sudden movement outside his window. The deer was crossing the road at a blind spot in the turn. He craned back to watch for any traffic and, sure enough, an oncoming car was approaching from his left. The car was traveling much faster than the road's stated twenty-five mile-per-hour speed limit.

Buchanan flipped on his emergency lights causing the deer to stop midway across the road.

"Crap," he said to himself. The car approaching slowed but wasn't stopping because of his lights.

Buchanan opened his door and stepped out onto the road. He flagged down the driver, pumping his hands palms down and flat in front of him. The car stopped. It was the son of a hard-working single woman. Her son had somehow turned into the local riff-raff and lived in a ramshackle house on a piece of property, the entrance which was about a third-mile from where he stood.

He motioned for him to roll down the window and said, "Bailey, I take you in one more time on this road for speeding, you won't be incarcerated here. I'll send you to Island Jail. Not for just a few days, either. It'll be a month or two. You're putting people's lives at risk speeding. And with these blind turns? Come on. Don't be stupid."

"Sorry Lach. I mean, sorry, Detective Buchanan."

"Get," Buchanan said, motioning for him to leave.

Another car approached behind Bailey and he rolled up his passenger window.

Buchanan cupped a hand over his eyes though the day wasn't cloudy. He was trying to spot where the deer had gone. It was in the process of scaling a barbed wire fence. It jumped over a rickety stretch of fence that held a NO TRESPASSING sign. The fence had been there since well before Lach had arrived. It was rusty, probably fifty years old by now, and surrounded a large swale of farmland that Mr. Johnson owned before he died. When Bailey past it, the deer sped off, bounding deeper toward the middle of the grassland. She stopped and began snagging the yellow tips of dandelions with her teeth.

Buchanan gestured for the next car to pass. He yelled to a young woman driving, "Twenty-five miles per hour, ma'am. This is residential. Slow down." He gave her a serious look and heard her call out that she was sorry. Then he checked for the doe but, in her natural surroundings, she'd become camouflaged from sight.

He got back into his car. Now, he needed to figure out what to do with Peters' request, "Use Turner to track the husband," the message ordered. It was the first time he'd suffered an ethical dilemma at this job. He marked the moment as the beginning to an end. But what end? His job? His on-and-off-again relationship with Turner? Both?

He spent the next few minutes awfulizing—worrying about what the future held. How badly things could go. If he didn't comply, Peters could fire him or, worse, he could regret for the rest of his life possibly making the wrong decision.

"Shit," he said. Finally, he flipped the car into gear. He spun a one-eighty down False Bay back toward Cattle Point. He'd left his cigarette burning in the ashtray. He crushed it out, pulled out another, and fired that one up also.

MEG

10

Meg Storm kept her eyes closed longer than usual, working hard to ignore Jay. When she opened them again, her view settled on something quite a distance from where she sat at the kitchen window. Out back, one of two turkey vultures shredded the remnants off bones of something dead in the field. Meg lowered her eyes to the point that she could see only the top and bottom rows of her lashes. For far too short a time she remained distracted and felt compelled to gaze out at the scene again.

The second vulture posed, thrusting its rooster-pink head in and out, trying to snatch a piece of their kill. It held its wings unfurled, stretched wide. From tip to tip, the wingspan measured around six feet. The second bird began to hop around the bird feeding but the first held its ground. The second, continued to perform its dance in deference to the more dominant bird.

Jay's words broke her concentration. "Good lord," he said. "They bombed Syria again."

A doe darted out disrupting Jay's words and halting the vultures' meal but only for mere seconds. The female deer pounded her front hooves, kicked up her hind legs, and shook her head, trying to threaten the vultures off. As it turned out, it was all show—a futile display with the doe trying to spare the ravaged body of the fawn.

God. How could it have happened? It was a just-born, the first she'd seen this season, the only baby deer this May—when fawns get born.

Meg sat there secretly mourning for the doe relating its death to her own daughter, the one she'd just buried.

It's no good when a child dies before a mother. No good at all.

The monster birds returned. Seemed determined and before long they returned to their kill, taking turns now, tearing its body apart. Meg wanted the vultures to die—to flip the outcome, to preserve the fawn, and to relish watching the killers be killed, if only this one time. Did her desire insult God? Were her thoughts wrong—to wish for the death of something evil? Forget nature. Forget survival. How can a person turn a cheek and allow evil to continue when you could as easily pull out a gun, then and there, and end someone's pain, someone's suffering?

"Where's the gun?" Meg said.

Of course, Jay would be confused by the question and asked, "What?" She knew the gun was in the box inside the upper drawer of their chiffonier. She wanted him to move off his butt and retrieve it for her.

*

The steel felt cold at first but, within seconds, the handle warmed to the body temperature in her hands.

53

She'd been wise to slip on a pair of sloggers. The weather had made swiss cheese out of the back field, pocking it with small pools of rainwater. That's how wet the earth was. That's how much it had been raining. She wiped her eyes and cornered the backyard fence, which created a smaller, enclosed yard behind the house.

When she appeared, the more submissive vulture fluttered up a few feet above the ground then landed, but in the process, it had alerted the one feeding of danger. She could only imagine what Jay was thinking. Meg cocked the gun. The clicking action alerted both birds. Each lumbered off away from the fawn, bolting off toward the cover of woods.

She pointed, watching each scramble toward flight. Their bodies clambered low, in take-off, bouncing up then down again above the earth, their movement resembling two giant ducks waddling their fat butts into the air.

When she squeezed the trigger, the jolt spasmed in her hand. The strength of the gun surprised her, so she gripped the handle more firmly and shot again. Each blast whizzed over the pond and dissipated through a thick stand of half-naked alders. She heard the smack of each bullet hitting tree trunks. She was shooting blind through the woods and toward the far side of the pond. She worried about killing someone but remembered the judge who lived on the other side, had moved back to Seattle, and abandoned his property.

She took another shot, worrying less about injuring a human being. The bigger vulture cawed, shrugged once, and nodded its ugly head but continued to flap. A small spray of blood dribbled from its wingtip. It stumbled back to the ground.

Meg thumbed the cocking mechanism once more, but nervous sweat had made her grip unsteady and her fingers slipped around the handle. She stuffed the gun under an armpit and wiped her hands on her pants.

By the time she regripped the gun, the vulture had gotten its balance back and managed to take wind. The injury was superficial, nothing that would kill the bastard. She tracked the muzzle on the bird as it lifted into the air. She pulled the trigger and fired again but missed when the bird dipped from its path to the right in a turn away from the fawn and made off toward the other bird which was well above and beyond its mate.

Meg lowered the gun in front of her legs still holding it in both hands. The birds would be back. Murderers are like that—liking to stay close to a trove of their trophies. As she watched the birds fly south out of sight, Meg imagined the damn birds taking a selfie when they landed and posting it on Twitter—the social media preference for birds. But, yeah, they'd be back. Especially when a trophy provides nourishment, even a piddling of food like the dead fawn at Meg's feet.

She bent to touch its stiff body but the doe reemerged. It was standing off and away in a north side stand of woods. She moved tentatively, inching out from behind an old Geary oak, one that always reminded Meg of a Halloween witch with its gnarled arms lurking as though wanting to snag any passersby who might walk near her. Then, at once, the doe darted. Only a mother would race headlong into the end of a gun to save its child.

The doe's frenetic actions colored late spring and washed a sense of gloom, of sadness with full intention to spread throughout the rest of the year—summer and fall, winter, and well into next spring.

*

Meg hadn't planned the morning to end up this way. But fantasy is like that. It comes on sneaky-like, rises on a slow tide, and when you least expect, mushrooms into conspiracies you would never act on in real life... or... you don't think you would.

Meg drew her eyes off the scene of the vultures tearing at the fawn. A bright shred of sun carved a blade through the kitchen window where she sat fantasizing about a death of vultures.

Sunshine blinked through creases of accordion clouds and spilled out of a mix of alders, Douglas fir, and wild cranberry that made up a ridgeline of vegetation growing along the pond's berm. One million molten miniature stars shattered off the pond's surface in a blinding glare each trying to imitate the Sun.

Meg covered her eyes. She couldn't have planned it better—to end up right then right there, at that precise moment, staring through the window at a breaking sun, sipping coffee, witnessing the kill of vultures, and wishing, wishing with every molecule in her body that she might act against the virulent beasts—to save the fawn. To save Lily. But, instead, there she sat, doing nothing. Save for pressing one finger into her upper lip so hard the moon in her nailbed blanched under the strain—to the point the imprint of her teeth fossilized onto the inside of her lip.

She leaned back in her chair twisting a coil of streaked hair, trying to struggle it back into a clip made from mother-of-pearl or, at least, a rendition of mother-of-pearl. But her hair wouldn't behave. It kept pulling loose from behind her ear. Futility would mark the day. She could never willingly kill an animal. Not an animal.

The photos lay before her—some in color, some black-and-white—covering every inch of their mahogany table. The flat, cold wood under each photo seemed like the only sturdy thing left in their home, when she felt wobbly, and she thanked God for the table.

Her coffee had gone cold. A new pot brewing distracted her when it burped and wheezed but she returned to the photos of Lily. A sudden, brief wind pushed a stand of tall tiger grass outside the French door, and once again she allowed the distraction to drag her attention away from one shot of Lily as a teenager, one Meg could barely set her eyes on. The time Jay took the photo was around the same time everything turned sour for Lily.

She was wearing a cat mask, one that stopped just below her nose. The mask had bendy pipe-cleaners meant for whiskers. Lily was posing in front of the North Seattle High School theatre where the drama department was putting on their annual fall recital.

She had on a black leotard, black tights, and a short, black cashmere cardigan-and-sweater-skirt combo. The recital's theme that year was domestic pets. A ghost of frost filled the air in front of Lily's smiling lips. Meg shivered, remembering about how chilly that evening had been.

Jay had taken the picture. He'd said, "Okay, honey, start purring."

Lily laughed. Jay snapped the photo. Magic. The perfect depiction of how she wanted to remember her daughter.

When she laughed, Lily lifted her lips, like a cat baring her teeth. Jay said, "Purr-fect," after taking the shot. Meg was smiling as she revisited the moment.

Jay took the next photo after the recital. By then, Lily was crying. She'd told Meg that she was terrible, just terrible, and Meg tried to console her, recalling how she told Lily that her solo had been flawless, not one misstep in choreography, and that her voice was beautiful. But Lily was inconsolable when her drama teacher, Ewan Dorico, whisked her away for a group shot with the other performers, he'd said. As he pulled her away, Lily's hands reached out to Meg, their fingertips glancing off from each other's grip.

"Momma!" She cried. A word rarely used by Lily—one that had become more mother and mom by then. Meg's hand rose, reaching toward nothing but a dead fawn on the ground outside. If she'd only gone after her.

Things went upside-down right after for Lily with her returning home drunk graduation night but, thank God, Ewan had driven her. She'd thought back then.

Jay called out something from inside the laundry room, something about getting the laundry done, but his voice was muffled by the rolling dryer. She slammed a fist next to the cat photo. Dorico had been so understanding and the kids seemed to adore him for that. Lily had spoken highly of him, especially when he'd said, in front of the entire drama class, that her looks would take her far, but her talent even farther. He added, again in front of the whole class, that Lily had "star quality." But her praises of him stopped after the recital when darkness began simmering in Lily.

The dark moods came on fast. Meg brushed it off to hormones. Before long Lily was smoking pot, and soon after she took to snorting cocaine, all the abuses seemed to lead into an experimentation with heroin.

Meg wanted to go back to the days before Lily's darkness set in, to redo the fifteen years since, recycle them, all the way to seventeen days ago when Lily was still alive. To perfect each moment to a time when none of the bad happened. To right each wrong turn, sidestep pitfalls, and avoid people who prey on teenaged girls like Lily.

She was only thirty when she died. For Christ's sake. She cursed God for the senselessness of it all, the useless loss.

Meg rose to get a fresh cup of coffee, but her head spun. Blood seemed to drain out of her. She grappled for the chair but landed on the floor. Jay ran in from doing laundry. It was crazy that she noticed, but he held a bleached towel slung over one of his shoulders. The stark white highlighted the flecks throughout his black hair and reminded her of snow. When he bent to help her up, the towel slipped off and fluttered to the ground—a dying ghost. It settled in a heap next to her legs.

"Babe." His voice held a pathetic note that irked Meg, one that didn't match his actions. Instead of reaching to help her up, his hand wandered toward the towel. He snapped it off the ground then tossed it over his shoulder again. Moisture trimmed the base of his eyelashes, which irritated her more. Once he'd retrieved the towel, he opened his palm to Meg, but she pulled away.

She screamed for him to never touch her again.

She needed to be alone. Needed him to stop doing stupid laundry and, instead, sit with her. To try to understand the depth of her sadness. To get out. She couldn't stand to see his face.

It was the third time since Lily's death that she'd screamed at him this way. But this time, Jay acquiesced. He backed off, picked his keys off the buffet in the foyer, and set out through their large set of double doors. Jay pulled the door shut with such force the glass rattled within its hickory frame. Sure, he was angry. Meg was, too. And a mother's anger trumps a father's. Doesn't it?

But in a moment of weakness, of sudden compassion, she started to go after him. Why was she trying to hurt him? When she made her way to the door, Jay's car rumbled to life. Her hand barely grazed the doorknob, when she stopped. What would she say if she called out to him?

Come back? I'm sorry? I'll stop.

When she wasn't sorry? When she didn't know if she could stop screaming at him.

Pain burned in her gut. It burst up into her heart, spilled down her arms into her fingertips. The metal doorknob was molten to her. Meg retracted and pulled her hand away.

He would be back. Certainly, he wouldn't leave her at a time like this.

JAY

11

"For better or worse" didn't sit well with Jay. Clothes lay in heaps around the washer and dryer in dirty but separated piles. Jay's worries didn't numb by white noise droning on-and-on by clothing tumbling in the dryer. A chemical-sweet infusion of softener billowed into every inch of space the room offered. He cracked a window and sipped some coffee. He'd allowed the coffee to cool plus he hadn't sweetened it enough. He liked two teaspoons and a thimble-full of cream, enough to take any bitterness out. Why couldn't he fix it right this morning?

He pulled at his earlobe and sat on one of three stools Meg had purchased online. Each offered a bucket seat and resembled a saddle. Tacking that trimmed the leather upholstery added a cowboy feel. He pulled a white towel off the pile of clean clothes and flung it over his shoulder. The folding counter ran the length of one entire wall. He swung his legs partly under the counter and folded the towel in half, in half again, and then in thirds just the way Meg liked.

The folding counter had turned out to be a great place to think. A large window had been built into the middle of the east wall. Meg said, "to catch the sunrise." She was right. The whole room was alive with morning sun. She had made a point of telling the architect that she wanted a "wildly, sunny laundry room." Back then he wanted whatever she wanted. New love is like that. There's a certain stupidity in new love that is quelled by the years.

Familiarity breeds contempt? Not exactly the subject of marriage vows but, howdy boy, ain't it the truth. Familiarity plus a child dying breeds hostility. A dull ache churned in his gut. The growing pain kept him from crying. He hated to cry and turned his pain into anger. Everything pissed him off, lately—if the sun rose, if it set. It was easy to feel anger. To channel it. To be ticked off when birds chirped by a window, if they stopped, or when they flitted off.

"Be nice to get this laundry done!" he called from the room. He knew she could hear him with the door open. He wanted to start a fight. A big one. He hurt, too. Lily's death wasn't only hers to feel. She didn't respond, not after his rude voice broke the morning quiet. He noticed two vultures out back. It wasn't unusual for raptors out in the field. He could only see half of their bodies because from where the laundry room window was situated, a hedge along the back fence prevented him from seeing the full scene.

He huffed around the laundry room, and hauled out another load with everything from darks, whites, and in-between. This was Meg's job. She enjoyed doing laundry. When did he end up with this crap of a chore? As if it could go any lower, his mood tanked. He slammed the dryer door harder than he had intended and went at a wad of warm, crumped clothing.

Meg had been running on neutral, barely making it. Her engine had all but stopped. So, why was he trying to start something with her? With this shell of a woman he hardly recognized any longer? Her demeanor had become robotic. She moved around, speaking when spoken to. Her soul had flown out of her. Things that had brought out a sense of humanity in her before were substituted by a cold, impervious shell. But then maybe she was feeling the same surge he was—a torrent of unrelenting anger.

A breezed drifted into the room from the open window causing a current of miniature lint whirlwinds to skate across the Saltillo tile. Dryer dust made the floor look paler than usual with its natural state a burnished tone. He noticed footprints from his mocs in a tango throughout the tile. He couldn't help thinking his steps had been charted out by some schizophrenic choreographer. But the sound of something heavy falling rumbled under his stool and shook Jay out of his trance. He rose, pushed back the bundle of half-folded clothes, and rushed to the living room.

Meg was on the floor. She had fallen. She was crying.

At first, he thought she'd hurt herself, but he noticed her crying wasn't really crying at all. The sound she made was like that of a wailing cat, one being torn apart, leg-from-leg, by a pack of dogs. Her moans lasted long, trailing off until they made no sound at all lacking even a molecule of oxygen, until becoming perfectly silent. Through the whole scene, her chest still heaved in and out until she had gulped down a gallon of air, and then the crying would start all over again.

His anger evaporated, and the angel empathy shot an arrow through his heart. Meg had covered the table with photos of Lily. Lily as an infant, as a toddler. The photos charted all the stages of her life. How did she find them? He thought he'd hidden them where she couldn't. But how do you hide a bloody hunk of meat from a rabid dog?

Some photos had fallen to the floor and surrounded her feet—those beautiful feet. At once, Meg's pain was Jay's and their united pain was the only thing informing them that they were alive. And he was alive. They were both alive. They needed each other. People would call them "the survivors."

He figured their marriage had become like a set of dancing bears on a cuckoo clock. Together, in syncopation they dance through time, never allowing their grips to falter. They cling against the future.

But, right now, their shared present pain was "their life." They needed to hold fast to each other or perish. They had to hold on if they ever wanted to climb out of this present misery. And Jay wanted to climb out with Meg.

When he bent down to help her, the towel on his shoulder fell. He tried to catch it before it landed but couldn't and swiped it off the floor, then put his hand out to help her up.

"No!" she said. Her hands fisted in rage. She flailed at him to move away and, when she did, her left hand caught his cheek with her wedding ring slicing skin just under his left eye. Blood oozed out of the cut. Jay stood, shock stopping him.

She screamed at him. Cursed. Called him a bastard. Blamed him for Lily's death. Told him that it was his fault.

"Why couldn't it have been you?"

Jay stepped back. He still held his hand under his eye. He couldn't believe what he was hearing. He stood above her. And, from that vantage, he was seeing all their differences.

Her grief, an unforgiving grief, had consumed her. It had become the one thing she was holding fast to. She was giving up. She had joined the damned who feel grief without a shred of hope.

She couldn't have meant what she had said to him. "Don't say that," he said. She couldn't really want him to be dead. But she nodded.

"I do. I do." Her nod was as exaggerated as were her tears. Then she said, "If I could, I'd give you up to get her back."

He backed further away from her until the wall stopped him. In prisons, they put people like Meg on suicide watch. Calling it, "failure to thrive."

Pain rushed into his gut and coalesced with hers but for different reasons. Jay wanted to press through the pain and Meg wanted to end it. And as he stood staring down at his wife, Jay realized he was afraid Meg would take her life.

MEG

12

By evening, Meg spotted the first mouse-eared bat. It fluttered against the window moving from the bottom sill to the top as it worked through a cobweb, snatching from it a spider much the way a goldfinch will go at a moth caught in a web. Owls, hawks, snakes, and raccoons were the main predators of bats—birds that prey, they that slither, and thieves. The irony—of preying-things set upon weaker creatures, as with her daughter, didn't escape Meg.

With its belly against the pane, the bat reminded Meg of a freaked-out little mouse that had somehow gotten itself laminated inside a square of brown parchment paper causing the webbing that connected its forepaws to its hind. Four vicious fangs protruded from its jaws. The bat snagged the spider, using its tiny pair of skeleton hands to rip the spider to pieces and stuff the arachnid into its mouth.

Not unusual for sightings like this to happen around this in-between time of evening, when the sky is still light but sinking ever-close to a bruised hue, one that, if you blink, the day might troop off without you—a time when dark and light coexist so close to each other that it's impossible to fully hide. Twilight had long since left. It was a point in the evening Meg called pre-night—a sliver of time that handed off indigo skies, sorts you might find in Disney movies.

The bat thrashed against the windowpane when the last of the gawkers took their leave. After, people slipped out of the Storm residence and into their cars. She wasn't saying "goodbye" to any of them.

Meg closed her eyes and saw a vision of three men at Lily's graveside service. They were standing apart and away from everyone else. Her attention left them after Pastor Battles began his reading, after he sermonized and read scripture Meg and Jay had selected. When she glanced back to where they had been standing, all three were gone.

They hadn't shown to this, this, this—what? What do they call it? A reception? Didn't feel like a reception. It felt more like a deception. Like a con job. Like some weird astral projection. Like floating through someone else's nightmare, horrifying and hopefully, fake.

The affair took on an ugliness. Like that bat's vicious face. Meg was moving through a freakish halfway house of suspended belief—a place where the heart rejects what the mind discerns as real. And, these people, these mourners, they play a good part—acting sad, here and there. Crying on cue. But what do they really care?

At least that pig drama teacher of Lily's had the decency to stay away. What would she have said to him if he had shown up? Nothing good. She knew that she might just clock him in the jaw, even though he deserved a lower punch, and not to the gut.

She was fuming and noted how some guests had the gall to laugh as they enjoyed each other's company. This wasn't a party. How dare they? Couldn't they see the rift in her soul? Understand the hole in her stomach? Were they soulless, empty of compassion? Of empathy? How could they ever understand that the only thing holding Meg upright was a miracle of will, of muscle-memory that bid her to stand, sit, or lie down?

She was happy to see them go. She needed to be alone again. To return to the floor, a hard spot of marble by the fireplace, a solid piece of ground to support her. A place where she could return to staring at a geometry of ceiling tile, to feel the patterned of stone etched into the side of her face. She knelt on the floor and crawled over to the marble.

"I'll see you when I see you."

Meg turned to Jay's voice. It was a voice that had been so recently familiar but now sounded so distant. She didn't think she would ever be able to look him in the eyes.

He stood next to the open door. He was the only man she had known so intimately, held in bed, fought over stupid things married people fight over, angry about nothing important, cried with—happy tears and sad. Now, he was walking out. Her husband of thirty-two years, who told her in the kitchen, before people arrived, that he was getting a place of his own. Some cheap apartment in town. Said it was a monthly deal, "just in case." In case things went back to normal for them, is what he'd meant.

But how on God's green earth could things ever go back to normal? How? When the child who had grown inside her—the one she raised, who reached the age of thirty—had been ripped out of their lives? How?

Meg continued to crawl until she found her spot. She didn't care what he did. Nothing was registering. Her ears blocked his words. Jay was a cardboard cutout. She was plate glass.

She'd stuffed a vial of Lilly's Lorazepam into a planter by the fireplace. The anti-anxiety med sounded good about now. And the floor, she needed the floor. And a drink. Vodka. Then sleep. She wanted to sleep and never awaken.

Meg checked to see if he'd gone. Now, he was holding onto the doorknob. His lips were moving in slow motion over a string of indecipherable words. *Blah, blah.* Whatever he was saying, she absorbed in the thick cotton of her brain. Why was he still there? Leave if you must.

Or, was he a figment? A wraith? She watched as she stood up and walked over to him. She extended one hand and it slid inside his chest cavity. Jay looked down, then up, into her face. His eyes rolled back. He coughed. His knees gave out and he staggered back, then retreated. Her hand slid out as easily as it had slipped in. But he didn't die. He had escaped the death of her touch. She should've left her hand inside him. Then, he might have died.

The marble on her face felt good and cold. She wanted him to simply shut up and go away. If, right now, someone shot a bullet through her heart, the lead would exit her body as cleanly as before it entered.

"Did you hear me?" Jay asked.

Meg curled into a fetal position but was watching him.

Quit badgering me.

"Well, lord, Meg. Guess I'll see you around? Is that what you want me to say?" he paused then said, "I don't know how to do…this anymore."

He lifted his arms when he said "this." Shrugged his shoulders, too. He wiped at his nose, she supposed, for added emphasis. Could a father feel the same as a mother who lost her only child?

No.

Maybe.

Who knows?

She refused to take ownership of his emotions. It was already too much to think about her own.

A quick *thump, thump, thumping* drew her attention to the window again. The bat was back. It had begun to attack another insect now, another moth lured into the light by the table lamp inside the window. Its body left a gray powdery streak on the glass where the bat was chasing it into its jaws.

Her timing sucked. She had glanced away at the same moment Jay was pouring out his soul. It was bad form, worse timing but she couldn't control her eyes and looked away to watch the bat kill the moth.

The front door slammed. Jay was pissed.

Deal with it. She wasn't sure if she meant him or her.

She dragged her body upright and walked in his direction but instead ended up in the kitchen. People had stocked the refrigerator with food in every corner and in every drawer. Reception food. Villages of starving children could eat for weeks from that refrigerator. When the doors breathed open, the air inside felt like a late fall morning pouring down around her shins and ankles. Goosebumps prickled up and a chill coursed over her. A mélange of smells wafted out of the cold interior, emitting twenty different kinds of food.

Meg slid her hands along the cold glass…a casserole dish piled high with scalloped potatoes.

She heard the engine of Jay's car turn over. The rubber tires skidded loud enough to leave black marks on the driveway. They crushed along errant pieces of gravel sending some of it in a spray onto the house, some hitting the window. But his car paused for a few seconds making Meg pause what she was doing too. Then the engine revved. Again, gravel crunched under his tires then diminished down the road as he drove away.

Suddenly there was only silence. Jay was gone.

Her attention went back to inside the refrigerator. She fingered the edge of the casserole dish of potatoes. She pulled the rim to the edge—easy, fast, and hard—and let it fall. Its heaviness landed like a brick on ice. The dish shattered, splintering glass everywhere, and vomiting potatoes onto the floor. Next went a pan of meatloaf. The metal clattered against the tile, crumpled one side and sent mush and pieces of Ketchup-covered meat next to the potato casserole. Then came a cherry pie. It added color and texture to the mess.

Meg continued until she had emptied the refrigerator. She pressed the doors closed, dragged each shoe through the slop, flipped off the kitchen light, and tracked down the hall to bed, leaving a trail of muck where she walked.

SPECIAL AGENT TURNER

13

"Undercover," Lach Buchanan said, sighing through his cell phone when he spoke.

"Sounds bad, Lach," Special Agent Turner said. She had known Buchanan since before he came to live on the island. They met through a DEA Special Response Team they'd both served on when he was working for the Whatcom County Sheriff.

"You'll be lead."

"Now, it sounds good," Turner said. Another feather in her cap added to her CV. With her sights closer to DC, this job would be a good move for her.

"Peters wants you here yesterday."

She chuckled. "His same old self."

"I'm not okay with you tailing this guy. It seems…" Buchanan's voice drifted away in thought.

"Noted."

"Talk to your supervisor first and call me back. If you can't get away, you can't get away. That'll be it."

"Ten and four," she paused then said, "sugar baby."

She clicked off the phone. It was still early. Her coffee tasted sweet and hot under the cool air of her apartment. Bellingham was sitting inside a rain cloud today. The forecast expected rain tomorrow and the next day.

She loved jobs on the islands if for no other reason than its odd climate within a rain shadow, some called the "banana belt," of the archipelago. Prime real estate, there, if for no other reason than the lush cool climate and warm summers surrounded by water. She'd called San Juan Island home once, but a career had dragged her away. Living there among people with names like Lumpy and Droopy had lost its appeal well before she was eighteen. That's when she started studying for the FBI entrance exam. With top grades and no legal violations, Turner was a perfect match—a strong, young mind eager to learn law enforcement from the top echelon of government. Career was of the highest import for Turner. Each step along the way was in furtherance of getting closer to DC. She had DC in her crosshairs.

Her ambitions remained fixated on a possible directorship. Hell, she had met Jana Monroe, no less. There had been plenty of names bandied around to replace Director Mueller when he left in 2013. But Monroe, a top female agent and a former Director of a big city division FBI. She ranked high on the list to replace Mueller. If Monroe, a woman, could nab top posts, then so could Turner.

She took a fast, hot shower, threw on a pair of gunmetal gray slacks, a white dress shirt, a pair of black lace-up Doc Maartens ankle-high boots, and towel-dried her hair before biting into an apple. She grabbed her attaché and headed out the door holding the apple between her teeth. She didn't care about the rain today. Nothing could dampen her spirits.

When she arrived at the Bellingham HQ, her first stop would be to Director Dagnon's office. She was going to bypass Susan Milcott, her immediate supervisor. If Dagnon agreed to the temp post in Friday Harbor, Milcott would have no other option than to acquiesce. It might piss off Milcott but after this job, she'd be aiming at DC, making plans to exit Bellingham.

She knew Milcott would call Dagnon and say the team couldn't do without her. But Dagnon will have already agreed. It was a slam-dunk. And Dagnon liked Peters because of serving together before they both parted ways for different careers. Peters liked Turner because she was a woman. Sometimes a little T&A worked to an investigation's advantage. This was one of those times. What could go wrong?

MEG

14

It was Wednesday morning. The kind of morning that offered up one of those thick days, days that hold a mix in the air between chilly and warm—weather the islands experienced during El Niño years—when the summer sun brings on its rise a layer of humidity that would soon smother out cooler air that rises with the sun.

A male mallard flew up from the lower pond and rose, arching its path up high enough to glide over the roof. Two more females followed, heading off to the neighbor's pond, or perhaps to another lake west of there, one the geese fancied. After the ducks, a chittering of quail broke the morning silence. Meg had been watching the morning come on its gradations through the black of early morning to a cresting golden sunrise. The sky held no clouds and when the sun finally made its way high enough to peek onto land, it shattered any doubt of bad weather the previous evening's forecast had warned of. But in this slice of island, weather forecasts were more like throwing dice. Forecasts were crapshoots. You never really knew what you were going to get.

Today, she decided to box up some things of Lily's, but the job was slow-going. She had already finished boxing a few things Jay and she had given Lily and things Lily had given to them. Meg had separated items in organized piles to store, that is, until she built up the courage to either give them away or throw them out. She placed knick-knacks, cooking utensils, and some journals in stacks on the dining room table. Over the back of an upholstered wingback chair, she hung articles of Lily's clothing. And against an empty wall where she intended to hang them, Meg leaned Lily's art. She arranged the collection from Lily's happy pieces to her blue pieces, as Lily had referred to them. Lily had secured a strip of masking tape on the back of each canvas with a title. For instance, one of the blue pieces Lily had simply titled, Blue Piece #1. She liked Lily's blue pieces as much as the happy ones but for different reasons. Lily had a talent for arranging design and color in such a way a piece looked fluid, moving. And, of course, for no other reason than Lily's hands had been the ones to create the art.

One of her blue pieces depicted a woman slung off a couch with several knives stabbed into her left arm. The knives stair-cased up, deepening with each stab, and moved over the curve of her shoulder, then into her neck where all one could view was the butt of the knife.

Another piece depicted an image of a woman pulling both nostrils out as wide and large as elephant ears. And placed before the woman lay a small mountain of white powder. Tears streaked her face, showing clean stripes under a layer of mud. In that same piece, the woman had another set of arms. The arms reached out as though trying to pull the viewer into the scene.

A third painting portrayed vivid, sexual images with body parts Lily had worked to obscure. She distorted the bodies and, without studying the piece closer, a viewer received only the subliminal message of sexuality. Puzzling together the peculiar array of its shapes, the painting looked geometric and modern, and reminiscent of Picasso's style with ovals, dashes, triangles, and squares of red, cream, yellow, and green. And with an eye for texture, Lily had piled oil paint on many of her pieces like pats of butter. In places, she'd pressed the pallet knife dangerously close to the canvas, enough to pick up its primed white woven texture.

Meg peeled off her thin cotton cardigan and placed it over an armchair. The cardigan was a gift from Lily. She didn't know how her daughter could have afforded it. They had been out of touch for nearly a year when the FedEx package arrived. But Lily's hands had touched the fabric, had folded it, placed a ribbon under and tied it to the front of the sweater. She'd purchased it from a local shop in town. At some point in her day, Lily had taken time out of writing, painting, and her heroin to get Meg a gift, which meant she had to walk into town, get the gift, foot it over to the post office, press a mailing label onto the package, do the same with a return address sticker, walk up to someone behind the counter, and get the present into the mail. For Meg, the sweater felt as though Lily was hugging her.

She smoothed the cardigan flat with both hands. The white cotton waffled under her fingers over other items she had placed over the back of the same chair. But she didn't want to stop touching it and she lifted it off again to put it back on when her cell phone rang from inside her purse. She had chosen a ringtone which sounded like bleating sheep. Bleating sheep alerted her of an incoming message, not of an incoming call. Meg pulled out a tissue from her jeans, wiped her nose, and stared at the cell.

"No," she said, her voice less than a whisper.

The notification was a message from another one of Lily's overtures. They came at the worst times. The month between each of them felt like a slow drip, the way water torture must feel to a prisoner. She could never get through one in its entirety before reaching for a bottle of vodka. Meg hurried her cardigan back on and walked out of the house, powering off her cell behind, and slipping it into her purse.

Kneeling at her daughter's plot, Meg stared at the bronze nameplate. They had dug down a couple inches below the level of grass to set the metal marker, low enough for a mower to glide over. She placed a single peach rose across her daughter's name. Then Meg sat crossed-legged on top of the plot facing the marker.

The day had turned muggy with the threat of rain at the edges of the sky. The sun felt warmer. Meg pushed her sleeves up to her elbows and began to speak. She needed to tell Lily how she felt about her, from the second she lay eyes on her after she was born to the last moment they saw each other alive—six hours before Lily died—that last time they spoke. How through everything—the bad times too, Meg's love had grown stronger.

"Why did you do it?" she asked. Then, Meg turned on her cell phone and read the overture.

15

The warbled trill of a Swainson's thrush drifted down to the house from a high limb of the alder berry tree out in the backyard. With a box of tissue situated close to her right hip, Meg sat on a cushioned settee— a settee purchased a few years back when both she and Jay had tested it out in the store's garden center.

It was late-morning and if not for the covered cabana, Meg would be drenched by now. The day had brought with it a constant spitting drizzle from a system that moved in while she sat at the cemetery.

Meg held her phone away from her mouth. She could barely form a word, when Brian Battles stepped in to console after her voice cracked.

"There's nothing worse," he said, his voice sounded small through the phone's receiver.

She made a throaty noise meant to agree with him. Silence followed, then she swallowed down her tears, and spoke, "I want whoever is responsible for her death dead."

"Don't say that, Meg."

"Why not? What? Will God strike me down? I hope so. At least someone will pay for this."

"Didn't the sheriff say it was suicide?"

"I won't believe it."

"When did you talk last?"

"With Lil?" She took in a series of rapid breaths. Lil and she had spoken only hours before she died. "Oh my God. What have I done?"

"Meg. They said suicide." He paused and added, "Had she lived longer, it would have been an overdose. You know that. She was gone the first minute she started doing heroin. If that sounds harsh, well, I'm sorry but this... I'm telling you, Meg... this is not your fault."

"What if it is?"

"No. Stop."

She sniffed and wiped her nose. Battles had no clue how their last talk had gone. Meg held out hope that Lily had not committed suicide because of her.

"Then who's fault is it?" She asked.

"The drugs," he said, "she was vulnerable to them. To the dealers."

Her face cringed. "It's too much." It took a while for her to speak again but she asked, "dealers?"

"Yep. Dealers."

She said, "Then Pastor, that's who's going to pay."

PASTOR BRIAN BATTLES

16

His office smelled dusty. Battles wondered if Angie Mistofolos, the new office manager did much of anything besides answering phones, before she stepped into his office. Instantly, the dustiness of his room subsumed amid a smell of cheap cologne.

Battles angled the phone's mouthpiece away from his chafed lips. He nodded at Angie. Her eyes seemed to reflect her dull fashion sense. Were her irises brown or dark beige, like today's hair color. The outfit she wore reminded him of a style called a shift—a shapeless dress that flattered no one except perhaps Twiggy when she was eighteen. Angie was about four decades away from eighteen and about one hundred pounds away from Twiggy—in the wrong direction. Adding to Angie's dull fashion sense was a pastiness lent by the fluorescent lighting, which bleached out all color from her skin.

He bit at his lower lip and fought back the urge to roll his eyes. She'd been there two weeks and Angie hadn't yet figured out the intercom system. The intercom system, for Christ's sake. He drew in a breath and paused. He sped through a truncated version of Psalm 23 and made a mental note to explain the system to her once again when he got off the phone with the sheriff. She needed a cue to leave.

He mouthed, "Okay." He waved one hand at her for her to leave.

She nodded. And yet, there, she remained.

He mouthed, "Go."

She tipped her head as though a dog might when you say, Want a cookie? And still, there Angie stood.

"You can go," he said, full-voiced. She turned to leave but stopped when Battles said, "Not you," to the sheriff.

"Me?" She asked.

"Good lord, Angie." He covered the phone. "Go. I need to speak with the sheriff. Please shut the door when you leave." He waited for the door to close completely, then went back to his call, "Lord. This one," and responding to the sheriff's comment, said, "as a post." Then, "Hold on, Josh. Let me ask the new girl." He put his phone on hold and called out, "Angie?"

She crept into his office and pointed to her own chest. Again, she mouthed, "Me?"

"I said, 'Angie,' didn't I?"

"Yes, Pastor. What do you need?"

"Mrs. Storm?"

"Oh yeah. I forgot. She's here." Keeping her voice low, Angie asked, "What should I do with her?"

"I'll be out in a few. Have her wait in the reception hall," Battles said.

Angie blushed and nearly forgot to close his door. But she snuck her hand around the doorframe, found the knob, and pulled the door closed.

"Sorry, Josh. I swear her brain's the size of a grape. Anyway, yep. She's here. So, what's the plan?" He waited briefly, then spoke. "Like I said, vulnerable. At-risk vulnerable."

Battles' eyes bounced from the note he was scribbling on his iPad to the shelves of his library. Copies of varying Bibles filled one entire section. Another section, with a white pasted-on label, read FICTION housing books from the classics to contemporary. Same with the nonfiction section. A fine layer of dust was collecting on the shelf in front of the books. His eyes landed on a copy of The Chronicles of Narnia. One of Battles' favorites of C.S. Lewis. Battles often compared himself to Aslan, the great lion. He had the heart of Aslan. How many lost souls had he led from the fire? How many ways did he help people understand the true meaning of Christianity? With his ministry at the church, the numbers equaled a few hundred. Not to mention people from before his current congregation—the bigger ones from the Southeast U.S. to the North, and everywhere in between. He must have helped thousands of souls over the years, by now. Tens of thousands.

Battles nodded, agreeing with something Sheriff Peters had said. He hefted his legs up onto the desk. "Yep. I'll call after the seed is planted."

He swiveled his chair to reach the phone's cradle after they ended their call. Keeping his legs up he set the receiver down and crossed his arms over his belly. He was getting involved with a major community problem at a deeper level now. That was good. Battles rationalized his collusion with the sheriff. He determined his actions fit his calling, which was to save souls—those he could save—and to condemn those who defied the will of God. That small voice told him to act. So, act he would.

He glided both palms over his gut and grabbed a handful of fat on each side of his waist. He needed to get on an exercise regimen, at the very least his treadmill in the garage. He couldn't wait for golf season to resume. The gym was overpriced. He might ask that walking group of guys if they wouldn't mind him joining them on occasion. One of those guys owned the small corner store. They played golf on occasion together, and the guy sometimes attended church services, but Battles couldn't remember his name or his tithing, which meant he hadn't been tithing all that much to forget his name. He lugged his legs off the desk and rose, noting a new pain develop in his left knee. He'd have to rethink walking or golf. Maybe riding a stationary bicycle or spinning classes, which brought him back to the cost of the gym in town.

He murmured a quick prayer, stood, and grabbed his robe. The team was doing this for her benefit, the sheriff had reminded him. As pastor, he needed to be counselor and consoler today.

He was slipping his robe over his clothing as he stepped into Angie's office. "Let's talk about the phone again. After." He tipped his head toward the woman waiting in the reception hall.

Angie whispered, "Oh, okay." And gave her head at least a thousand tiny nods before he walked off.

The woman sat faced away from him on a folding chair near the kitchen pass-through window. She wore an outfit to die for—dressed to the nines, as usual. But something appeared off. Totally understandable, given all this woman had been through. She looked thinner, frail. He suspected her face would be gaunt and her eyes, sallow.

Her back was slumped into a question mark. A deflated tire. He could easily count the bones in her vertebrae through the red cashmere cardigan she wore.

As he approached, he spoke, "How are you doing, dear?" His head tipped to the right in a show of compassion. His voice mellowed to a practiced concern.

Tears immediately welled forth from Meg Storm's eyes.

"I know, dear. I know. Come this way." He'd helped scads of folks get through times like these, but the death of a child was always hardest.

He placed one arm around her shoulder as she rose to greet him. Meg caved into him. Battles pulled her into his chest. When he felt her heart beat next to his, something stirred in him.

"Angie," he called out, before entering his office. "Don't disturb us."

Then he led Meg inside, closed the door, and locked it.

THE SHERIFF

17

Peters hung up the phone feeling grimier than
when he'd taken the call. But that's how law
enforcement was. You got your knees wet and your
fingernails dirty when grub-hunting. He'd bagged
street people all the way up to residents of
McMansions. Didn't matter. When people went bad,
they went bad fast. It wasn't so much intent that
interested Peters but motivation. The why's about
their criminality—the psychology of it. He'd enjoyed
studying psychology in the required classes attending
UW-Tacoma for his criminal justice degree. They'd
studied Jeffrey Dahmer to exemplify nuances of
extreme sociopaths. He tried not to make an issue of
the damming sense of guilt he felt. He instead focused
on college courses that resonated in him, courses he
enjoyed more than others like *Addictions and Mental
Illness in the Criminal Justice System*, *Police and
Society*, and *Adult Corrections*. The addictions course
seemed particularly relevant these days, due to the
ever-growing rate of opioid users. He'd been watching
drug usage numbers eclipse prior years by the
millions, which now hung around twenty-six million
people addicted. In the U.S. alone, more than two
million were abusers with half-a-mil hooked on

heroin, specifically, not prescription drugs. The problem wasn't going away, not without extreme measures.

Peters was thinking "task-force measures." He broached the subject tenderly against standard practices to battle drugs and for a new narrative—one using less orthodox means. He often wondered what his ethics professor, Glimes, would say about his tactics. Most likely he'd repeat the adage, "the end never justifies the means." That holding two dead birds are never better than setting free a live bird. But that's how Glimes talked, in ethereal terms—in supposition but evidenced by not one iota of actual experience. The real world wanted people to act, people who stretched the limits, who tested the fuzzy edges between ethical and unethical, people who jumped through loop-holes in the law.

He rolled his chair away from his desk and in front of the window, then paused before picking up his phone. He knew people. People at the federal level who might help. People who wouldn't want anything but to sweep in and out undetected. Spooks and ICE fit well into Peters' picture of a productive task force. Of course, he'd have to contact the AG-USA. That little squirrel would require involvement but at the approval level only until they made an arrest.

FBI had a field office in Bellingham. The building was on Barkley in a weathered brownstone that appeared as part of the business next to it, a Title company. The buildings were attached to each other. Anyone who didn't know, wouldn't know the old brick building was FBI HQ in Bellingham.

Peters chuckled. The damn driveway didn't even have bladed tire barriers, better known as, *Road Sharks*. In fact, you might think of using the driveway as a decent place to turn your car around if you didn't know better. That's how nothing-much the place looked. A perfect hide sitting in clear view.

His fingertips felt cold, but his palms were sweaty. He lifted the desk phone. The receiver slipped in his hand. He cradled the phone between his ear and shoulder and wiped his hands on the front of his uniform shirt. The cotton khaki took on a darker appearance where his palms had smeared. The smears reminded him of hand paints.

He took a swig of coffee but coughed when a drip tickled his throat and went down the wrong tube. Then he poked an inner-office extension on the phone's keypad.

"Buchanan here," Detective Lach Buchanan's voice still held the sound of youth.

"It's me," Peters said. "Call her?"

"Like you asked," he said. Through the phone, Peters heard Lach breathe out and his swivel chair squeak.

"We need a cover, Lach," he said. For whatever reason, Peters sensed a need to defend his position. "She okay with it?"

"Seems to be." His answers sounded tight, short.

"Always a trooper." Then Peters added, "Stupid can call if he needs to."

Lach Buchanan smothered back a laugh. "She said she was going over Milcott and straight to," he paused, "stupid. Oh, I told her ASAP." He added, "I'm a body if you need."

"Thanks, Lach, but everyone knows you. Plus, I want to keep this one off-budget. If possible. The Feds can pay, after all. They like getting into other people's biz."

When Peters hung up, he knew it was one of many white lies he'd tell people. With his outside man on board and the inherent confidentiality that came along with him, Peters knew he could keep the operation under the wire, off books legitimately.

Denise Whitlock sat immediately outside his office. As Chief Civil Deputy, she took her job seriously. Maybe too seriously. Like a Marine, Denise was a bulldog. You throw her a bone and she'd jump a fence and dig to China to retrieve it for you.

"Whitlock!" Peters called.

He heard the worn feet of her chair scrape the floor as she pushed back from her desk. The deep tread of her sneakers slapped the floor then there she was. She opened the door wide enough to press her moony face within the opening. With her shoulders barely visible, Peter strained his eyes above the plump girth of her gut and her bulbous breasts.

"Sir?"

"Discretion is key," he said.

She looked behind her as if checking for eavesdroppers, then entered his office by sliding between the jamb and door. After entering, she pushed the door closed behind her, leaned against it and smirked.

LILY

OVERTURE TRES – February 14, 2017

18

Hey, Dad. So, when I tried it myself—H, that is—for the first time, I snorted it. Putting a needle in my arm seemed, I don't know, way extreme. And, whoa. Let me tell you, just snorting was awesome. Is this the sort of thing you wanted to know? It's weird that you asked but I guess you're trying to understand what happened to set me off down this road of addiction. If I explained the trigger—that thing that set me off (that still sets me off) in the first place, you might do something stupid and get yourself hurt. I couldn't handle that. I would kill myself if you ever got hurt because of me. Physically hurt, is what I mean. No one gets out without a goodly amount of trauma to their psyche, does one?

Okay. So back at it. I didn't throw up or anything like when I first spiked. But after that first snort, I knew I'd be hitting a vein soon. The feeling was, is, too good—like with sex. Like those identifiable pangs of pleasure just before the big moment. That sweet shivering and takeover of your system. Your mind clicks over to some Do Not Disturb setting and you can't turn back. That's when you're spiking, but with snorting you can turn back. You still have a way out— you don't want a way out, but you have one. From watching others spike, I knew their bodies hadn't denied them that sweet explosive sensation the way heroin gives when it hits your blood. I stayed tentative about using the needle for about a year—like a virgin before her wedding night. And when the wedding came, wowee, I knew I was in love with the groom and the groom would be with me forever more.

Okay, so, about the last time I used? Well, that would be this morning. A few hours ago. So, yeah. I'm high right now. We heroin addicts like our love daily. The problem with daily fixing is you run out of veins in your arms because they either get too sore or they collapse. That's a pain I never want to relive. But there are other creative options. In between the fingers and toes, behind the knee (you need a helper for those veins), the ankles, wrists. You make the most of all your veins but the best one is the arm, IMHO. It doesn't hurt nearly as much as going into leg veins. And shooting into the wrist is just wicked weird. Today's vein of choice was a vein in my hand. Right into my cat tattoo.

So, that's all the news that is the news. It's weird writing this stuff to you. But, hey. You asked, so there you go. Love you, Dad. More than you'll ever know. See you on the flippy.

PART TWO

TODAY

19

By late-morning, the sun was piercing the windows and bringing a sweltering heat into the small kitchen where they sat. Shadows from the miniblinds spilled in long stripes onto a matted area rug, then cascaded up onto a black leather couch where the sun's brilliance seemed to balance on an end table. Meg Storm couldn't help but think the sun sparkled, looking like a starry ornament that some extraterrestrial creature had placed there.

The lead guy had stopped talking to concentrate on whatever he was typing into his thick, black laptop. You could throw a laptop like that across the room, Frisbee-style, and it wouldn't bust up. His eyes flitted across the screen while he read silently what he'd just typed. When he finished, he lifted his cup to his lips and took a gulp. He cleared his voice and continued asking more questions.

"What did you learn from all of this?" He asked Meg.

"That's a strange question."

"Color me curious." There was zero humor in his face. The guy wasn't intending to screw around.

Meg smirked. *What a dick.* She knew the question went to intent, to motive, and culpability. She tipped back the last of her lukewarm coffee. The lead glanced to his assistant and gestured for him to refill her mug. She allowed the halt in action to pause with a response, watching steam rising off the coffee as it cascaded into her cup. Several drops spilled on the table when he lifted the pot to stop pouring. He used the palm of his hand to wipe the table then walked the pot back over to the coffee maker and set it onto the warmer.

"What did I learn? That's your question?" She was digging at a ragged cuticle and wouldn't look him in the eyes.

"Humor me. Like, you'll be dead tomorrow and want it off your chest."

Meg stopped digging at her nail and slipped each hand under her thighs. Then she faced him squarely and said, "A person never knows what motivates someone. You know?" He sat back. She continued, "Could be love. Could be money. Hell. It could be cheese puffs. People rarely know what motivates themselves let alone another person. But here's the thing, until you get a sense of compassion, some empathy. You know, take ownership of your heart? Well, you can't really call yourself a human being. Can you?"

"And yet," he said, letting the sentence drift off to the cloud of tension filling the room.

She looked down into her lap. With her eyelids partly closed, she said, "Compassion took a powder, slipped." She lifted her hand and extended her arm, rolling her hand, as though on a wave.

"The human being thing?"

"Like becoming a werewolf."

"And turnabout? You know, what goes around, and all? What about that?"

She grimaced, then said, "I'm waiting for a shoe to drop. Or all of them," she said, then added, "At once."

JAY

Late Spring at Lily's funeral

20

The crowd had thinned considerably after church, but people still milled around the food table, snacking, and drinking coffee. The ladies of the Women's Auxiliary kept in steady motion, racing between the reception hall and the kitchen as they picked up coffee cups, dirty plates, basically keeping the place tidy as guests messed things up.

People were beginning to filter out of Lily's funeral service by now. Jay noticed how more had attended the reception than the curbside cemetery service where Pastor Battles had given his sermon to a meager few.

Here at church, most in attendance were friends, although Jay spotted a few folks who were not. Those folks were younger. They stood huddled by near the door just outside the sanctuary doors where Church greeters stand handing out programs before service. Two of the girls wore thick, charcoal liner around their eyes. If they were going through some outdated Goth phase, the least they could do was not apply their makeup as though they'd used a crayon. Both, girls, and guys alike, wore jeans where dressier clothing would have been more appropriate. So much for parental guidance. Their clothing looked like they'd all rolled out of bed, together, in time to get to Lily's funeral. These were Lily's group. Her friends. Riff-raff. Wanting the skinny on the remains. The leftovers of Lily's life. There clustered together, most with their hands in their pockets. The tallest boy was rubbing one hand up and down the opposite arm in a series of itchy strokes. They were speaking in whispers when Jay approached them. One girl nudged the other, turned her body face-forward to her, trying to act discreet. But discreet didn't appear to be in any of their wheelhouses.

"We're tired. Is there something you want?" Jay wasn't trying to be a good host when he asked. He wasn't smiling. The thickness in his heart allowed him to be blunt. A headache was building behind his right ear and he just wanted to be alone. For everyone to get the hell out.

"No, man," the main guy looked at his group, "we're just goin'."

He gave a subtle snort, but Jay caught it. He grabbed the guy's arm, and said, "Problem, son?" He moved closer to the young man. Their chests nearly touching one another's. "What's your name?"

"Will," he said.

"How'd you know Lily?"

"Around," he said. His lip shivered before settling out of a smile.

"Something seem funny to you?"

"Hey man. We're here for Lil. Okay?"

"No. Not okay."

When Jay didn't stand down, Will said, "Come on." And they funneled out, pressing their hands deeper into their pockets.

Thankfully, they took the clue. It would have been objectionable to slug another human being inside the church. Jay considered all the variations of the word, smite, and how the boy might use it in a court of law. "He smote me!" Or, "He began smiting me!" "I didn't smite him first!"

Jay had made his way back to people piled in to give their sympathies. But Sammy startled Jay when he slipped in beside him. "I'm just right next door, Jay," he said. He grabbed him by the shoulders. Sammy was Jay's one and only neighbor friend. He moved around to face Jay, grabbed his hand to shake it, and looked him in the eyes. "Call me," he said. "I mean it. For anything."

Jay was nodding to Sammy when he locked onto a young woman who was speaking with the pastor and sheriff. It seemed the sheriff was introducing her to the pastor. They shook hands. She swiped a strand of hair behind her ear when the pastor asked her a question. Then she nodded. The woman turned to the sheriff, asked him something, then they all shot their attention to Jay who suddenly felt embarrassed, turned to the next person in the receiving line, and accepted that person's condolences.

Sam was still standing next to Jay, stopping the next person in line coming up to speak to him. He turned to face Jay. Holding his gaze locked on him, Sam said, "I don't want to say, 'this too shall pass.' Seems overdone. You know? Cruel."

Jay dropped his eyes. "Thanks, Sam."

Sam patted Jay's shoulders then headed for the door. Before he exited, he snugged his golf cap down over a growing bald spot that had become his crown. Sammy was a monk, in demeanor and appearance. He was a good man, one of his few, true friends.

Jay rubbed both hands through his cropped shag of hair. He always went through this ritual, rubbing a hand over his head around Sammy. It had become an action, he figured, as a check to see if he too had gone bald by mere association. He had wanted to go to the barber, but everything was a whirlwind with Lily, everything happening at warp speed after her death, he hadn't been able to manage to get there before the service.

A thin stream of people followed Sammy out the door. It was an after-funeral exodus like any of a dozen funeral services he'd attended, when folks segued from the pain of a surviving family, back to their lives as they had been before the funeral. Jay wanted to go home too. He wanted his old house back, where death hadn't touched them. He wanted to be back to before—with a wife who still loved him, and a daughter who was still alive. He wanted to go back before Lily's overdose.

An overdose. Bullshit.

He didn't buy it. The finality of her death still had him reeling.

"Mr. Storm?" A woman's voice asked. She had walked up behind him. "I'm so sorry for your loss." It was the woman who had been speaking with the pastor and sheriff. She was around Lily's age. Pretty like Lily, too, an elegant, almost masculine air about her with her bronze hair pulled back, no-frills style. He'd seen her before around the island but couldn't place her. Her skin was porcelain perfect. Her eyes round and inquisitive, laughing eyes, happy and bright, but today they were sad for him.

She must've sensed a lack of recognition in him when she added, "I'm Leanne. I went to high school with Lily. We were in drama together." She grabbed his hand in both of hers. She was wearing a navy-blue suit with a hemline landing just above her knees. The skirt had a short split in the back. She wore matching pumps.

"Look at you." Jay wanted to smile but couldn't. Her face glowed with the rich tan of someone who spent days running outside, who still had youthful blood coursing through her veins. Still childbearing age, he assumed.

Lily should've had children. How did he let her die?

"Thank you for coming, Leanne."

She nodded, let go of his hands, and walked to the exit. Before leaving she paused, held the door ajar, turned back as though remembering something she wanted to say, and glanced back over her shoulder. He was expecting her to return. Instead, she dropped her gaze and walked out of the church.

"How you holding up?" Pastor Battles said. He'd appeared with two cups of coffee—his and one for Jay.

"Been better."

"Expect things you would never expect. To feel. To remember. To act. It will all feel at odds with everything you've known up to now."

Jay hadn't yet taken his eyes from the door. "Just a sec, Pastor."

He handed his cup back to Battles and hurried to the door. He was about to apologize for taking off so abruptly, but Battles' attention was on Peters, who was giving him a thumbs-up, so Jay left without saying anything.

Outside, the air smelled of honeysuckle and gasoline. A stiff wind had come up from the marina and bent the shrubbery and tender trees around the entrance inland. He spotted the heel of Leanne's navy-blue shoe turning the corner down Blair Street toward the market.

"Leanne!" he called. He waited for her to respond but she didn't. She must not have heard him. He wanted to know her last name, wanted to know if someone hurt her in high school, too. He didn't want to suffer the stuffy interior of the church any longer. Someone, he didn't turn around to see who, creaked through the door behind him and let the door fall closed. Then he took off in Leanne's direction.

The chill in the air was undeniable. Cold stripped away all inner heat that had built in him during the service. His face went moist melting in a cold sweat. Wiping the tip of his nose, he searched in his left coat pocket for the handkerchief he'd remembered to bring. Just in case.

He blotted his face after, again, wiping his nose then took off in a sprint stopping at the end of the road, at the corner of Blair and Spring. That's when he saw the hem of her navy-blue skirt flit up to the rhythm of her gait, where he noticed the curve of her tanned calf just as she stepped out of view. She had turned left on Caines, heading for Argyle Street.

"Leanne," he called once more, but this time not loud enough for anyone to hear. It was as if the breeze had spoken her name, the trees rustling in such a way simply for the sake of hearing their windy voices speak. Certainly not loud enough for someone a block ahead of him to hear. He sprinted after her but reached the end of the sidewalk when she was pulling her leg into her car, a small yellow Mini Cooper with black-and-yellow-checked side mirrors. Before he took one step in her direction, the engine thundered to life and the car pulled away from the curb.

Then, she was gone.

He repeated her name, there alone on the street, right as Meg rushed up behind him. Had she been following him? Guilt painted his cheeks red. A rush of heat spilled out of his neck and down his body over his shoulders, back, and chest.

Had Meg heard him calling for Leanne?

"Jay, what are you doing?" She asked and glanced down the road. Then Meg slid both arms around his waist. She lay her head on his shoulder. "Are you okay?"

Up to now, they had spent their days like all the rest, with Jay reading the morning paper, working out, golfing, coming home, eating, and sleeping. Up to now. Now was the absence of time. There was no before that mattered. Certainly, no after. His baby was dead. What marriage could withstand the death of a child? The inevitable next main event would most likely be one of their deaths. He knew these morose thoughts grew from a deepening depression and grief.

A surge of anger swept over him. He peeled Meg's arms off.

"Why do you care. We're living separate lives now." He knew the words sounded cruel, so he stopped. "Look, I'm going to the course." He avoided her eyes.

"You don't think we should be together today? Today of all days?"

"I want to be alone."

Meg reacted as he guessed she would—eyes squinting, turning away from him, trying to puzzle pieces together in an orderly fashion. She was so predictable.

He'd watched as she'd planned everything—from the casket to the scented tea. She appeared determined, competent even, arranging for party favors. Party favors. For her daughter's funeral reception? Miniature books for people to write in about Lily and either keep or leave with Meg. She could handle the reception they'd be having at the house in a few hours without him. He refused to let her drown him.

Up to now, their Sunday mornings were slated for Meg and him, waiting for the infrequent call from Lily. Maybe he'd scratch Meg's back. Maybe they would make love.

But now? He couldn't imagine touching her, he couldn't imagine making love to her. She'd become wild and venomous toward him. Someone he didn't recognize anymore. So, an act as exquisite and tender as lovemaking, his desire for her molted from him like snake skin, falling off into an abyss.

Questions still vexed him. Why was she naked? They'd told Meg and him they found Lily naked. Three stoned guys were there, too, but they hadn't told him who. Said, they were passed out—one on the bed with Lily, one slung across an upholstered chair in the same room, and another guy on the floor. Initially, they thought the guy on the floor was dead. And when they rushed him, his eyes opened as though he'd come out of a long nap. He pointed to the bed. Why did he point to the bed if he didn't know she was dead? He pointed as if to say, "Up there. The girl. She's the goner. Not me."

Someone had complained about a neighbor's dog—about the dog's incessant yapping provoking her to call the police. The caller, a woman of questionable means, called to complain about the dog. But when they learned who she was, the dispatcher shrugged her off as just another one of his looney calls. Still, later when detectives and deputies began filing in to work the next morning, he told them. Just to follow-up, they went to her house and she pointed them to where they found Lily.

Jay wondered if the woman had called when Lily was dying. Maybe the dog barking was a coincidence. When they checked the time of the call to the estimated time of Lily's death, the times matched up. Why did the dog bark? What did it hear that disturbed it to the point of making a nuisance out of itself? They knew the dispatcher had made a mistake when he didn't act, because the woman was an assumed drug dealer.

Part of Jay wished Buchanan had kept the information to himself. So many questions circled her death, but he kept coming back to that one detail about their baby's naked body with three men lurking around her. What was wrong with him? Why couldn't he stop thinking of that? Who was the woman with the dog? Did the dog pick up the scent of a dead body or did it hear something? Why was she naked? Why weren't those three men dead, too? Why only Lily? Again, why was she naked?

"Jay?" Meg said.

But he didn't respond. He was planets away.

Meg had blamed the drugs and the dealers. It was their fault, by his wife's account. She had "never been surer," she'd said, which amazed Jay. He never felt more unsure about anything in his life. But now he felt like he had something to grab hold of.

He turned to leave. "I have to go."

"Jay," she said, objecting.

"No," he said, lifting both palms in defense. "Don't. I need to get out of here. Ask Sherrie to take you home. I'm leaving." Her expression sentenced him. He placed his hands over her eyes. When she flinched away, he pulled her back by the shoulders, planted an obligatory kiss on her forehead, then brushed past, and walked back toward the church. If leaving was a problem Meg would be ranting by now.

A fat cloud scudded overhead. The wind carrying it cooled the nape of his neck. He didn't notice if it was a turtle-shape or a shark. Nothing had shape anymore. The cloud acted merely as a prop, one to set the coming lonely scene, one he happened to spot a second before jumping into a trot. By the time he reached his car, he was panting. Tears chilled his cheeks.

Golf would be a welcome friend. And he needed a friend.

As he closed the door to his car, he whispered, "Leanne."

MEG

Early Summer, June 1, 2017

21

Although she was not quite a widow, Meg related more closely now with them since Jay left. She had begun to sit on the same pew as a few other widows.

Few parents in the congregation had lost children. Those who had, didn't know her all that well, nor she them—an added qualifying factor allowing her to continue to sit with the widows. She had sat with these women on and off for years now but since Lily died, they allowed her a spot with no reservations.

Meg wore a scarf adorned with a white watercolor floral pattern. She worked at securing it by wrapping it in a coil around her neck. Her hair began to dampen under the scarf and she worried she was about to have a hot flash. She hated hot flashes. Fanning herself was a give-away to anyone of the same age, women and men alike. Still, she uncoiled the scarf, letting it fall loosely in front of her outfit.

The air inside the church helped soothe the flash. The church was usually cool. The stained-glass windows didn't keep out the weather, and the high ceilings made it difficult to heat.

She never understood why someone didn't turn on the heat as soon as they showed up. She'd seen it herself. The new girl, Angie, would come in, go to her office, and brush her hair. It was odd that she brushed her hair in her office when the bathroom was only a few feet farther down the hall. Not until fifteen minutes before service, when people were already gathering, did she turn on the heat.

Meg slipped her jacket around her shoulders and, curiously, the act made her body shiver.

"It's cold in here," she said to Sheila.

Sheila and a handful of the other widows were close friends with Meg. They often referred to each other as family even. Jay would sit with them as well, but not today. He hadn't for a while, not since he had left and gotten his own place.

She sometimes worried how odd it looked, her sitting there with Jay and five widows. Jay was the token man in the pew, but he hadn't been to church since Lily's funeral. He hadn't attended since he'd left her. He'd taken only a few things with him—essentials, he'd said—his shaving kit, and a pair of tennis shoes and dress shoes. He took some memorabilia—an old photo album full of pictures of his father in service utilities at boot camp, and of himself from Desert Storm. He took the Mauser S/42 Luger his grandfather left him, the one he'd taken off a Nazi in World War II. So his father told the story.

Jay took his father's old Brownie—the camera that flipped images upside-down when you looked down into it. He took a few shirts, some pants, and his shampoo. Things like that.

"Maybe you'll want me back," he'd said.

Meg enjoyed the quiet brought by living alone and was taking the time as a respite. They hadn't discussed divorce but they both knew they each needed to be without the other, for a while, at least.

She thought he would return on his own, without an invitation. Thought that he'd saunter back through the door as if nothing had separated them, like returning home from golf. That he would've changed. That he would hurt like Meg hurt—that they'd have something in common again, they'd become more understanding about their feelings after the loss of their child. The one someone killed. Gave her heroin for God's sake. How? How had everything turned to dust? The second Lily died, each corner of her life fragmented. Light became dark. Red, black. Happy, glum.

The sanctuary door swung open behind the pews and creaked. Meg involuntarily turned, hoping to see Jay to walk in. But it was someone's baby—a four-year-old. She had dark bouncy hair and was wearing sparkly shoes, a pink chiffon dress, and a sparkly hairband that matched her shoes. Pickle, or something like that—a condiment name. Olive! That was her name. Olive. The prettiest little thing this side of the Cascades. Still, Meg didn't smile. She only watched as little Olive ran up the aisle. She dashed into the pew ahead of the widows, sidled up to her mother and father—a dusky blond. Olive took after her mom.

Pastor Battles was droning on when Meg's attention fell elsewhere—somewhere outside the holy walls of United in Christ Church. Blah, blah. But it wasn't the message or the messenger. Her attention was flagging because her commitment to the Word was flagging. She had begun to question God. Didn't trust Him anymore. Anger burned through every pore, every follicle in her skin. She swiped her forearm and hadn't realized she'd started perspiring. Was she sitting under a sunbeam? How could her internal temperature soar from freezing to hot in seconds? She fluttered the hem of her blouse to get some air onto her skin.

It was three weeks ago, Saturday, in this very church, in the reception hall outside the sanctuary, where they had held Lily's funeral. The flowers had smelled like decaying honey. Attendance was slim. People tended to stay away from tragedies like children who overdose, unless the tragedy happens to them. Only three lined pages of the small guestbook had names written in. The catered food arrived lukewarm and tasted like sawdust. The coffee was weak. She needed a drink—a Screwdriver. Why hadn't someone thought to bring vodka and OJ? There weren't enough tissues. The one right move was foregoing mascara and wearing only lipstick. And she was right. She would've cried away any hint of eye makeup.

"Are you hot?" she asked Sheila.

Sheila patted her hand but was trying to focus on what Battles was saying.

Lily lay there in a white casket—Meg's porcelain doll encased in a shadow box. The horrors of the funeral filtered through her mind, blocking out whatever Battles was sermonizing about when someone distracted her. Meg turned. It was Jeri. She was crying about something.

"Jesus, Jeri," she whispered. Meg spent her days in cruise control. No synapses were firing correctly. Tact and diplomacy were nonexistent.

Directly in front of them, Samantha stood. Meg's eyes darted when Samantha turned to face her. How forlorn she appeared. How tender. How fake. Then she was saying Meg's name and asking for prayers now.

"We're so happy she's here with us today, Brian, especially after, well, what she's been through. A prayer of thanksgiving to lift Meg Storm up to the Lord."

Brian nodded, raised his arms, and led everyone in saying, "Lord, hear our prayer."

Did Meg roll her eyes just then?

The pig. What had he tried with her? Had she overreacted, or did he become aroused the day she went in for his help? Then her lame excuse—saying her stomach felt off, like she might have an accident—and running out of the church. And instead of feeling blessed she felt embarrassed, ridiculous. Damned. Her legs went numb. Her heart began to race. She fluttered her blouse with more furor and blew air against her chest and stomach.

My palms are damp.

Meg lowered her eyes. She'd clenched her knuckles tight enough to make them white from lack of circulation, each nailbed blanched under the pressure she exerted clutching the Bible on her lap. Someone touched Meg's shoulder, startling her, and making her jump. It was Sheila, sitting right next to her. She grabbed Meg's arm and squeezed. Did she do it to stop Meg from falling apart or simply to let her know she was there for support?

Meg's face tightened. She cringed. She tried to fight away the sharp, dull pain stabbing her behind the eyes. She flinched and grabbed the side of her head. A pain like an icepick drove through her temple. It coursed across her brow, from her right ear into her left. Her sinuses thickened. And her throat tightened. She couldn't breathe. A vise grip had squeezed off any air out of her lungs.

As suddenly as her pain came on the parishioners moved on to a new prayer, someone else's prayer—a person needing a job. She was asking if we would all, lift her up to the Lord?

A job? A job!

Compared to a dead daughter? How could they move on?

Next, some strange woman's cat was ill, and she needed prayers for its healing.

Dear God, help me.

She began fiddling in her seat. The temperature had to be nearing ninety-five in there. Had someone turned on the gas stove in the back?

Someone was pulling her up and saying, "Peace be with you."

Crap. The passing of peace. When did time skip forward?

There were throngs at the end of the pew. All there to give her condolences and to offer a blessing of peace. Meg wanted to scream. Any peace she ever felt had been drowned by a roiling sea of rage complete with needles and syringes, drug dealers and police officers, undertakers, with a funeral on top. Turmoil moved in when peace was evicted.

Was He a good God, or was all this heartache and suffering His fault? If He made us in His likeness, then we have His traits. Does that mean that God is careless, cruel, and evil?

Meg used to hate when people questioned God's character. But now? Well, now… she understood how the great Almighty might be confused with a less than kind god.

Why couldn't it have been someone else's daughter?

Sitting there was crushing Meg when her body took over. People had returned to their seats after passing of peace. She heaved up, using the back of the pew in front of her as an anchor. She now only needed to get to the end of the pew. Maybe make it eight steps and she was free. Sheila and Sandy leaned back and shifted their legs in the direction Meg was heading as she slipped out of the pew.

Her lips pressed into a tight line and she darted toward the kitchen—a shortcut to the bathroom. But in the kitchen, the church's resident bag lady, Maizy, was slurping down a cup of coffee and emptying a plate of cookies, cookies meant for everyone who attended the after-service social hour. Meg couldn't tell what she felt. Whatever it was, fell somewhere between loathing and pity.

The woman looked up at Meg.

Busted, thief.

Crumbs speckled her moist, painted lips. Meg had surprised her, but the lady showed little guilt of committing one of the ten commandments while in church. She certainly didn't offer Meg any condolences.

Heathen.

Instead, the lady squinted. Meg took it as a dare, and she froze.

One of the woman's eyes protruded larger than the other. Had she applied her makeup in a sweeping wind? Her lips pinched into a ragged, closed circle.

Witch.

Yet, as quickly as she'd glanced up, the woman returned to her plate of cookies. Meg took the opportunity as a chance to slip by her where she rushed into the restroom.

Thank God.

No one else was in there. She checked for feet under the door of each toilet stall. She was alone. Meg locked herself inside the bathroom and slipped inside one of the stalls where she crumpled onto the toilet. Within seconds someone else was jiggling the handle. Then they were pounding.

Let them pound.

"Hold on," she called out. Her voice quivered.

She pulled herself up using a long metal bar on the wall and exited the stall. She checked the pleat in her pants, walked to the door, and flipped open the lock. Two young girls flew past her, giggling. They couldn't have been older than eight or ten. In fact, they might have looked like Lily when she was their age. One raced to the sink, used her foot to hook the plastic step-stool below the open pipes of the plumbing, and climbed upon it to reach the sink where she washed her hands. When she finished, she hopped down from the stool, and wiped her hands on her skirt leaving a water spot in the front of her yellow cotton dress. After realizing her error, she spun out a few sheets of paper towels and dabbed at the blot, but her friend came out of the toilet and they both dashed out the door again. The girl in the yellow dress dropped the wad of paper towels on the floor before exiting.

It was raining again when Meg got inside her car. She had forgotten about the girls in the bathroom and, instead, was thinking about the bag lady. Her snarl. Her odd eyes. The woman's black hair streaked with a thick band of white lining her part and dandruff chipping off from her scalp in flakes. The cookies she hunkered over. The woman's wet, red lips.

Meg threw her car into drive and got out of the church parking lot, never feeling further from God or Jesus or His church or any of that religious mumbo-jumbo than she did right then and there. What had He done for her anyway but rip apart her family?

Jay figured it out a while back. "What was the point?" He'd asked.

Meg knew it would be a long time coming if she ever returned. She turned the car away from the building to head home. And although a pang of guilt hit her heart, she whispered, "Screw it."

LILY

OVERTURE QUATRO – March 6, 2017

22

You never know who's a cop and who's not. That's Wes's latest wisdom. He's been edgy lately. I try to calm him down. He's almost as yummy as H and, trust me, he'd agree that nothing or no one comes close to being as yummy as H.

Wes says anyone in a city could be a cop, but not here on the island. Everyone knows everyone else, especially we of a certain element. And our element has its finger on the who's who of law enforcement on the island, if for no other reason than for how small the place is.

I remember thinking how, after high school, I was going to move off the rock because everyone was in everyone else's beeswax. Apparently, I didn't follow through on that promise either, Mom.

Remember how you told me you wouldn't fund my leaving, said, "I'd get into bigger trouble in a bigger town." 'Cause folks, that's how much she trusted me. Bitch. Sorry, Mom, but maybe I could've gotten straight in a place where there were more opportunities. Did you think about that or was your knee-jerk reaction first to doubt me? Like, you knew what was better for me. Right. Maybe if you'd helped me again, I would have made it. Don't think you can boast my successes as yours and not be somehow complicit in my failures. One doesn't come without the other.

That's what the therapist told me. She's right. And, she noted, that first-time tries often become successes but only after a few tries. That you needed a solid support team in place to get through all the failures. Where was my support team, Ma? It's not only my fault that I turned out to be such a prize and your biggest embarrassment. Please.

Oh, screw it.

Anyway, Wes went on about the cops, saying, "On our Podunk island, the cops sometimes employ CIs—confidential informants."

"It seems so Law & Order," I said. I laughed when told me about the CIs. What a mistake. Wes and Lee both jumped on my case, screaming at me, telling me how stupid I was. Randy didn't say anything. He just kept out of the crossfire, but I could see he wasn't pleased either. I tried to explain the Law & Order thing, but no one would listen.

Here's Lee's wisdom on the matter: "Junkie's gotta know is: watch your back, your front, and your kit."

MEG

23

"Look at you. You're a mess." Meg's mouth constricted in disapproval. There Lily stood. Sure, she was an only child—one she raised in a loving home, a home environment offering good values. There she stood, wiping her nose, rubbing her arms, and twitching for her next fix.

"Please, Mom. It's the last time. After, I'll go to DSHS for help. They'll get me into a program." She paused, then said, "You can take me. I promise. I'll go."

She hadn't allowed her daughter to come inside the house, since they had kicked her out years before when she admitted to using. But they knew about Lily's using before that, saw the signs. A mother knows things about her own daughter. And yet, it's funny how denial will blind the critical eye of parents.

Still, for some odd reason, today was different. She'd lost more weight than when she last saw Lily. She couldn't have weighed much more than one hundred pounds now. Her skin had a gray tinge to it. Her sunken eyes made Meg sick.

Lily shifted from one foot to the other, tapping a toe with each sway side-to-side. Her clothes were stained, her sweatpants frayed along the hem in back.

She smelled like pot. For a top, she'd decided on a sloppy tee-shirt that said, SERVICE HUMAN, PLEASE DON'T ENGAGE ME.

Great choice, Lil.

"You're disgusting," Meg said to her daughter and started to shut the door, but Lily's hand grabbed it before it closed. Her chipped nails were grimy and caked with something brown. A series of purple veins covered the thin skin of her knuckles.

"Mom. Please."

Meg wanted to howl, to reprimand her thirty-year-old daughter for bad decisions, for bad, stupid decisions. "How could you end up like this? After, the way we raised you?" She paused. Regained her composure and spoke sternly, "No, Lily. Not this time. It's got to stop."

She peeled her daughter's fingers from the door's edge. Each dirty finger she touched caused Meg's emotions to boil, to bubble over, to feel disgust. When she removed Lily's hand, Meg closed the door, and leaned against it on the inside.

Lily started to cry but then began screaming. Calling Meg names, saying things for everyone in the neighborhood to hear.

"It's your fault! You did this to me!"

Meg ran to a faraway spot in their home. She ducked into the pantry closet where she closed herself off from the rest of the house, where she hunkered against a cupboard and covered her ears.

She couldn't listen—wouldn't listen. Not this time. Not after seeing Lily in this state.

Meg wouldn't allow herself to fall for it, not again. This time marked the end of their relationship unless Lily cleaned herself up. If she chose not to get clean, then she refused to see Lily ever again.

SHERIFF PETERS

24

The room reeked of burnt coffee. Paper cups from the six members of the *Joint Border Drug Trafficking Task Force* sat on top of the office table where each member had convened in Sheriff Peters' office. They all stood around the table for the meeting.

Sun broke into the window but a layer of fat clouds sprinting across a late morning sky snuffed it out. Rain shimmered off the concrete sidewalk outside the courthouse building. The rain darkened the pavement to deeper black hue on the road down Court Street. Peters touched his cell phone. It was acting up. RockIsland, the local internet business, sat directly across the street, two minutes from his office. But would he make the trip to see what the computer people could do for him? Probably not.

"Look alive," Turner whispered. She stood next to Peters when she saw his attention lag.

On the other side of Peters stood an agent from U.S. Border Patrol. He was second-in-charge. His U.S. Marine Corps chop job showed flecks of blond and ginger running throughout his hair. Peters noticed the USBP's pink scalp his hair was so short. Chop Job leaned on a hip-high, wooden pointer as though it were a golf club. Peters tried not to stare at Chop Job's hair when the Assistant U.S. Attorney started in.

"Thank you all for coming," he said. His voice reverberated in the confines of the meeting room. "This is serious business. Showing up in a place like this means these bad hombres will try anything," the A-USA said.

Peters figured him to be a drill sergeant at some point in his life. Peters didn't appreciate the insinuation "a place like this" or the hombre comment. The A-USA, the USBP, DEA, and ICE agents stood to the left of Peters. Rounding out the "team" was FBI Special Agent Turner from the Bureau's Bellingham satellite office. She stood closer and to the right of Peters. Turner and Peters had been on the problem since its inception—since Peters realized the bigness of the issue a few years back. Since he called Bellingham FBI for guidance, Turner had been coming up on occasion to assist.

Island law enforcement didn't much like hosting outside authorities. Peters rarely called other agencies in, but sometimes an extra eye was a good thing. Plus, the anonymity Turner brought, helped. Turner was an unknown. But the problem with bureaucracy was that it brought with it a straggled chain of command that Peters deplored. Not only that but the FBI, ICE, ATF, even the A-USA's office were over capacity with misogynistic idiots like Chop Job.

"We have intel that Zambada's planning a move. Not sure if it's a drop or something else. Or, why he's making the trip but he's planning his holiday in your neck of the woods." He looked at Peters. Then said,

"Through B.C., Puget Sound, and down, or via the western states and up. We know he left Sinaloa, but eyes lost him at one particularly sketchy pick-up point near the border in a bitch of the desert." He paused nodded to Turner, and said, "Sorry ma'am." Then continued, "So we don't know how he's traveling—by land, sea, or air. Air would be bold. Sea, obscure. He's likely visiting San Juan Island with a stop from B.C. or Seattle.

"Land travel would make a safer route but Zambada's spoiled and doesn't enjoy the long, arduous trip. He's all about comfort so, if by land, he's gonna arrive cranky. And that means dangerous. My guess is sea. Air is too ballsy. But eyes are on all avenues.

"We reinforced manpower. Dragged men from lower-risk ports." Now, he used his pointer for something other than a prop. "In Seattle, here." He tapped the pointer to the map. "Brought in some on-call reservists. A couple of weeks is all we can give the reservist. Most reservists have day jobs. This is dangerous work, men, ma'am." He nodded again to Turner. "And they're some good men, people." He paused dropped the pointer between his legs and stood at attention while he looked at Special Agent Turner. She nodded her unspoken forgiveness about the slights in gender, so, he continued, "Representatives'll be covering all shifts. Dogs, too. If he has product in tow, the dogs will prove an invaluable asset." On the map of Washington State, he tapped the wooden pointer at four red thumbtacks, each marked points of entry into the state. "Here, here, here, and here." He pointed, calling off four stations in the Blaine Sector which included Blaine, Sumas, Bellingham, and Port Angeles stations. "'Course, that doesn't account for ferry traffic." He set the pointer on the ledge of the stand and stood back at ease, hands crossed in front of the fly of his pants.

Next, Special Agent Turner chimed in, "We have undercovers for Sidney travel to and from, plus the airport." She rubbed a polished pink nail under her nose. "Fifteen new people, total. Three at the airport, the others on a perpetual ferry ride."

The men chuckled at Turner's comment. Then the ICE agent laid out his plan, which was to supplement CBP.

DEA followed up. Watters was his name. "Look, folks," he said, "Zambada is sneaky. Trained by El Mayo himself. Mayo's prodigy, Zambada knows the terrain. Knows players. Lays low. Usually has a lackey, or few of them, doubling for him. That's probably how you lost eyes on him. Am I right?"

"A fake double, yes sir," Chop Job said.

"What's troubling?" Watters went on, "This place. It's an up-and-comer territory for Zambada which means it's his new baby. He's sees potential here. I consider the problem, here, here on this island moving from code yellow to orange. We need to stop this criminal in his tracks, or sink. No question. This crap is killing our children. And you all know Secretary Sessions and the President made the opioid issue top priority." He stopped talking, which allowed every member of the task force to take in the volume of the problem. Watters crossed his thick arms in front of him. His white dress shirt couldn't hide his dark skin. He looked like a football player, a front guard. His wide nose, cheeks, and forehead gleamed with oil. He puckered his lips and nodded, a signal to everyone he had finished with his segment.

Peters fumed. He knew how bad the drug problem was on the island. Hell, he'd been asking for help for years but only got it now because of this Zambada – Most Wanted character. Several children, island children he'd known, had died from this crap. Some had been put in jail for it. The hair on his neck stiffened at their slow response to a problem that had been brewing for years. Peters had had zero luck getting these mahouts to act before Zambada entered the picture. But the fact was this: having the feds show up was a feather in the island's cap. Bodies were bodies. He wasn't going to let snubbing his previous requests get to him. Right now, Peters needed the added weight.

"Okay, then." The A-USA clapped his hands. "We know what we have to do. Let's get busy."

Agent Turner glanced sideways at Peters, who hadn't spoken through the whole thing. She grabbed his hand and gave him one firm shake downward. "Sheriff," she said.

"Turner," he responded.

Peters didn't like the A-USA. He was short and pushy. Smart, though, and had a good sixth sense when it came to people—a sense that says you either trust them or you don't. The A-USA waited for her with one hand on the knob holding Peters' door ajar. FBI Agent Turner passed between the door and the A-

128

USA. She slipped on an official FBI cap and walked out, leaving Peters and the A-USA in the room alone momentarily. The men nodded to one another and the A-USA walked out, following after Turner.

ZAMBADA

25

Benito, Ismael's driver, swung the armored car through a set of enormous automated, metal sliding doors that started to open when Ismael's car began its approach. Daylight lit the warehouse interior from a single row of hazy, rectangular windows set so high on the walls that even drones couldn't catch images of the goings-on inside the warehouse. Additional light came in through eight massive, translucent skylights centered thirty feet overhead, at the pitch of the roof.

It was hotter than hell in Sinaloa, but the car's air conditioner made the drive comfortable in the backseat where Ismael "El Mayo" Zambada rode checking his cell phone. With his flight out of Mexico delayed, he reorganized his plans for the next thirty minutes. Of course, he had to do this one thing before travelling but then he had enough time to top the grueling task awaiting him with something wonderful.

A fresh coat of shellac on the cement caused the car's tires to squeal when Benito turned the steering wheel. He pulled up in front of another set of interior doors and parked. Zambada pocketed his cell and slid down the window between him and the driver.

"Dame el arma," Zambada ordered. Benito slipped El Mayo the Uzi through the window's aperture. "Gracias."

The driver unlocked the doors and jumped out to open the passenger area for his boss, who didn't thank Benito but kept his mind on the weapon. He removed the clip, checked the bullets, then returned the clip back into the butt of the handle. A faint chemical odor wafted through the cavernous warehouse.

Benito skipped ahead of Zambada, rapped his knuckles twice on the door, he flung the door open, allowing Zambada entry to the office. Then, Benito closed the door behind Zambada, who walked between sheets of plastic. Each sheet hung from the ceiling inside the door and along the perimeter of the small room. Everything was in place.

Pietro, one of Zambada's henchmen, stood behind the infiltrator, Joaquin, a Sinoloan and the father of his own granddaughter. Pietro had secured Joaquin to a metal chair where he'd wrapped duct tape around his wrists and ankles, and covered the man's mouth with tape, as well. Today, Joaquin wore a loose orange and yellow Hawaiian shirt, jeans, and open-weave shoes with no socks. Zambada never understood his son-in-law's choice in fashion but then, Zambada was old school. He liked a military look.

Plastic sheeting covered a single window and was laid over the floor. Pietro had also draped sheets of plastic over the chair where he'd tied up Joaquin.

Pietro wore a clean-suit. His goggles sat on top of his headcover. He wore a surgical mask hung at his chin, so he could speak. Pietro handed Ismael another clean-suit to zip up over his shoes, clothing, and head. Zambada slipped on a surgical mask and goggles over his eyes. He ticked up his chin to Pietro, who slipped on his surgical mask. Then he ripped the tape off the young man's mouth.

As soon as he could speak, he was stating his case. "El Mayo." He paused, and said, "Papa, you're wrong. I'm not informing on you. Think of Juaquita. I love her. Think of Miriam. She's the love my life, Papa!"

"Quiete!" Zambada yelled. He ticked his head at Pietro, who wheeled over a set of varying sizes of scalpels on a surgical tray.

"No, Ismael. Come on," Joaquin begged. Zambada had included Joaquin on more than one tongue removal of people he learned who had informed on him. He did, as a deterrent for his employees, to keep them from talking to the wrong people.

"I said, quiete!" Zambada needed to get going. He didn't have time to play with his idiot of a son-in-law.

Pietro lifted an inch-long blade and handed it to Zambada. Pietro yanked back Joaquin's head who was now openly weeping, begging even. What an embarrassment. And, instead of slicing open a cheek to cut out his tongue, Zambada ran the blade lengthwise along his jugular. Joaquin's eyes flared. He pulled against the restraining tape until he could no longer fight. Blood burbled rhythmically out of his neck, painting his Hawaiian shirt deep red. Blood drained down his chest to his waist, and onto the front of his denims.

"I gotta go," Zambada said. He handed the blade back to Pietro, bent down to the man and spoke to him face-to-face. "Joaquin, esta estupido hombre." He handed a gun to Pietro. "Terminas. Dump his body in Tijuana. A little gift for Border Patrol." He stopped before leaving and said, "Make it look like an accident." One side of his mouth curled into a sneer.

Zambada slipped off his surgical gloves and clean-suit, letting them drop onto the plastic-covered floor. Then, he exited the door between the curtains of plastic. Benito was standing at attention next to the car. A blast from the room let Zambada know Pietro had finished Joaquin off.

"Benito, enciendo el auto. Tendre me puerta." As he ordered, Benito jumped behind the wheel. Zambada opened his own door. He needed to leave. He needed to get to the U.S. to fix a problem that was brewing up north.

Zambada retrieved his wallet from his back pocket. He shuffled through one of several U.S. forms of ID. He found a Washington State two driver's licenses and five US-issue social security cards.

His attaché case sat in the back. "Vamos," he ordered Benito. Inside a hidden base of the briefcase, he withdrew several passports and found the blue one with a gold eagle emblem and lettering. He checked the name, Israel Guerrero, stuffed the other driver's license inside, and placed the passport into his wallet. He stretched one leg to get the wallet back into his back pocket.

"Benito. Stop at Lalle's."

He needed to work off a little steam and Lalle knew how to calm him. He poked her number into the cell, "Lalle, bebe. I have five minutes. Nah. 'At's all. Cinco. Te amo, mi azucar." He ended the call, shoved a piece of gum into his mouth, and checked his hands for blood spatter.

26

The old woman, Mrs. Izzy Adaba, struggled out of her seat after telling others in first class, with a shaky voice—for the entire trip, that one of her sons had purchased her ticket so she might see her grandchildren in Seattle, "One last time," as she put it. After a spell in Seattle, they were planning a short trip to the islands to see the Pig War Museum. She chuckled at the name and asked the young woman seated next to her if she'd ever heard, in her life, of such a museum. She pondered aloud, after leaving Sky Harbor International Airport on route to SeaTac, if the pigs actually took up arms and fought one another—if it was a war of pigs. She laughed at her own words, while a young woman in the seat to Izzy quailed and angled her legs toward the aisle, away from her.

The young gal opened her laptop and told Izzy she had to work or else get fired. Izzy told her she had the prettiest lips. That once upon a time Izzy herself had lips like that. She also advised her to take lots of vitamins, and lots of photos to preserve the memories of her youth.

She had a figure, too, Izzy told the younger woman. "Hourglass," she said, like those girls in the WWII posters, saying she could have been a pin-up girl herself, had she not met her husband and had children—all boys! Five glorious boys. "But now," she said, "she had lips like worms and hands like a ditch digger. Just look at 'em," she said, as she held up her hands, each finger painted a sherbet orange. Izzy giggled. "They're mitts! Look like a man's now." She shook her head. "No amount of lotion can turn back these hands of time," she said. Then elbowed the gal. "Get it?" she asked, "Hands of time?" And laughed again at her joke.

Izzy had flown in from Phoenix. It was too hot there this time of year and, at the beginning of summer, she was already sweltering under that oppressive sun, as she put it. Izzy, like many old people living in the Southwest, was Hispanic—a transplant from elsewhere. Her sons and she were U.S. born citizens but not her husband who—God rest his soul—died in a car accident, nine years before. He was only sixty-nine. "Just a young man still," she said, and dabbed a tear from the corner of her eye. Izzy tried to exchange niceties with other passengers, but no one seemed to want to talk with her.

She wore a scarf around her neck, a chiffon peacock scarf emblazoned with the orange that matched her nails, and with pinks like the pillbox hat she wore. She wore a classic worsted wool jacket that she'd seen in a magazine and, what the heck, you only live once, right? So, she spent the money.

Everyone within earshot of Izzy knew her story, even the man with the wheelchair waiting outside when they de-boarded the plane. Her oversized white molded purse became a pendulum with each of Izzy's labored steps toward the wheelchair. She balanced herself by using a fake wooden cane. Izzy thanked him for helping her and dropped into the bucket of the chair in a breathy heap. She set the purse and cane on her lap. The man knelt, flipped the chair's footrests down, and lifted each of Izzy's feet in place.

"Ready?" he asked. He battled against a wide grin, appearing ready to laugh at any moment.

"Oh, yes. Thank you," she responded. "And what's your name, young man?"

A chuckle slipped out, and he said, "Fernando, ma'am."

He disengaged the brake on each of the wheelchair's back wheels. The chair bumped across each seam of the plane's exit ramp. In the terminal, Izzy noted how the air inside the exit ramp felt markedly cooler than the where she'd come from.

"Yes sir, ma'am," Fernando said, each word quivering to hold back his laughter.

They continued to roll toward the gate, out toward baggage claim. It was a good way's away down a wide corridor. In fact, Izzy noted corridor might be, "two-thousand feet from the gate!"

"Yes, sir, ma'am," Fernando said.

They passed gift stores selling books, Seahawks pajamas, caps, and snacks. They passed two cafeteria-style restaurants selling green juice. To that, Izzy said, "Oh, Dios mio!"

There was one sit-down-style place serving beer with sports glowing on each of three TVs of the open-faced restaurant.

"Fernando. Cervezas?"

"Si, sir. Excuseme. Senora," he replied.

After downing a beer each, they left where soon, they reached baggage claim.

Federal agents flanked five posts surrounding the baggage claim for Izzy's flight. Each agent wore a nondescript charcoal grey suit, tennis shoes, and a coiled earpiece that looped around the back of their right ear. Each stood alert as they scanned the area. In syncopated random waves, the lead agent would lift his wrist mic, whisper into it. The action instigated the other agents to respond in kind, each lifting a wrist, and replying, "Roger."

Izzy loved lip-reading. She'd spent a good amount of time in the '70s training for what would turn out to be a life of work reading people's lips. It wasn't a requirement for the job she'd had, but more a hobby.

The five agents stood around and between carousels twelve, thirteen, and fourteen.

"Everyone is in place, Mrs. Adaba." The man pushing her lost his laugh—his voice taking a serious tone.

"Oh lovely," she said, then, "and the twins?" Her voice quavered.

"Si, Señora. They're here too. As you asked."

Izzy gazed back and forth across the vast hall and the man pushed Izzy close to carousel thirteen. "Now would be wonderful," she said, her voice warbling with age.

Fernando bent to untie then re-tie his shoe.

All at once, each of the five "twins" revealed their faces. One dropped a newspaper he'd been reading. Two lifted their sunglasses and slipped them on their heads. One took off his golf cap. Another exited the bathroom. Each man stood about five-foot-nine, weighed around two-hundred pounds, and had sullen, deep-set eyes. All the men looked remarkably like her. Izzy thought, "the spitting image of herself." Of course, in men's clothing and not old lady clothes, the wig, and the pasty tan of the bottle makeup she wore.

The Feds responded as trained. They approached the twins, dragging each man into one of three private detention rooms situated within the interior wall of baggage claim.

But one agent yelled, "Dammit!" He held the shoulder of his guy, shoved him inside a door, but turned when he heard a woman yelling behind him.

"Oh!" Izzy called.

The young woman who'd been sitting next to her in first class had shown up and was standing behind the growing crowd.

"That's my bag, Fernando, the one with the red bandana! Oh, miss!" she called to the woman, "Young lady! Have a lovely time in Seattle!"

The girl swung around without responding. And the main Fed entered the detention room and closed the door behind him.

"Guess, she didn't see me, Fernando."

"Guess not, ma'am," he said, and chuckled. He snatched the old woman's luggage off the conveyor belt and dragged the bag in one hand while pushing Izzy's wheelchair with the other.

Outside under the high cabana of the arrival area, Fernando hailed a car. A long black town car zipped in, next to the curb where they stood. Fernando stowed Izzy's bag in the trunk, then guided up off the wheelchair by the elbow as he assisted her into the backseat. After she was inside, he got into the front seat next to the driver.

From there, they headed off to a smaller terminal where she would board a charter flight, one, Izzy noted, that had "literally zero safeguards." Certainly, fo TSA.

After which, Izzy would fly thirty minutes north to Friday Harbor, on San Juan Island where she would spend a few months, getting business in order.

She considered the other passport. Would she give birth to Enrico del Torio? Or, would she remain Izzy? Well, there was enough time to worry on details. Either way, she knew one thing—she would take up residence in the house she'd purchased online, where she could take off her ridiculous outfit, wash the makeup off, and change back into slacks and a military-style shirt. Where she'd fix the mess the idiot dealers had gotten into.

LILY

OVERTURE CINCO – April 14, 2017

27

Wes' friends are jealous of me. LOL. Only Lee follows my blog so, Hey Lee! I'm onto you.

Randy could give a shit. He puts up with me just fine.

My whole thing with Randy and Lee, well, that stopped a while ago when I decided I was in love with Wes. Guess you could say I was testing the waters. 😊

Wes and I talked about getting married. He bought me a watch so that I could mark time toward a day that we haven't yet decided on. Isn't that terrible!? LOL. Terribly cute. I love my watch. It's white with a glittery face that goes all opalescent in the sunshine. And it's solar-powered. Who knew they made this stuff, right?

When Wes gave it to me, Lee said, "A present?" And then they shuffled off into Wes' bedroom, our bedroom, for a talk. I heard Lee call me a skank.

Randy was fiddling with whatever gadget he was working on. He heard, too. His eyes flashed over in my direction, but he went back to work on whatever mechanical goo-gaw he was fiddling with when he heard Lee call me that name. I lifted my shoulders like, whatever.

When they emerged, I jumped down Lee's throat. Gave him my whatever. Told him he was the skank and if he didn't stop wearing such tight clothes his balls would become raisins.

He called me a bitch and things went downhill from there.

But, honestly, I sort of think they're jealous of Wes and me. To that, I say, get a flippin' life, losers.

MEG

28

Roberta Flack was singing Midnight Train to
Georgia out of the sound system and Meg's feet
caught the song's beat on the treadmill as she ran.
With each step, the treadmill's belt bounced, giving
slightly under her weight. For the past five minutes,
Meg had walked a moderate clip, so she increased her
speed from three -MPH to three-point-five-MPH, then
switched on the fan in the control panel. A flash of
cool air hit her throat and chest and swirled around her
neck and under her ponytail.

The black, razor-back sports tunic she wore felt
like a vise around her breasts. The undergarment bit
into the skin around her underarms, her midriff, and
her stomach. The leggings she'd chosen gave more,
but the give lent a few extra pounds to jiggle her rump
at each footfall. But wasn't that why she was at the
gym in the first place? And she was happy the people
at the gym had faced the treadmill toward the center
of the room and not the other way around.

Meg poked at the incline control, adjusting it from
a two-degree slant to three-degrees. She intended to
alternate between two and three, up-and-down, for
periods of three to five minutes at each go. After ten
minutes, she would increase her speed again to four-

MPH and, after another ten minutes, she intended to jog at a rate of four-point-five-MPH, alternating between speeds just like she'd read in a June Glamour article called "How to Lose Weight & Get into Shape Faster!" Meg normally didn't spend much time read articles like that but when loneliness and the empty house began closing in on her, she'd snout through the recycle bin for something. She called it, mind candy.

This was month three since…well, since she'd stopped saying "Lily's death." She hated connecting those two words—hated that the words might be in the same proximity of one another, so instead, she said, "Since Lily left." The word death rang like an explosion going off in her mind.

But, she was fifty-two, heading off the peak of menopause, with a strong urge to regain her once-upon-a-time physical state. In fact, she'd once told Jay, before Lily left, that she wanted her "ass back." Living a healthier lifestyle had become important, almost urgent. And, without, Jay at home, she figured she could plan her days around going to the gym.

Two machines whirred in the main workout area of Best Body Fitness. The clank, clank, clank from a woman using a set of free weights was mitigated by more monotonous hums offered by the treadmill and an elliptical. The weights clanked each time the woman lifted them over her head. The clanking picked up speed as her repetitions increased. Finally, the woman set the weights back onto the rack. Meg wanted defined arms like hers someday. The definition from her arms traced up her shoulders and up along her neckline. And even with more than twenty feet between them, Meg noticed a small red heart tattoo on her neck under her left earlobe.

To the left of Meg, in a row running the length along the street-side window was a series of ellipticals where a man, around thirty years old, maybe, had worked up a sweat. His skin welted in blotches of pink that intermixed with his freckled skin. Sweat seemed to leach out of his follicles like a soaker hose. The front of his cotton shirt was drenched and had turned a darker shade of the shirt's original pea green. He blotted his face with a gym towel every few seconds, hanging the towel back around his neck each time. His name was Louis. Meg knew this because he wore a shirt with words written on it that said, BECAUSE, I'M LOUIS, THAT'S WHY!

Meg wondered how long Louis had been working out. Was it months or days? He didn't appear to be fit like the woman in the corner with the free weights. Would he buff up or did his DNA preclude Louis to a lifetime of pudginess? Then, she gazed down at the slight paunch in her stomach and wondered the same about herself.

The woman placed the weights back onto the rack, picked up a jump rope, and started repetitions— singles first, then doubles. Meg thought she knew the gal but couldn't place from where. Meg figured her to be about twenty years younger—around Lily's age.

Sweat glistened off her tan stomach—her tan, flat stomach. But Meg noticed the slightest bulge immediately below her belly button, which showed above her low-slung workout pants, most likely caused by the elastic waistband of her pants. She had long, lean legs that curved and caused a gap between her thighs. Her calves were shapely with well-defined calves. Basically, she was Meg's worst nightmare. At least she had a sweat stain like Louis's, letting Meg know the woman wasn't perfect. The stain made a dark swatch in the shape of a 'V' that trailed from her neckline down between her breasts, which weren't too big but were perfectly shaped.

When the woman gazed up, Meg dropped her eyes, trying to act like she hadn't been staring all this time. She knew she had seen the young woman around the island. They didn't run in the same circles. Not that Meg had any circles left since Lily, well, was gone and since she'd quit going to church. She remembered that the woman might have worked at the library for a spell, but Meg couldn't remember for sure. That's how the island was—filled with people you either saw all the time or occasionally and didn't know well.

Meg poked the +sign on the speed button three times to pick up her pace and began to run. If she was ever going to look remotely like that woman, she'd best up her game.

Her breath caught a faster rhythm to match the pounding of her feet, when Cat Scratch Fever by Ted Nugent blared through the gym's sound-system. The system's speakers loomed high on zinc brackets in each corner of the room against acoustical ceiling tiles. The porous eggshell white tiles alternated with fluorescent lighting, which left a sallow tinge on everyone's skin.

While the song blared, Meg whispered the words. Nugent had been a favorite of hers in high school until he became a radical and outspoken in his politics. She loathed radicals—conservatives and liberals alike. Radical equaled crazy. Anyone committed to any idea so strongly, leaning to extremist ideologies, had to be crazy. Right?

She pressed the button for the fan. A flood of air instantly cooled her neck and chest. She upped the speed again and her feet landed in double-time on the rubber treadmill outdoing the song's rhythm.

No matter where you stood, a mix of coffee, sweat, and glass cleaner permeated the air inside gym. Someone in the adjacent room started up the blender at the juice bar. A smoothie sounded like a perfect reward after her workout.

Endorphins ping-ponged throughout Meg's system sending a wave of fire into her brain. She glanced again at the woman in the corner who had moved to a training machine housed with a series of pulleys and cables, which ran the weights up and down. The gal sat on the edge of the bench with the pulley grips securely in her hand and Meg was noticing this when their eyes connected. But this time, Meg didn't look away and smiled at her, who nodded at Meg and Meg nodded back. Then, she stopped the weights after a few rapid successions and walked toward Meg.

As she passed in front of Meg's treadmill, the woman nodded again, and said, "Hi."

"Hello," Meg responded.

The woman stepped up onto the treadmill next to Meg and went right into a jog.

So, Meg poked the speed button on hers to a higher setting but began to struggle right away. Still, she didn't want to adjust the speed lower because how would that look if the woman noticed? So, she continued to jog at the higher rate clocking the time by each second. After one minute, she lowered the speed to a fast walk. And, after another five minutes, she was walking to cool down. She'd hit the showers afterward then get a peach smoothie with soy.

Yes. Shaping up, losing weight had taken on a new fervor. It fed her will and her battle against a more complacent life she'd become accustomed. It was her new addiction. She hated that word. It reminded her of Lily.

But she figured that after a month of working out, signs would show—the loss of weight, a glow to her skin, firmer muscles, her clothes would hang better. She had to wonder what Jay would think after seeing the changes in her.

She threw a towel around her neck, grabbed her bottle of water, and headed to the showers. But she spotted the back of another man who had just entered the building and did a double-take. Meg thought she recognized him too. The young woman noticed Meg staring at him and stopped her treadmill. There, she stood looking back-and-forth between Meg and the man.

He wore a pair of tight, black bike shorts that showed off a pair of overly shapely legs. He was trying too hard. Meg knew age was a futile fight to

148

hold onto the past. It was ridiculous to try to stay young, a game you'd lose every time, one that tries to stop time.

But she did know this man. It was Dorico.

Meg's jawline twitched, and she squinted. She wanted to charge him, to tackle him, beat the living crap out of him but, at the same time, she wanted to hide. Not for fear of being seen but, instead, to spy on him…unnoticed. Track his every move. Catch him committing one more abuse and send his lousy butt to jail for good.

Only after several girls came forward, the high school fired Dorico. He still had balls enough to follow the Storms to the island. He couldn't get another teaching job in the Seattle area but neither did he seem to need the money. It was only after she understood Lily's connection with him that she tried to get him off the island. But her efforts turned out to be a total fail. Unless law enforcement caught him in the act, they couldn't do much. FBI had already posted his name and location on their sexual offenders registry. It was when Meg began placing signs on light poles throughout town, that Dorico complained and she was instructed to remove them—which she refused to do. So, someone, probably Dorico, took them down.

Instead of the workout area, he walked toward the indoor pool.

A swimmer. Figured.

He was slippery, like a snake.

The pig.

She watched him through the windows. He climbed onto the diving plank. Without moving his arms away from his sides, he jumped off feet first into the water and disappeared under the crystal blue surface. She wanted to jump in after him and hold him under.

Meg snagged the bottle of glass cleaner that sat on a shelf behind the treadmills and sprayed off the handles and control panel. Then she walked in the direction of the showers but stopped at the pool room door.

29

"I need paper and something to write with," Meg said to the clerk at the desk, whose tight ponytail reflected her efficiency. She didn't miss a beat and reached into a drawer near the cash register, pulled out a yellow pad of lined paper, and handed Meg a black marker. She slid the pad of paper across the counter, which Meg caught before letting it sail off onto the floor.

"Thanks," Meg said. Nerves shook her hands

The lady nodded. "What do you want?" she asked someone standing behind Meg. It was the girl from the workout room.

The gal said, "I'll take one of those." She gestured to the smoothie Meg balanced in her left hand. She backed away to let the woman order. Meg placed the writing paraphernalia on a small round table, took one long draw off the straw in the smoothie, and began to write. Her hand pressed hard writing in angry strikes with the thick black marker. When she finished one page, she flipped to a new page repeating the same message.

"Soy?" Meg heard the clerk asking the woman.

"Nah," she responded.

The clerk engaged the blender, which stuttered when she added frozen fruit into the juice just as it did when she'd prepared Megs, dropping in pie cherries, wedges of peach slices, and blueberries. The blender went from low to high spun in a loud whir until she flipped the switch off. The smoothie glugged into a cup, a lid snapped into place, and the clerk asked, "Straw?"

"Sure," the woman responded. When she did Meg glanced over right as she was slipping a fat straw into the hole in the lid.

"Membership number?"

"12-61," the woman said.

Then, she walked past Meg and gal headed off toward the women's lockers and showers but stopped when Meg asked for scotch tape.

The woman had bent down to untie a shoe when Meg walked by her to the shower doors. She taped one of the signs on the interior side of the door and one on the outside. Meg saw the woman's face fill with surprise.

"He is," Meg said, in defense of the sign.

"Is that legal?"

"Why not? It's true. I can't believe this pig isn't in jail."

"Aren't you worried he'll sue for defamation?"

"He won't sue me. Besides if it's been proven true then it can't be libelous, right?"

The young woman blurted out a chuckle. "You have some balls, lady."

"They grow with age." Meg smiled at the gal. She was pretty and funny. Probably smart, too. Her eyes sparkled, and Meg replied, "Jay says, 'I'm entertaining.' I guess there's that."

The gal laughed again and asked, "Need help?"

"With the signs?"

When the woman nodded, Meg said, "Sure. Why not?" And handed over three sheets, all with the same message:

EWAN DORICO IS A PEDOPHILE!

*

Both women watched him from outside a window where the high open room housed the gym's swimming pool. Dorico pressed out of the pool, up to his torso. Water sluiced off his chest and he paused flipped his head flinging water spreading out in a circle.

"Oh lord," Meg said. "He thinks he's so hot." She puffed out disgust.

Meg had taped up a sign on the outside of the window facing it inside toward the pool. He noticed the women watching him and gave a slight nod when he smiled but his smile melted from his face, and his eyes flashed with horror when he read the sign. He scrambled out of the pool slipped on a wet spot of the concrete floor and nearly fell.

"Wouldn't it be justice if he broke his neck?" Meg whispered.

The young woman's chuckle turned into a moan.

His face flushed white when he stopped at the window. He was re-reading the sign. He placed both hands in front of it and glanced behind him to the left then right. A teenaged girl who was swimming laps, no doubt on the high school swim team, wore a washed-out, adobe-hued swim cap, shiny swim goggles, and a bright blue nose clip. She wasn't paying him any attention.

But Meg and the woman saw him mouth the word, "Shit," as he walked toward the exit. They were tracking his movements to the door. He flung the door open and charged toward them.

"Did you do this?" Dorico asked. He ripped the sign off the window with his fingernails, leaving a corner of paper shredded under tape still stuck to the glass.

"It's true," Meg said. Meg stood her ground. In fact, she leaned in at him.

"What the hell…" He spotted one on the door and ran toward it. "Take them down."

The other woman stepped up next to Meg but didn't speak.

"I'm posting these everywhere in here," she rose her voice, "the gym doesn't want a pedophile patronizing the premises."

Meg, and the woman with her, turned back. The clerk had paused when Meg's voice got louder. She had been wiping up a mess from smoothies but now stood alert to the hubbub brewing inside the place of her employment. The clerk narrowed her eyes at. No doubt, she heard the word "pedophile."

"I'll sue!" Dorico warned.

"Go for it." Meg held her arms down and tight, her hands were fisted when she walked up to him. "You hurt my daughter, you bastard. Led her down a path to no return. *You're* responsible for her death. So, no. I will never leave you alone. Not until I see you leave the island or die trying."

Meg kept her face so close she could smell chlorine on his skin.

But he didn't respond, Instead, he dropped his gaze.

Shame is like that. Makes you take your focus off the target.

Then she spat. "You're filth," she said.

Saliva dribbled down the bare skin of his chest. He placed one hand over the spit but couldn't seem to wipe it off.

The young woman sneered when Dorico turned his attention to her.

"You heard the lady… filth," she said.

And Meg walked off so fast that the other woman had to skip into gear just to catch up.

30

The young woman took a deep sip through the fat straw then sat back and squinted at Meg. The look was laced with humor. She dragged one hand through her hair combing it with her fingers. She started at the temples dragging her damp hair back behind her ears. Then she coiled a fat strand hanging by her cheek behind one ear but the hair didn't stay. It fell swung by the side of her face.

"You're a badass, Meg."

Meg laughed. "Hardly," she said.

The girl took another long suck off the straw. "I'm getting a brain freeze."

The girl was funny to Meg. "Slow down," she said. "I didn't get your name. And, by the way, how did you know mine?"

"Leanne." She paused and drank more wincing at the coldness from the smoothie. "I know you from the island."

"I see." Meg smiled and paused, then said, "by my reputation." She chuckled, and said, "Well, it's nice to meet you, Leanne."

They sat silently for a beat when Leanne remembered. "Oh! I know who you are. You were at the service."

Leanne nodded. Then said, "I love these things," she lifted her smoothie, "but I could do without the grainy thing."

"The soy powder?"

"Yeah. I like the taste fine but not the grainy."

Meg took a long draw of smoothie. "It interferes."

"Think he's going to file charges?"

"How can he? He's a criminal," Meg said.

"He still can. Probably won't but he can." Leanne's eyes danced away, trying to land on something other than Meg's face but, finding nothing, she turned her attention down in the creamy concoction inside her cup.

"You know for a fact?"

"Just seems he could, is all." She said, still drawing smoothie into her mouth.

Meg nodded and took another sip of her own smoothie, noting how the peach taste was fresh and light, set off by the yogurt, and the "grainy" thing.

"You know Lily well?"

Leanne looked away. "Just from around."

"Around, huh?"

"Didn't hang with the same crowd."

Meg sat back. She pushed her drink near the center of the small two-top where they were seated.

"I've seen a few girls, like Lil, get hurt," Leanne said.

Meg's skin brightened and turned pink. Her jaw tightened. "Did you do anything? Say anything?"

Leanne nodded her head. "Got the authorities on it." Her tone changed, took on a tougher air. "They were all over it. Families got involved. Once that happens, lawyers come next. Moms and girls start coming out of the woodwork. You been watching the news?" She asked Meg, who nodded. "It's like the O'Reilly thing, the Cosby thing, Weinstein, the judge. What's his name?"

"Moore. Roy Moore."

"That's right," Leanned said. "Once the first brave few come forward, then all the others tend to. Soon, there's a pile-on. They feel safer in numbers. You can't blame them. Most have been abused by men their whole lives. I remember once before," she paused, chose her words, "before I got into shape—took self-defense lessons and everything. But before, a guy attacked me. He didn't rape me but he got close. I screamed my head off. He couldn't shut me up. I just freaking screamed and screamed."

"Oh my goodness," Meg's face cringed at the story she was hearing.

"Well, my point is this, you think you can handle yourself in a fight but if you've had no training, you can't against a man. Even a man like that." She tipped her head up referring to Dorico. "You need to learn to fight. Most women don't train for battle. After my attack, I went straight into training mode."

Meg shuffled in her chair, took in a breath, and gazed to a wall where, behind it, the gym housed the Olympic-sized swimming pool.

"Dear God."

"Look, Lily didn't have a chance against that sick creep," Leanne said, "What's better is, they got him. He served back-to-back for three girls—served a total of nine years. Paid out some big bucks. He's got old, wealthy parents. They tried to stuff it, but he still ended up doing time and paying fines," she said, and sipped her smoothie. Then she added, "Justice for all."

Meg glared at Leanne. "Not quite."

"Sorry. I didn't mean…" she said.

Meg waved it off and Leanne took another sip.

"We can put up more signs. You know. Official sex-offender signs."

"I need to hit something. Like his face."

"Just hurts your knuckles. Look, it's over. He paid his dues. I know Lily got the crap-end, but he isn't offending anymore. The meds make him limp." She giggled. "Brad, the probation officer has him on a short leash. Weekly probation. Used to wear a bracelet."

Meg squinted. "How do you know so much?"

She glanced to her lap. "I was one of the lucky ones and, I guess, sort of feel guilty."

"Lucky? How?"

"Girls fawned over him. I didn't. I thought he was a pig from the get-go. He tried to corner me once. That's when I knew. I got away. Figured he wasn't on the up-and-up. Anyway, I'd heard the rumors. How he took girls into locked rooms."

"How'd you hear that?"

"Court. Allocution."

"Allocution?"

Leanne blushed. "Guess I'm into the law, a bit. My favorite shows are the reruns of *Law & Order* with Sam Waterston. I love him. Please don't tell me he could be my father. He could be my grandfather. I don't care. I love him with a sweet, sweet affection."

She bobbled her eyebrows, smiled, and took another drag from the straw. Then she said, "Well, thank you for the smoothie. My treat next time."

"You coming tomorrow?"

She nodded. "Gotta stay in shape." Her skin blushed fresh and plump. Not a trace of age. No wrinkles except when she smiled, which she was doing now.

"I'll take you up on that smoothie." Meg rose first. "See you then."

"Later," Leanne said. But before she walked away her eyes dropped near her foot, near the gym bag next to her leg. She lurched forward to recover whatever had slipped out and began fightingt with the zipper to close the bag. "Crap," she whispered.

"What's wrong?" Meg asked, twisting around the curve of the table to see what was happening, but Leanne had already stuffed something deep into the bag, which she now balanced on her foot.

"It's nothing."

"All that trouble for nothing?" Meg chuckled. "Okay," she said, then, "You know, Miss Leanne, you are one interesting young woman." Meg turned to leave but stopped again. She said, "What say we a proper farewell?" And held out her hand to Leanne who rose and, when she did, the bag rolled off her foot, spilling out of it what looked like a leather jacket wedged within a half-open zipper. She saw gold embroidering on the jacket but could only make out one letter. It was the letter B.

31

Meg wore a different razor-back tunic—a solid teal top that matched the style of her black leggings, with white-piping that ran along each seam. She'd wanted to wear a yellow top but when she held it in front of her in the mirror, the color washed out her skin. She didn't know why she was so concerned about what she wore there, but every time she got ready for the gym she seemed to pull out every article of clothing. She knew she wanted to look her best and what she lacked in fitness maybe she could make up for in style.

The same clerk worked behind the counter today. And after acknowledging each other, Meg walked into the workout area. As promised, Leanne was there again too. She'd piled her mop of brown tresses into a gnarled, lemniscate of a twist, which she'd secured with three yellow pencils. A rolled yellow bandana around her crown kept her hair out of her eyes. Her tights screamed out an array of rainbows, which contrasted by a slack gray shirt with a low neckline showing off a fuchsia push-up bra underneath. Blood pumping through her system flushed her skin nearly as pink as the bra. She worked hard against an elliptical trainer, the same one Louis had been using the day before.

"Hi," Meg said, as she stepped up onto the treadmill. "I have a yellow top you might like."

"Cool," Leanne said, her breath puffing with each push of the elliptical. She smiled but forged forward, her legs forcing the pedals in a circular motion. Her quads bulged each downward strike. She was keeping the machine at a steady pace.

"Speed?" Meg asked.

"Five-point-two."

"Wow."

Leanne's legs striated in ripples of sinewy muscle. Meg switched on her machine and asked, "How long have you been working out?" Meg's feet caught the rhythm at three-MPH, where she liked to start her workout.

"Today?"

"No. How many years?"

"On and off," she puffed, "twelve years."

"Kids?"

"Not yet."

"Want them?"

She cocked her head. "Maybe. Someday."

Meg wasn't focused on the treadmill control panel but could tell from her voice Leanne was smiling. Then she asked Meg, "Any kids other than Lil?"

"Just Lily," Meg replied. But after a few seconds, Meg spoke up. "Everyday since she passes is like a hundred years."

Leanne paused to stand on the elliptical. "I'm so sorry," she said.

"Damn drugs," Meg said. Working out on the treadmill today compared to a walk in pool of taffy.

"Want to talk about it? We can skip this, go sit down," Leanne said. She began adjusting the speed, slowing it down.

"I'm okay," Meg replied, then added, "Don't stop. We can't give up."

Leanne nodded and increase the speed again and slowly caught up to the speed she'd been working at before.

Meg spoke louder over the buzz of their equipment. "There's only some things we can control," Meg said, "Just love your family and don't ever let them forget that."

"I don't know what I would do," Leanne said. Her voice strained with each movement of on the machine. "I mean, even though I don't have any kids, well, I can't imagine the pain."

Meg didn't respond. There was nothing to say. You never understand until you experience it yourself. And the pain? Unbearable.

Forget the damned warm-up.

Meg kicked the treadmill up from three- to five-MPH. Her feet tripped up at first but became caught the rhythm and steadied. Her heart beat with each footfall. Her legs burned. But she kept on.

And she ran. She ran for Lily's life.

LILY
six hours before dying

OVERTURE SEIS – May 9, 2017

32

I can't believe my mother. She should have been in theatre.

First off, ma, my life is not your life. You have your own so please refrain to tell me how I've screwed everything up. How dare you. How about this, you sold yourself out. Went for cash not love. Dad always wondered why you married him. Did you know that? Sorry dad for outing you like this but, good freaking God. Mom went way out of her way to let me know how much she disapproves of me. How I've let her down as a daughter. Your thoughts are yours. Mine are mine. Stay out of my head, ma. Yours isn't all that great, you know? You could use a good shrinking, in my humblest of humble opinions. So, there. How does it feel to have someone you thought loved you tell you what a loser you are?

Ma, you're a peach—a real, freaking peach.

JAY

Summer 2017

33

Jay sat low in the front seat of his car. He took a swig from a water bottle, then nibbled out of a full-sized bag of potato chips he'd purchased at The Little Store. He hadn't yet lit into the double-pack of land jaegers. He liked land jaeger more than jerky. Jerky was stringy and dry.

Hail came on fast, cracking onto the hood and ricocheting, pinging and tinging as pellets struck the metal of his pine-green SUV. The hail reminded Jay about a bag of frozen peas he'd opened and rejected after seeing they'd been burnt with frost. Now, a blast of slush pelted the hood.

He had parked in the opposite direction and three houses east of a house where Wesley and the two other guys had parked. He canted his rearview mirror down in a way that he could spy on them and not be seen. As fast as the downpour came on, it stopped, leaving behind a snowy sheet on the glistening ground where it hail swept up in shallow dunes along a chain-link fence. Yellow grass poked through the fence and trimmed the front yard of the house. Stalks of wheat-colored thistle shot up in stalks, the tops appearing black and seedy.

Inside the yard, A dog lay chained to a post and huddled near the side of the house. It didn't move when the three men entered the gate. The dog's brown hide sunk in between each of its ribs.

A plastic macaroni salad bowl had tipped over. He assumed it was the dog's water bowl.

In what was probably a drop, the smallest of the three guys carried a satchel. They stepped inside when a woman smoking a cigarette opened the door—the bones under her loose clothing as visible as the dog's.

She stepped one foot out of the door, using her body as a stop, and leaving the other foot on the threshold. Her hand rested on the knob. She blew smoke from her nose and scanned the area outside, past them after they entered.

Jay slunk down into the seat further but watched through the mirror as the three men walked inside. The woman wore dingy tank top and didn't appear fazed by the weather. She took one last look around the area, then dropped the cigarette onto the cement porch, ground it under her shoe, and pulled the door closed. A snake of smoke spiraled, twining away and off the concrete. But soon the ember extinguished under a grizzled mist setting in.

Jay had made it a habit to end up wherever this Wesley guy went. It wasn't like he'd planned it. In fact, the first time was by accident. Only after, did he feel a compulsion to follow him.

He told himself he needed something—something for breakfast, something for dinner. He realized he was going to the store two, often three times a day.

First, he sort of blamed Meg. He didn't understand how much work went into maintaining a house until he moved out. It was sort of her fault he moved out. She'd kept the house stocked with fresh fruit and veggies, meats, cold cuts, bread, milk, coffee, sugar—toilet paper, paper towels, cleaning products. And even still, there were more items to round out a household—paper plates, cups, and cooking utensils.

Part of him knew he hadn't appreciated the smaller details of housekeeping.

So, it came as a complete shock that while Jay shopped, Wesley appeared. The store had opened an hour earlier. There were maybe five other locals there.

The store's floorplan, which resembled a warehouse, made the interior vacant and tinny. A junco had entered the store and was trapped inside. It flitted over each shelving wall of items chittering as it searched for somewhere to escape. Jay began to follow the bird. He turned down one row when the bird bowed, dipping low after clearing the household items shelves. The junco pulled up to avoid flying into a second person who stood staring at beauty products. It was Wesley. He had stopped more than half-way down the aisle.

Jay swerved his cart out of the aisle to avoid being seen. A flash of cold sweat washed over him as he hurried to the natural snack food section. There, Jay waited. He parked the cart at an endcap next shelves filled with bird bells and plastic sacks of birdseed. One sack had a hole pecked out of it. Jay assumed, the trapped bird had perpetrated the crime. Millet and milo scattered covered the floor. Some seed lay crushed from shoppers' carts. Jay noticed shells stuck to his own cart. The hard rubber wheels held smatterings of grain. The bird swooped down near Jay's feet to snatch up some seed. It picked up two tiny pellets then scampered taking flight when Jay moved. He snuck a peek around the endcap to see if he could locate Wesley. Right then, he emerged but was heading away from Jay, in the direction of the checkout counter. Wesley was bent over, leaning his arms onto the push bar of his cart.

At the checkout counter, he pawed at some gum, then some breath mints, then went back to some gum in a white and green package. Next, he picked up a box of matches and began twirling it between each of his fingers on his right hand. When his turn came, he asked Nyna for some Marlboro lights. She moved from behind her station to retrieve a pack from a locked cabinet situated behind the customer service desk. When she walked away, Wesley pocketed the pack of gum. He spun to the left, then right to see if anyone noticed but didn't spot Jay. Jay had stepped into the aisle behind the endcap as soon as he saw Wesley pocket the gum.

Nyna held up the Marlboro's and called back, "These?"

Wesley nodded then Nyna relocked the cigarette cabinet and returned to the cash register.

"Find everything okay?"

"Yeah."

"$47.32," Nyna said.

He opened his billfold and pulled out three twenties.

"Receipt?"

"Nah," he said, but took his change, bagged the items he'd bought, and walked out.

Jay didn't remember when his heart had started pounding. Heat rose into his chest and settled there. His breath sharpened.

He rolled his cart to Nyna's station, set out all his items, and opened his wallet.

"That all, Jay?" Nyna smiled.

"For now."

"That'll be $74.64."

He inserted his credit card in the chip reader and waited. Nyna hadn't seen Wesley steal that pack of gum. The reader buzzed, and Jay removed his card.

"Thank you," she said, and handed Jay his receipt.

He stuffed the receipt into his pocket and pulled out a reusable bag he'd brought in. "You know," he started to say but another shopper interrupted him.

"Nyna!" said a woman who worked at one of the island's insurance companies. He always forgot her name.

"Hey, Sharon," Nyna replied.

That's right. Sharon.

She winked at Jay who smiled back at her. Then he walked to the end of the register's running conveyor belt where all his items sat piled one on top of the other. When he had finished loading grocery items into bag, he didn't bother saying goodbye. Nyna and Sharon were exchanged in a lenity of chatter. Instead, he rolled out his cart, climbed into his car, and set off to find Wesley.

That all happened two weeks before and Jay still felt guilty for not saying anything to Nyna about Wesley stealing the gum.

He looked into the rearview mirror when heard voices drift around his car. Wesley and the other two guys were leaving the woman's house. The woman didn't bother showing them out.

The metal gate clanked open and closed and he slid down the car window to hear them better. Lee, the slimiest looking of the three, was talking.

"When's he get in?"

"2:05," the small one said.

"Kenmore?"

"Nah. Charter."

"Shut up," Wesley said. "Keep it inside the car."

They piled into a yellow and black El Camino. Wesley gunned the engine and skidded the tires. A puff of smoke spewed out from under each wheel when the hot dry under his tires hydroplaned over the cold wet ground surrounding the car. Finally, when rubber caught road the tail swiveled, settled, then squirreled away. Wesley didn't stop at the corner. Instead, he sped through the turn and lit the road with more smoke when he gunned the engine again.

Jay sat up in his seat and adjusted the rearview mirror. He opened the packet of land jaeger, grabbed his sack of potato chips, and the bottle of water.

Outside of the car, he nudged the door closed leaving it cracked in case he needed to make a fast return. He hunkered down as he ran toward the house. When he got to the gate, the dog shifted its brows at his approach. Jay lifted the metal latch trying not to make any noise. He slipped inside the yard but left the gate open. There, he stood eyeing the dog who was eyeing Jay.

"Hey boy." Jay's susurrus tone meant to soothe the dog. But the dog didn't flinch. He lay there judging the strange man entering his territory.

Jay sidled closer and noticed the dog's shoulder twitch. A fat mason bee buzzed the area and was pestering the dog, landing then flying away, keeping up its abuse at the dog. The dog twitching each time the bee landed on the dog's muddy coat.

"Here you go," Jay said, hoping not to rile the dog. It sputtered out a short growl when Jay tossed a land jaeger near its front paws. He chose to stay where he was and dumped the chips onto the ground. The dog lurched up but smelled the meat and went at it, devouring it within seconds. Jay tossed over the second one. The dog devoured that one, too. Then it moved forward, closer to Jay but instead of attacking him, the dog slid next to his leg for the chips. While it ate, Jay righted the plastic container and filled it with water. He set it against the house to keep it upright.

But the screen door creaked open. "What the f—?" The woman said.

Jay spun in her direction.

"Get the hell out of my yard." Her tiny eyes took on a viciousness that outdid anything he'd gotten from the dog.

"Your dog—" he said.

But the woman cut him off and held up her hand, pointing her finger to the road. "Get out. I'm calling the cops."

For whateveer reason, Jay smiled, and said, "Yeah. Right."

Her eyes flashed opened wide enough for Jay to see the red line of bloodshot trimming her lids. The red contrasted her blue irises making her eyes bright blue. But the whites of her eyes were yellow, jaundiced. Blemishes scarred the skin of her arms with scabs trailing down to her wrists and on top of her hands. She couldn't have been older than thirty-two, but looked used up, was leathery and sick.

She pulled the screen door in front of her and snuck back inside without another word. Jay bent back down to finish filling the dog's water. It had polished off all the food.

"Here you go," he said, and pushed the bowl of water closer. The dog rose and started lapping. Then, Jay walked out of the yard, this time he let the metal gate latch drop in a clank, and he got into his car. He had another stop before heading home.

PART THREE

TODAY

34

"How long have you attended church here?"

"Years. I don't know." Meg frowned. She wanted to go home. "How long is this going to take?"

"How many years?"

"I said, I don't know. Eleven years? Maybe? Twelve?"

"Before Battles?" The man asked and jotted something down on a pad of paper. He handed it off to his assistant.

"Yes. A few years before."

"Battles is a peach, isn't he?"

Meg turned away. "I don't know what you mean."

The assistant walked into the kitchen to get his jacket and called back to them, "I'm heading out for pizza. Any preferences?"

Meg leaned back in her chair and folded her arms over her chest. "We're having dinner together?"

"Consider it a treat—for us," the man said.

"I don't want anything."

"Need to keep up your strength. Not sure how long this will take."

"It's getting late. You can't keep me here."

"You can always lawyer up but then you'll look pretty guilty if you do."

"Great," Meg said, and then "Pepperoni. No pineapple."

"I'm a pepperoni man myself," the younger man said and, "pepperoni, it is." Pepperoni man held up a shiny object in his hand that Meg recognized as the key to the door. Pepperoni man twisted his wrist in the air as if to secure some invisible lock.

"Yeah, I have one too," the man interviewing Meg said.

Meg shook her head and noticed that they'd been at it, now, just under fifteen hours.

"More coffee?"

"Wine would be nice," she said. Her mood had soured hours before, which didn't appear to be changing anytime soon. However, she was surprised when the man got up to retrieve a bottle of Barefoot chardonnay.

"Your favorite white, right?" He said.

"I would ask how you knew that, but I don't think I really want to know."

He laughed and poured wine into a stemless wine goblet past the hip of the glass. She raised her eyebrows, surprised by the healthy pour. "You deserve it," he said, "plus it may be your last on the outside, should we decide to take you in."

Her demeanor darkened. "Aren't you a charmer."

174

"I've been called worse. What was the last question?"

Meg took two big gulps of wine, shook her head, then said, "I don't know. You tell me."

"Battles."

"Yeah, right. He changed things up when he got to town. Some good. Some not so good."

"Not so good? How so?"

"Most, rumors."

"You know what they say…"

"He fooled around with one of the elder's? One of their wives? Is that what you want me to say? Yeah, I heard it too. Again, a rumor. No one left the church or got fired. No one divorced anyone. Maybe people assumed his *gestures* were more than they actually were."

Meg took another sip of wine. She felt her cheeks flush. A sudden band of warmth rushed into her chest.

"Weren't you an elder?"

She nodded but realized what he was insinuating and glared at him. "Hold on a minute. You're not implying…"

"Jay left you, didn't he?"

"That was because of Lily."

"Was it? You had marital problems."

"Jay and I were fine. We just flatlined. It happens. Neither one of us… well, not before Lil, anyway," she stopped talking.

"So, there were extramarital relations?"

"Good lord. What the hell does it matter now?"

Anger surged in her. All of it felt like a sick plan to destroy their reputation. Her hand shook and

175

tightened around the goblet. Before she could stop herself, she threw the glass of. It smashed against a wall. Wine splattered, and glass sprayed across the floor. "Son of a bitch!" She stood up fast and clenched her fists.

"Mrs. Storm, you need to sit."

"I'm not a dog. Don't order me like I'm a dog."

He didn't respond verbally. Instead, he pushed his chair out and set one hand on his firearm. "It would look bad to shoot you."

"Unbelievable." She laughed but anger dribbled from her lips, "You bastard."

"Please," he said, then ordered, "sit."

When she did not, he stood in front of her. He had a good ten inches of height over her. She sat down hard, keeping her eyes locked on his.

"You got a bit of a temper there, ma'am," he said. He walked into the kitchen, pulled out another glass, and filled it with wine. The man set the glass on the table and pushed it closer to Meg. "Try not to spill this one," he said, and sat back in his chair. He spoke in a calmer tone and said, "Let's start this over. Now, exactly, how well do you know Pastor Battles?"

Meg wrung her hands, studying them as they lay in her lap.

SHERIFF PETERS

Summer 2017

35

It wasn't all that unusual to see the pastor and sheriff together eating lunch. It just looked odd—the pastor with his stiff white collar, every other article of clothing black, sitting next to the sheriff in his khaki uniform. Let's just say they stood out from other combinations of people sitting in Mike's Café & Wine Bar.

Others grouped there at lunchtime sitting with their workmates. Painters and plumbers donning in their own brand of work clothing—spattered shoes, ratty jeans or coveralls.

Mike's patrons were a mish-mash of construction workers and women fresh out from behind their desks in downtown Friday Harbor offices. The women wore business clothes and casual shoes.

A muggy breeze blew through the restaurant. Mike liked keeping two front doors open street-side and another one in the back that lead to a sunny deck. But today the deck was anything but sunny. A marine layer was sifting up from the marina from the Strait and buckled onto shore, pressing across land like a massive ice floe. The restaurant's interior took on a mist that might've been mistaken for smoke coming from the kitchen. But the mist smelled of saltwater and slimy driftwood.

Pastor Battles stuffed a nugget of fresh-baked bread into his mouth and spoke, "How she doing?"

"What do you think?" Sheriff Peters said. "You haven't seen her?"

"Not for several weeks." Bread crumbs covered his lower lip.

Peters squinted and switched his focus outside of the restaurant. He stabbed at a leaf of lettuce on his plate but was searching the street. He lifted the fork and turned back to the pastor who had thankfully wiped his mouth and was shaking out the napkin, allowing specks of food fall onto his lap and the floor.

"Distraught," the Sheriff said, then "this can't end well."

Battles shrugged his shoulder and took an enormous bite out of his portabella mushroom burger. Juice and oil oozed out of the bottom into his plate. Searing steam puffed out of his lips and it was everything Battles could do to keep the bite in his mouth. "Dammit," he said, the word distorting from a mouthful of food.

"Blow on it first."

Battles chewed fast with his mouth open allowing air to flow in and out to cool the piece.

"Jesus, Brian. You eat like a pig."

Still speaking around the food, he responded, "Don't use the Lord's name in vain."

"It's a bad idea."

"Everything that happens, happens because the Lord has set it in front of us." Battles' eyes shifted down fast.

"What?" Peters asked.

"Nothing," Battles said and continued to eat.

"It feels wrong."

"How can the Lord's work be wrong? We have been given this beautiful woman as an opportunity."

"Beautiful woman?" Peters placed another forkful of salad into his mouth. He bit down on a cherry tomato and it sprayed out of his mouth before he could close his lips.

"I'm the pig?" Battles said. A grin spread and revealed particles of food between his front teeth. "Yes. She's a beautiful woman." He bobbled his eyebrows.

"Lord, Brian. I hope…"

"Look," Battles said. "She's ready. Women are easily excitable, highly susceptible. She's no different." He looked down again.

"We need to go over a few details about this. The feds require extreme caution."

"Let's pray." Battles blotted oil juice off his mouth, bowed his head, and grabbed Peters' hand. Peters pulled his hand out of Battles' and glanced around to see if anyone had noticed. He pushed his chair out, stood, and tossed his napkin onto his salad plate.

"Call me at home. Tonight. This isn't screwing around. It's serious."

Battles chuckled.

And Peters snugged his hat onto his head and walked out.

JAY

36

Hiding again, Jay dipped low behind the steering wheel and watched. Today was going to be nothing but drizzly. A chill had fallen the night before moving in like an uninvited relative. Mist speckled his car and made the sidewalks and pavement appear a darker gray. A marine layer cloaked the island in stratus clouds that hung high enough to allow small planes to fly in and out of the airport where Jay had followed the druggies.

They shifted on their feet where they stood behind a stretch of chain-link fence in the open waiting area for arriving flights. The tall one, Lee, rubbed his hands together and blew into the ball he made with his fingers. All of them were wearing gloves, all of them with their collars snapped tight around their necks.

Jay had slipped on a pair of sunglasses and a Seahawks beanie cap he'd taken from his glove compartment. And even though he was out of the drizzly weather, the outside air seemed to seep through to the inside of the car. He sipped at a paper cup. The steam from the hot coffee warmed his upper lip.

Then, there was movement. The three straightened up, with Lee nodding to the south. Jay's eyes followed their attention to an approaching plane making a turn. Jay estimated the plane's position crossing over South Beach. On its nose and wings, the small aircraft's anti-collision lights blinked red and white as it began its descent.

Jay realized this wasn't one of the usual island flight airlines, it was a charter craft—a jet. The high-pitched scream of the Lear engine shook the chassis of his car. Its speed was mesmerizing. One second jet had been hovering over South Beach, seconds later it was lowering its landing gear and alighting on the far end of the tarmac. The yelp of tires, a single bounce, and the jet settled into a speedy taxi but slowed near the turn. Then, it glided to a stop, twenty yards from the waiting area where the druggies stood at attention. The whirring engine spun to a stop with a set of cooling engines continuing to hiss.

Jay watched the pilot as he fiddled with the panel in front of him. Then, he slipped on a cap and lifted the intercom mic to his mouth. Then, he slipped the mic back into position and stood. His back hunched over to accommodate the lowness of the jet's ceiling, he walked to the passenger area, lifted the door, and set out a folding set of stairs. With a clipboard in his right hand, he jumped out taking all three stairs at once. There, he met an arrival clerk and handed her the clipboard. She ticked something off and gave the clipboard back to the pilot. Then she grabbed a flat cart she rolled to the opposite side of the jet. There, she opened the baggage compartment, unloaded a few bags, set each onto the cart, then rolled to the airport baggage claim.

The pilot had reached inside the aircraft where he set the log somewhere inside the door. Then he bounded up the stairs and shook one of the passenger's hands. They exchanged some chatter and were still talking when he led a stocky Hispanic woman, ten-to-fifteen years Jay's senior, to the top of the stairs. She was stocky and short.

The older woman looked around and murmured something to the pilot, who chuckled. She handed him a cane, which he looped over his forearm, then he assisted her out of the jet and down the stairs. Her skin took on the dark gray of the sky, and her hair was the color of grease fire smoke.

The druggies raced in to help her, two of them tried to take her hands in theirs but she slapped them away. She took the cane off the pilot's arm and nearly dropped her purse making Lee grab for it but the woman put up a fight so, Lee let go. It appeared she was the only person flying the charter.

The pilot gestured to the north end of the terminal where the clerk had taken the woman's luggage. Lee hop-stepped it away in that direction and the woman and two other men followed.

None of this was what Jay had expected but then he didn't really know what he expected. He certainly hadn't expected the men to be meeting someone's grandmother.

The dark woman stopped suddenly. She spun to the left, then the right each time making a one-eighty, skimming the area with squinted eyes. She reached in her bag and placed a pair of reading glasses onto the bridge of her nose. Then she paused for briefly when she spotted Jay's car.

He scooted down below the driver's window. He didn't think she'd seen him—he was almost certain. After a few moments, he snuck his eyes above the bottom rim of the window enough to see. The group had left the waiting area where they now stood clustered around the north end of the terminal. Each of the men picked up a piece of the woman's luggage.

Lee pointed to his car. She had a stopped, opened her arms as though taking a deep breath, and laughed. Jay could hear the deep rumbling of her laughter within confines of his car. The others joined her in laughter too and led her to their El Camino. But the woman balked and raised her cane to the car. It appeared she wasn't pleased.

Jay chuckled to himself. "Dimwits," he said.

But after a moment, Wesley opened the front passenger door and helped the woman get in. Lee and Randy jumped into the back, and when Wesley got in, the car rolled off, turning left, and continuing out of the terminal's parking lot.

Steam from Jay's breath was sluicing in rivulets down the interior of his driver's side window. His half of the windshield was foggy. He cranked on the engine, turned the air up to high, slapped the wipers across the window, then zipped in behind the El Camino, tailing it until the car stopped at the airport exit.

Wesley exited the car. He held his cell phone up and was pointing it at Jay's car. The auto-flash blinked in three quick successions. He was snapping shots of Jay in his car.

Wesley got back inside the car and handed his cell to the woman. Then, the car lurched forward and took off, leaving Jay where they'd sighted him.

37

Jay was rattled. A thin film of sweat coated his palms and he was about to wipe them on his pants, when he spotted the girl, Leanne in his rearview mirror. She was exiting the north side of the Friday Harbor Airport terminal. Jay put his car into reverse to a few yards from where she walked. He rolled down the window and called her name.

She was far enough away from the car that she had to crane to see who was driving. A glimmer of recognition crossed her eyes and she smiled. As she walked toward him, she was bending to see inside. Her eyes flitted between the airport and into his car. She wore a slicker that matched the flannel clouds, black jogging pants, and running shoes. Her hair was done in a single pony tail that swished back and forth when she walked.

"Jay?"

"Hey, Leanne."

"What are you doing here?" she asked.

Jay glanced around and shrugged. When she reached the passenger window, she rested her forearm on the car. "Just hanging out at the airport?"

"Want to go to Ernie's?" he asked. The question came out of left field.

She glanced over to the small restaurant there at the terminal. She pulled out her phone and checked the time. "Sure," she said, "I have an hour or so. You buying?"

He nodded. "Get in."

186

"It's only right there."

"Get in," he insisted.

"I usually walk back, uh, home," she answered. Her eyes darted left, opened the door, and got in.

"I'll take you back, uh, home after," he mimicked.

"I can walk home. My place isn't more than a mile. It's good exercise."

"Let's eat then decide."

The smell of Ernie's spilled out of the doors when they stepped inside. Christine and Paul owned the place. The two had moved to the island as young adults and had spent most of their lives on the island.

"Oh yum," Leanne said.

"I'm having a beer."

"Before noon, no less."

Jay chuckled. "I'm a wild one at heart."

"Okay. Well, me, too," she said. "Heineken."

"A lager girl." Jay retrieved the beers. He chose a Black Frog Stout made by the Snoqualmie Falls Brewing Company for himself.

"A black beer guy. You *are* trouble."

The chatter between them was fresh, teetering on flirtation.

Jay chuckled again. He liked Lily's friend. She had a natural and precocious way about her. "Popover?" he asked.

"Can't come here and not," she said.

"Soup today, Jay?" Christine asked.

Amused, Leanne chuckled, and said, "You're a regular."

"Clockwork. Tuesdays and Thursdays at noon," Christine said. She frowned when she checked the time. "You're early."

"Popover and chili, Jay?" Paul called out from behind the counter, where he was putting together a hoagie.

"Yep and yep," Jay said. "Leanne?"

"Same. Why not, right? I work out." Her skin blotched in a rosy pattern. "Beer at eleven-thirty. Good gravy."

"Good gravy, indeed," Jay replied. "Where do you want to sit?"

"Let's go to *your* table."

"Perfect."

He led her to a spot that was carved out from the rest of the room and set back from other tables, and the most intimate spot in the open, bright space.

He pulled her chair out.

"A gentleman."

"Old habits."

The beer went down fast and Jay order two more.

"I never drink this early, and rarely beer," she said.

"What do you drink when you're not drinking beer this early?" he asked, teasing her.

"Stop," she said. She chuckled and took another swig. "I like wine. White. Chard."

The same kind of wine Meg liked. When she wasn't drinking vodka, that is. He glanced away from her. He wanted to go back to Meg but kept finding reasons not to call or see her. The last time they'd slept in the same house, he'd stayed in a guest room.

The relationship turned sour after Lily's death. He didn't know how to talk to her anymore. But he also didn't know if he wanted to either.

"Did I say something wrong?" Leanne asked.

Paul walked up with their order before Jay could answer.

"Oh yes," Jay said. "What I live for."

Leanne laughed openly.

After lunch, they stood outside the restaurant. "Please don't deny me one more second of your time, Leanne. Let me drive you home."

She blushed looking uneasy by the offer but then she turned her eyes to him. They shone under the dim sky like the waters of Lake Mead where the Colorado swirls into an aqua pool becoming a shade of blue that no paint could replicate.

"God, your eyes," he said.

Her cheeks flashed pink, she slid her hands into his, and whispered, "Take me home."

*

Leanne slipped on a downy robe over her tan shoulders. The plush fabric draped in soft folds around her rump. She didn't bother tying the belt, which allowed Jay full sight of her stomach. He took his time viewing her chest, her stomach, her thighs. She was carrying two glasses and a bottle when she returned.

"I think this deserves wine," she said. "Don't you?"

Jay pushed himself up to a sitting position against the upholstered headboard. "The robe sets off your skin color. And, by the way, I think this deserves a marching band, baton twirlers, and a magnum of Champagne, but a glass of wine will work, too."

She laughed, unrestrained. "You're funny," she said, then, "it's teddy bear soft. The robe, that is."

"You're beautiful."

"You are amazing," she said. "I didn't expect, um, this."

"No commitments. I'm not asking for the world. I don't know. Maybe I am. Forever sounds good to me. What I mean is, a slice of you, this slice. If I could snatch the moon out of the sky. It's yours. I mean, if nothing else, nothing other than this. Well, I will die happy."

Leanne covered her face with both hands. "Stop," she whispered.

He hadn't meant to embarrass her. "Wow. I nearly proposed, didn't I?" He swallowed hard, remembering words similar to these when he'd asked Meg for her hand. "Let me just say this, it's the unexpected shred of joy a man remembers most."

"I'm going to the kitchen. The wine?" She handed him the bottle and a corkscrew she lifted from a pocket.

This time Jay laughed. He *could* die happy right now. He knew nothing could eclipse how he felt at this moment.

"Can we slot this under the label of kismet? I mean, why were you at the airport?" For a blink the slightest frown wrinkled her brow but then she recovered. Still, Jay noticed a darkness sink into her eyes and an uneasiness settled over him. "What did I just say?"

Leanne glanced left to a high tree lumbering outside her bedroom window.

"I work there," she said, then left Jay alone in the bedroom. Jay watched her hips shifting slow and easy under the loose robe, her bare feet padding on the rug and out the door.

"Are you embarrassed by that?" he called to her but she either didn't hear him or didn't bother to answer.

38

They kissed outside her door. It was a deep, slow kiss. Jay still tasted the wine from her tongue on his, still felt her warm breath linger along his upper lip, on his cheeks.

Moments before, he'd told her they had to stop or suffer another round of love-making. She had to get back to work, she'd told him. Maybe he would surprise her, he said, at the airport tomorrow, leaving out "with a gift—a bouquet of roses—two or three dozen."

This was love. A lightness moved him as he walked through the parking lot, as he got inside his car, which seemed to be floating on autopilot as he drove away.

Her body had moved in a poetry he hadn't known since before he and Meg had Lily—before, when their sex life was all about being carefree and fun—before caution entered their union, before a child cried in another room, or at the bedroom door disrupting any chance of spontaneity. As he pulled out of the apartment complex, he envisioned Lily as a child, calling through their door and Meg—in an act of de rigueur she'd set for herself—rolling out of bed, pulling on a nightgown, and tending to their child. His smile still there way back when—on the bed, blankets bunched around his girth, watching his wife with admiration and love filled with desperation to consume her but releasing her from bed nonetheless.

Love changes fast, all too soon becoming habit rather than need.

How does life end up so complicated? When does it become chore rather than blessing? \

Guilt flooded him. Prickles spread across his scalp. He had to break it off with one of these women. Jay refused to go behind either one's back. It was wrong he had gone this far with Leanne in the first place, but it had all happened so spontaneously, so naturally.

Good lord. She was twenty years younger than he was. What was he thinking? What did she think? No doubt, that he was an old fool falling headlong in love for a younger woman. He was a cliché. A fool. He knew he had to make a choice. He had to break it off with either Leanne or Meg.

His heart thudded. Dread filled him. Within seconds, Jay went from ecstasy to apprehension and he'd driven less than a mile. He wanted to turn around, make love to Leanne again, face his insecurities, and explore a long-hidden passion he'd forgotten but found with Leanne.

He yanked the steering wheel hard and right, down a twisting road off Lampard. He swung around and was about to head back to her apartment when he spotted Wesley's trash heap of an El Camino driving toward town. He sped out onto the road following when it turned left up Marguerite, toward the Episcopal Church. Jay sped and followed him cutting off a landscaper's wide flatbed. The truck screeched to a stop and the driver laid on the horn. His hand was out the window flipping Jay off. He was yelling something in Spanish. But Jay didn't care. He was on the Wesley's tail.

He barely noticed as visions of Leanne fell away to some outer region of his mind. He was now feet from Wesley's bumper when the El Camino turned right onto Guard. He hoped Wesley didn't notice Jay tailing him and let up on the gas pedal. He reached across the dash, flipped open the glove compartment, and retrieved a sun visor. Then he slipped on a pair of dark shades and continued to follow Wesley who slowed at the three-way intersection of Guard and Tucker. The left indicator of the El Camino blinked on. Just the two of them sat at the juncture. Jay figured if Wesley spotted him, he'd do something—take another photo or get out of his car to say something. Instead, he turned left down Tucker—down Jay's street.

The day turned from ethereal to dire. Things were getting away from him. He wanted to go back to the morning when he was with Leanne. Jay lifted his foot off the gas pedal and backed off Wesley. He decided to give up the chase. He wanted to call Leanne. He needed to talk to Meg. For now, he wasn't going to waste another second on. He had to call Robin's Nest and put in an order of two dozen pink roses—roses to match the blush of her breasts.

He depressed the brake pedal. Enough was enough. For the moment, he quieted his anger. He shelved his desires to track these thugs. For today, anyway. A sudden exhaustion enveloped him. He wanted rest. To dream about beginnings.

And he was about to turn into his parking lot when Wesley's car stopped in the middle of the road, blocking Jay's entrance into the apartment complex. Jay was forced to nudged up on Wesley's tail.

The car was idling. His brake lights flared red. Wesley gunned the engine. Black smoke huffed out of the tailpipe creating a dirty curtain between the cars.

Was this guy egging him on? Jay's cheeks went hot.

What's another dent in that piece of crap?

Jay tapped his gas pedal and edged up closer. Wesley's park lights lit and he gunned his engine again. More toxic smoke rose from the back of the El Camino.

Jay tapped the gas again. This time connecting with the car's bumper. Wesley shot out of his car. He was a lanky piece of dog crap.

"Hey man, what the…?" he yelled, still standing at the door, it wide open.

Jay mouthed two distinct words then flipped him off.

"You're gonna pay, jerk weed!" Wesley yelled.

Jay only flipped him off again but this time out the window. He lifted his arm high and repeated the barb using the previous two distinct words.

Wesley glared at Jay then dipped back into his car. He gunned the engine again. His tires peeled as he screeched off further down Tucker toward Roche Harbor Road.

Jay's heart was sprinting. He'd intentionally committed a traffic violation. He pulled into the complex's parking lot and into his space, sitting there while his nerves melted back to normal.

He gave a nervous laugh and said, "That little bastard."

A chill wound up from his gut and coiled around his heart. He'd never done anything like that before. Wasn't given to acts of impulse. He favored predictable outcomes, never gave in to confrontation. A cool head always won out and now this.

What about karma? What about love thy neighbor?

The words slipped out without thinking, "Who the hell cares?" Then he said, "This is now," and, "you're in my sites now, you little bastard."

39

The urge to learn more about Wesley, the other druggies, and their dealings returned full bore by the following morning. But first, Jay needed to pick up roses. He would set off in search of Wesley after, trail him then.

But when he opened his apartment door, there stood Leanne, her hand fisted, about ready to rap on the door.

He gasped, lifted his palm to his chest, and blurted out, "Oh crap!"

In the other hand she held a cardboard cup container holding two paper coffee cups, with a paper bag slung over her forearm. The scent of hot coffee blossomed up filling the space between them. Oil soaked the bottom of the white bag, which had the logo of a flourish around its label. Jay knew the logo, knew the bakery, Cakes by Felicitations.

"I didn't mean to scare you," she said, then added, "You know what they say…" Jay looked puzzled. "Beware of women bearing coffee and pastry."

Her eyes twinkled in the morning light. Peace washed over him. He opened the door wider, allowing her to enter.

"How did you find me?" He backed up, "Please, come in," he said. When she entered, Jay scanned the area outside in search of Wesley. Or, worse, Meg who might see Leanne there at his apartment. Which, he rethought because he knew Meg wasn't following him. By all indications, she care what happened to him or what he'd been doing the entire time they'd been separated.

He hadn't heard from her in over a week and when he did, she didn't speak with him, only at him. He had called for some things he'd needed. When he got to their house, she made him wait on the doorstep. When she reappeared, she held a brown grocery bag with the items he'd asked for. She set the bag on the mat by his feet, walked back inside, and closed the door behind her, leaving Jay alone. Still, a wave of guilt pulsed through him.

"Yesterday, was, well—" Her words came out fast, practiced but she didn't finish the sentence before Jay started in.

"I feel the same way." It seemed he had no control over his face muscles. He was beaming, joyful—a flood of emotions akin to falling in love for the very first time.

"Do you?" she asked. One of her cheeks twitched.

Jay tipped his head and placed both of his hands on her shoulders. "Spectacular, right?" Knowing something was off by the way she was acting.

Leanne paused, turned away, and headed toward the counter where she set down the coffee and sack of pastries. "Jay," she said with a somber note in her voice. "It was spectacular, but…"

At that moment, he knew he didn't want to hear the rest. Yet still, he asked, "But?"

"I'm terrible at this."

"Terrible at *what*?"

"This. This 'after-the-thing,' thing."

"It's a *thing*, now? Is that what you call what happened?" He felt his skin bristle and go hot. He was right. He'd been a fool—an *old* fool. She must've woken up this morning, realized he was just some old guy that had the hots for her, but in a weak moment, and after too many drinks, made a mistake.

"Jay. Come on. You know as well as I that it was a mistake."

No. He didn't really think she'd say the word, mistake.

She leaned against his kitchen counter like she needed support.

His pulse lodged in his neck somewhere between his windpipe and his mouth. He couldn't breathe. A surge of weakness spilled into his legs. Did he stumble as he walked away? After slumping onto the couch?

He lifted his arms and rested his head back. "A mistake."

"I know it's not what you want to hear but, well, we can't. We just can't. Shouldn't."

"What happened?" he asked. Her brow creased at his question. "Between yesterday and this morning?"

"Nothing." She slid from behind the counter and slipped next to him on the couch but sat at the edge as though ready to stand at any moment. "This thing, whatever it is, isn't right. It's not supposed to have happened. It's complicated. You're complicating things."

"I'm complicating things?" He shook his head and stood up. She rose too. "You sure it's not the other way around?" She wasn't that much shorter than he was, and she smelled so good, just-out-of-the-shower good—fresh, clean. "No. I'm neither complicated nor complicating. I'm me. Jay. And, you're—" he paused, "well, you're stunning."

He slipped one hand around her waist, dipped onto the couch, and pulled her down onto him.

She let him kiss her but acted like she wanted to object. When she pulled away, she said, "Jay." She stood, and said, "We can't." Her face wore the color of a setting sun, each cheek a California poppy, her lips strawberries in the morning mist. She must've recognized an admiration in his eyes glowing with intensity because instead of walking out, she sat next to him, then leaned in to kiss him.

After their lips separated, she started to giggle. "You're rotten," she said.

"I'm rotten? You're the one doing the kissing."

He ran his hands behind her neck. "My turn," he said, and pressed her mouth onto his. It was a small peck at first, as though they were each testing one another. He released her, leaned back, and rested his head against the back of the couch. She held her eyes closed. Her skin still the glow of a morning sun rising, spreading through his dim apartment.

It was her turn next. She opened her eyes. They sparkled with playfulness. She leaned forward and slid her hands around his neck and in one smooth motion she straddled his lap. Again, they kissed but this time he let his mouth slide from hers to her neck where he gently suckled her throat, letting his tongue guide him.

She moaned, and he felt his loins tighten against her rump. Her eyes opened, recognizing his body reacting to hers. It felt so desperate, so new.

There was no stopping this. "Jay," she whispered. "I have to go to work." Her objection rung with a definite insincerity. She giggled again and when they kissed, she flicked her tongue against his.

"You can walk out right now, if you want," his words hummed against their skin. If she got up to leave, he wouldn't object. But when she kissed him again, when her tongue pressed against his with the same intensity the night before, he tightened his hands around her waist, soon letting his caress fall onto her hips, down to her ass.

"You feel so good," he said.

"We shouldn't," she whispered.

"That's not a no."

"I'll be late."

Jay stood, holding her in his arms, then swept her up—an imitation of carrying a bride over the threshold. He headed into the bedroom and as he walked, he said, "I'll write you a note."

Then he kicked the closed the door with his foot.

LILY

OVERTURE SIETE – June 20, 2017

40

I remember waking after sticking that first time. I was so high. My body was floating out somewhere in the sky. I reached out my hand and could touch the blue backdrop. It felt like running my fingers through a waterfall of clouds. I was with God. His hand held me there, up there, up there so high, and pretty and I never wanted to come back to earth.

Someone's voice told me to get off the bed, so I sat up and began to laugh. But then I vomited on the guy who was talking to me. He began laughing too. We both laughed and laughed. He ripped off his shirt and tossed it to a corner in the room. I watched him. His body moved like hot caramel as he slinked over to the dresser and he pulled out a tee-shirt. The material was wadded and wrinkly. His chest and stomach muscles rippled when he lifted it over his head and slipped it on.

I loved watching him dress. I pulled my shirt off. I unsnapped my bra and let it slide off my arms onto the floor.

He didn't use his hands but his smile to push me down on the bed. His smiled helped him pull off my pants. Then he got on me. We rolled and bucked for only a few minutes before he stopped and fell off to the side of me. Then another boy got on me. He was beautiful. More than the first boy. His hair was this dusky, chopped mop. He was bigger, everywhere. Randy. I called his name. His skin was tanner than the first boy's, but the second boy was younger, around twenty-two, and excited by what he'd just seen me do with the other boy. I think he asked permission, if he "could, too?" I said, "Of course." Just like that. Randy lasted longer and we both reached a climax that I thought would never stop.

There was a third boy. Lee. He didn't ask, and I didn't offer. His always drew the ouline of his eyes in eyeliner. He looked ridiculous, clownish. He sat near and took care of himself on the chair while the second boy and I went at it. Lee wasn't pretty like Randy or nice like the other two.

But I was in love with all four of the boys, even Lee—the three boys and H. And I wanted to repeat the same thing over and again. Just the same way, every single day if I could.

So, sorry about the explicit details, Mom. But you asked. That's the euphoria you feel when you do H.

ZAMBADA

41

The fake click from the digital camera was all but hidden by Lee's laughter. Wesley had parked behind Jay's building. Zambada instructed Lee to hide in a natural screen of the complex's Salal hedge abutting the parking lot.

The day was cool. Lee was wearing camo-gear not by coincidence but because Zambada had instructed them to wear something that would act as cover. And Wesley had a cache of camo-gear. He had a small arsenal of weapons, several storage bins holding dried foods, and nine rain-catchment barrels on his property—fifty-five gallons per.

Zambada, who stood nearer Wesley and Randy, swiped one hand across his neck—a knife slice—a signal for Lee to shut the hell up. If these two lovebirds saw Lee, things would wind out of control, but would have to move fast. Zambada preferred setting a plan in motion rather than acting in slap-dash confusion. Planning worked to mitigate collateral damage. It worked to avoid collateral damage if you got boxed in. The girl would have to go, too, he'd thought he'd seen her down in Mexico. If this was the same woman, she was trouble. However, he might've been thinking of another woman. So far, they weren't boxed in. Assuming the biggest idiot of the three idiots could keep his pie-hole shut.

The girl turned away from Jay and blew him a kiss. She skipped down a set of stairs, slipped a white cell phone out of her back pocket, and punched at the screen, balancing the phone between her ear and shoulder while she buttoned her jacket. Her dress was casual in jeans, not like the woman in Mexico who wore the standard uniform, which exhibited to Zambada that he was wrong about her. This gal didn't work in an office or anywhere that required a uniform. Her shoes appeared as if they might better be suited for standing or a more active job, like a clerk at a grocery store, or the post office, or a delivery person.

Her satiny hair bounced with each step as she navigated through the parking lot, where she stopped at a Mini Cooper and disappeared inside. When the car rumbled to a start, Jay slipped back inside his apartment. The woman backed out and drove off, turning right toward town.

Zambada slipped out of a blue-gray rental car and met up with Lee, who showed him the images on his cell phone.

"Send them to me. Get some printed."

Lee nodded and stepped in behind Zambada who joined up with Wesley and Randy. They hid behind a marred blue garbage dumpster that stunk like death.

"What do you want me to do with the prints?" Lee asked Zambada.

"Just get them to me. And shut up." Zambada had no intention of discussing his plans with these morons. They had their job to do. He had his. If everyone could stay focused for more than three seconds, everything would go smoothly. If they became distracted, if they screwed up just once, Zambada would replace them. He had people in other states he could move around—some in Idaho and Oregon. People in Canada.

These three idiots showed little promise in the way of adding value to his organization. If Zambada were to bring on more bodies, more unknowns, it would attract unnecessary attention, attention he didn't need.

Either way, there was time later on to make staffing changes. Now wasn't that time.

MEG

42

An amber SUV with a Re/Max logo on the side and back doors pulled up in front of the house across the street. A youngish woman emerged and popped open the back door. Her hair was cropped businesswoman tight, shaved in the back, and slicked down on the sides. She dressed in a fitted red, power suit, tailored at the waist, cut above the knee, donning four-inch red pumps. Even so, she managed to muscle a "For Sale" sign off the property by straddling the ground around the sign and knocking it back-and-forth until it was as loose as a five-year-old's tooth. When it became dislodged, she tossed the sign into the back of the SUV.

As the door was closing, a U-Haul van pulled in behind the woman. A thick-bodied Mexican man was driving. He wore a tan baseball cap and was an older gentleman around Meg's age, maybe a few years her senior. He stepped down, out of the cab and slammed the door. If a tin can had doors, that was the sound the truck door made when he slammed it. He turned and stared right at Meg who was standing outside the front door watching with a cup of coffee clutched between both hands. Meg lifted her cup and tipped up her chin acknowledging him. She grinned when he nodded back.

"Hola!" The man yelled to Meg.

"Hola!" She called back, and, "Have fun!"

The man tipped his cap and trotted to the hind-end of the U-Haul van where he began unloading its contents.

She wondered when the neighbors across the street had sold their home. Of course, she felt nothing of them leaving—not one way or the other. No one on the street had been very neighborly to the Storm's since Lily had started using drugs. For fourteen years, she'd watched people trade walks back-and-forth, as neighbors will, not once had they included her. Maybe with these new people they might become friends, despite Lily.

The real estate agent fumbled with her cell phone but called out to Meg, "Ma'am, excuse me, ma'am." She had already crossed the street looking like a fairy princess tip-toeing in those heels. She was gaining on Meg in quick steps up the driveway.

"My stupid cell. I can't get a signal."

"We're in a dead zone. Mine has a booster. Want to use my land line?"

"Oh, bless you! May I?"

"Of course. Come in."

"I don't want to bother you."

"No bother. Happens more often than you might think." And she tried to think when the last time was but couldn't remember even one instance, and said again, "Come in."

The real estate agent made a mini-curtsy as she stepped inside. The house smelled like coffee and cut vegetables from last night's salad.

"Oh, that smells good."

"Want some coffee?" Meg asked.

"Only if it's not a bother."

Meg had seen her around. The real estate agents were pseudo-celebs on the island with their faces plastered on "For Sale" signs down streets, and in newspaper ads.

"You're Monica with the really long last name, right?" Meg asked.

The gal laughed and said, "Van Winkle-Blanchette. You have no idea how happy I was to get the name Blanchette when we married. Everyone used to call me, Rip." She laughed freely with an added little gritty end to it, which made Meg laugh also.

As Meg walked by the phone, she picked it up and relayed it behind her to Monica, then continued into the kitchen.

"I'll get the coffee," Meg said.

As Monica dialed, Meg pulled out a mug that looked a lot like hers.

"You're Lily's mom, right?" She called from the hallway

When Meg didn't respond, Monica said, "God, I'm sorry. That was a terrible thing to ask." But she cut her condolence short turning her attention to the person who answered the other end of the call. "Tamara!" She laughed again, in the same edgy way as before. "Mrs. Adaba's stuff arrived. Will you call her and tell her she will be able to move in after the moving guy unloads? No. He doesn't speak English well at all. Yeah. I'll be there within a half-hour. Tell them to wait."

Meg walked up with the gal's mug just before she ended the call.

"Oh, thank you." She took a big gulp and tried to hand the cup back. "I have to run."

"Take it."

"But your cup," she said.

"Drop it back when you can. I have plenty of cups. Or, I can pick it up at Re/Max. Don't worry," Meg said.

"You're a huge, wonderful angel. I so need it today. It's like everything is happening today, for whatever reason. Got someone waiting there right now to see a property."

Meg walked out behind her. She glanced at the moving van. Monica was draining the coffee as she made her way across the street. The man was on his cell phone when he noticed both women. He spun around and walked to the back of the truck. Meg thought his voice sounded odd, more high-pitched than when he said hello to her, but then he coughed and ended the call. Monica had reached her car where she inverted the mug into her mouth. Then she reversed her steps and dashed back to Meg. She held out the mug and mouthed, "Thank you," then leaned in and said, "The guy's a loon. I think he's a transvestite or something. He either talks like a Mexican, no Inglés. Or, like a woman." She paused and shook her head. Then as though considering her words, she said, "Takes all kinds. Right?"

"I guess," Meg said.

"Hey. Thanks again for the phone call *and* the coffee. You're the best," she said, then added, "Delicious, by the way."

She trotted back to her car and called out slowly to the guy, "Will. You. Be. Okay. Here? Aquí?" Gesturing as she spoke. The man gave her a thumbs-up. He glanced over to Meg, then stepped inside the back to retrieve more of the new neighbor's belongings and began unloading.

43

The moving van left three hours before. And the old woman who had arrived via Classic Cars Cab Co. crossed the street on her way over to her new neighbor's home. She moved with a precision of steps, each step emphasized by the *tick-tock* as the tip of a turquoise and gold striped cane struck pavement. She needed the cane to help her ambulate safely. As she scaled the steps up to Meg's front porch, she used the cane as a knocker giving the door three quick raps each hard enough to chip the blue paint.

She was humming a Spanish tune made famous by Pesado called *Mi Promesa*, when Meg opened the door.

"Hello. May I help you?" Meg asked. She glanced past the woman's shoulder then back to the woman standing there.

"Hello, miss," the old woman said. "I just moved in."

The woman had a good inch on Meg and was twice her size.

"Oh, yes. Hello. I saw the moving van earlier."

"Almost everything is in now." The woman patted her head and fanned herself with one hand.

"It's good to meet you. My name is Meg," then she added, "Storm." Meg held out her hand. The woman switched the cane from her right to her left hand and grabbed Meg's in a grip like a fish troller's.

"You wouldn't happen to have a glass of water for an old woman?"

"Of course. Come in."

Meg opened the door wide for the woman to enter. "What's your name?" She asked.

"Oh, I'm so sorry. Where are my manners? Adaba, Izzy Adaba."

"Izzy. I love that name."

"It's short for Isabella."

Izzy had switched the cane back to her right hand and *tick-tocked* her way into the kitchen where she dropped heavily into a wooden chair. Meg got two glasses of water and set one in front of Izzy then pulled out a chair and sat next to her at the table.

"The house has been for sale for a while. It was good to see it sell. Do you like it?"

"Oh, yes," Izzy said. She smiled and sipped the water. "Thank you for the water. You know what they say about water?"

"I'm not sure," Meg said.

"Fish have marital relations in it!" She laughed deep and loud.

Meg's eyes opened wider and chuckled. "I don't think I've ever heard it put that way before but, yes, I guess they must, right?"

Izzy laughed more at Meg and then said, "I prefer scotch."

"I only have wine and vodka?"

"Vodka works. Tomato juice?"

Meg laughed at how funny her new neighbor was.

"Tabasco too?" Izzy asked.

"Why not."

Meg walked to the cabinet where she kept her alcohol, pulled out the vodka and two short rocks glasses, and splashed in a little liquor. She had a six-pack of tomato juice in the pantry and when she returned, Izzy was standing at the kitchen window looking across the street.

"Ice?" Meg asked.

"No, thank you. The room next to this room?"

"The living room, across the entry?"

"Other side."

"That's the master suite."

"You married?"

Meg didn't know what to say and stalled on answering.

"Oh, forgive me. I'm a nosy Nellie," Izzy said. "I get nervous and say the most inappropriate things. You'd think a woman my age would learn by now."

Meg handed Izzy her cocktail, raised her own, and said, "Cheers and congratulations," but before Meg finished toasting, Izzy downed her drink in one gulp.

"Papa used to say, In a gadda de vida! Whenever he lifted a glass to his lips."

Meg was laughing at her and downed her drink too but had to battle the ice in hers.

"I'm going to need to go to bed at this rate," Meg said.

"I'll join you!" Izzy replied.

The response stopped Meg, but she was enjoying the woman so much that she simply laughed off her remark.

"Oh, Izzy. You are a welcome break for me. You have no idea."

"I get that a lot." Her face turned sour, "My late husband used to say that." She shook her head.

"I'm so sorry for your loss."

But Izzy recovered as if he'd never died, "Not to worry. He's been gone twenty-three years," she winked and said, "Never let the grass grow under your ass, is what I always say."

They both laughed when Izzy said she needed to go.

"The previous owners didn't know a thing about cleaning. It's a pig sty in that place. I should spray the kitchen down with a hose. Oh well." She paused but added, "This was fun. I'm coming back tomorrow. May I?"

"Now, wouldn't that be fun?" Meg said.

"Maybe I should call first."

"Hold on," Meg said. She walked to the buffet in the foyer, took out a sheet of paper, and wrote down her cell number. She folded the paper three times then handed it to Izzy. As they walked together to the front door, Meg thought she caught an air of men's cologne.

"Is that Aramis?"

The hand holding the sheet of paper went up and she covered her lips. Then she giggled. "I kept his cologne. Pathetic, isn't it?"

"Not at all. I get it."

Izzy lifted the folded paper in her hand and waved it and she balanced her cane against each step as she descended, turned back once to look back at Meg, winked at her, then walked back to her new home across the street.

SPECIAL AGENT TURNER

44

Given the thick odor of coffee that always seemed to permeate the interior of the courthouse, Agent Turner still noticed a dusty undertone. Probably from wet, soiled shoes entering and exiting the doors all day long, then drying before the cleaning people could mop up each evening.

The chill from outdoors left her body in a shiver as the glass door closed behind her. One of the dispatchers was on a call. His name was Jenkins, Tom Jenkins. Laced with a hint of paternal father in his tinny voice, Jenkins took on a pedantic tone about how shooting guns in rural-residential-agricultural neighborhoods did not break any laws. He wore a portable receiver-microphone headset and sat behind a bullet-resistant transaction window in a darkened room. The room had a single solid-core door leading into the secured area where the offices of the sheriff, deputies, detectives, and other staff worked. Several computers, phones, desks, and chairs filled Jenkins' enclosed area. He rose when he saw Turner step up to the window. He didn't stop speaking to the caller as he approached.

"Yes. It's terrible. The noise guns make," he said. He rolled his eyes and pointed to the phone then twirled his index finger next to his temple indicating the crazy caller.

Agent Turner chuckled.

"Yes, ma'am. 'Bye," he said, then spoke to her. "Hey, Turner. Need Peters?"

"I'm afraid so."

"Doesn't sound good." Then he said into the phone's intercom, "Turner's here. Okay." He hung up. "It'll be a minute."

Turner took the cue. She glanced at the poster hung on the wall of the FBI's Ten Most Wanted—three men of the ten shown had photos with a diagonal, red banner across their chests reading CAPTURED. She squinted, and she stopped on one photo: Eduardo Ravelo, an especially lethal criminal who went by the name of the Lumberman because he liked to beat his victims to death with a piece of wood. That's how he killed his latest recorded victims—a young pregnant woman and the woman's husband. They had been at a birthday party for their five-year-old daughter. She was a consulate for Arizona. She was four months' pregnant. The crime scene stayed with Turner for months. The woman had been bleeding vaginally due to the brutality of the murder. Turner couldn't stop envisioning the dead unborn child still inside the woman.

"Turner," Peters said.

She gasped and answered, "Sheriff."

Peters led her into a secured section apart from the visitor's area, and down a corridor to his office.

217

Neither spoke as they sidled around Denise, the Chief Civil Deputy, who was bending over her assistant's desk. Denise's large posterior dictated the need to walk single-file as they shuffled past her. Even after Denise glanced at them, she showed not one iota of courtesy—to scoot in and allow them room enough to get by. But that was Denise, Turner had learned—a person of low self-esteem and a propensity to dislike other women equal to her or higher than in rank. Word around the drinking fountain was that Denise had applied with the Bureau but didn't get accepted making Turner—a woman and an agent—especially despicable to her.

Turner closed Peters' door and spoke, "Sheriff, sir, a situation has arisen, and I may need to transition out of this tour."

Peters sat behind his desk in a swivel rocker and motioned for Turner to sit also.

"I prefer to stand, sir."

"Transition, huh?" He lifted his eyebrows. "A serious matter."

"Yes, sir."

He interlocked his long fingers behind his head and leaned back in his chair. "Spill it."

"I may be compromised."

"Compromised." Peters rocked forward and lay his arms across the width of his desk. "They make you?"

"I wish it were that simple, sir. No. It's, uh, more convoluted. In fact, sir, I believe I may have compromised the situation myself."

Peters frowned. "In English, Turner." He was obviously frustrated by the double-speak.

But before she could explain, Denise swung open the door. "Sheriff, we have a situation." She left her hand on the knob and motioned for him to come out.

"Can it wait? I'm in the middle of something."

She shook her head and strained her eyes at him. Denise, who Turner was now turning her attention toward, refused to give her any notice. "It's the Pram girl," she said, "she's a mess. It's bad. Real bad. Rick just brought her in."

"Son of a…" he said. "Damnit. Turner, we'll talk later. It's not a good day. Tomorrow first thing. Be here at nine." His words held weight.

He stood to leave.

"Sure thing, sir," she said and proceeded out, past Denise toward the exit.

MEG

45

After hearing knuckles rap against the door twice, Meg stepped out from the kitchen where she was drinking her second cup of coffee and gearing up to go to the gym. She opened the door, but no one was there, so she stepped outside thinking she might see someone walking off. But no one was around.

A boll of cement-colored clouds sat low above the earth, threatening to release a downpour of rain. A gentle breeze rocked a set of four sugar maples springing out in the front yard. A distant wind coming up from South Beach whooshed high above the woods to the left and wrangled its way across the north side of her property. At the corner of her house, two Picea shivered. The conifers grew so near to each other it was difficult to determine one from the other. When the trees rustled, Meg brushed it off to the weather, wind, whatever. She wondered if she'd heard the knock at all. Maybe a bird hit a window.

She turned to go back inside and kicked something she hadn't noticed when she stepped outdoors. It was a brown manila folder lying flat by the coir welcome mat. Flakes of grass lay on top of the folder, and when she lifted it she brushed off the grass. The blades of grass fell silently to the porch, floated, and disappeared between the cracks in the deck. Meg stepped out to the edge of the deck to check for whoever left the folder. A brief wind kicked up, rattling the folder in her hand as though a reminder she had gotten the surprise in the first place.

The paper folder felt cooler than she expected. She pinched the metal clasp that held closed the legal-sized envelope. The chemical smell of commercial-grade glue burst up when she ran her finger under the flap to pull out the document, then the smell dissipated among other odors in her kitchen like the coffee she had just poured. Meg slid out several sheets of printer paper between her finger and thumb. They were all grainy photographs taken in color with ink bleeding into the white margin of the paper.

Other than a tad of pixilation within the edges of each photo, the images were distinct. She certainly recognized one person in the photos. It was Jay. He was kissing another woman. Her back curved under Jay's caress. He was dipping her back, holding her around the waist with his left hand. His right hand supported her neck. They were standing outside of Jay's apartment, apparently in the morning.

Meg's heart thumped into a full trot. Her hands quivered. The paper shook wildly. Meg couldn't make out the woman in the first shot. She flattened the top photo onto the others and pushed away from the table. Before she stood, she raised both hands over her mouth. A grotesque noise exited her lips—a groan rumbling between a whimper and a scream.

They had only been separated a few months since Lily died. How could he do this to her? They weren't divorced. She assumed they were still working things out. Giving each other some space. Apparently, too much space.

She shuffled through the other shots, all equally damning, reprehensible depictions of longing captured by someone photographing them. His hands moved along her body with each photo—the first on her neck, the second cupping her breast, a third with both hands on her ass. There were eleven images. All sickened her. Meg knew the apartment complex, knew Jay's apartment faced the south. The sun hit the west side of his doorway, meaning the sun was in the eastern sky, meaning it was morning. Also, meaning they probably spent the night together. These weren't shots of people who didn't know each other intimately. She remembered how Jay's hands used to move over her body.

Then she spotted it. The giveaway telling Meg who this woman was, a giveaway that someone else, someone who didn't care might have been missed. But there it was—a small red shape below her left ear. The tattoo of a heart. She knew this woman. It was Leanne.

It was the ultimate betrayal. Leanne had befriended her. Jay was still her husband—legally, anyway. They hadn't yet decided to end their marriage. Not until now. Now, there could be no turning back.

46

"What the hell, Jay?"

"Meg," he said. "It just happened."

"Just happened? How does screwing some woman you're not married to just happen?"

He tried to explain but Meg dropped her arm, letting the phone dangle in her palm. Just happen. Did their marriage just happen, too? She called him immediately after she processed the images of Jay kissing Leanne, images that someone left on their doorstep.

Outside, the sun and blue sky were breaking through lumpy clouds. The wind had blown in a sunny day, but Meg's mood was anything but sunny.

How had their life become a farce? How could everything she trusted, simply fall apart? And in such a short amount of time. The precarious nature of life struck her. It's suddenness. It's fickle way. No one gets out alive. That's all fine and good, but can anyone escape without brazen embarrassment? Her shirt shivered with the intensity of her pounding heart. Her hands shook.

She breathed, using a Lamaze technique she'd learned when she was pregnant with Lily. She had lain in Jay's arms with her back to him, feeling his chest with hers heaving up and down in rhythm with his breath—how they concentrated on each intake, each exhale to help alleviate labor pain.

This new pain was like a shot to the chest, radiating down and dark, through the soles of her feet.

How could she, in her fifties, compete with a woman in her thirties?

Right now, Jay was trying to change the point, divert blame, asking who left the packet. He said he was worried about her safety. That whoever left the photos might be dangerous.

He should've thought about putting her in danger before screwing around with someone.

How could she ever look him in the eye?

When would her embarrassment subside? She was old, and the girl he was involved with was Lily's age. She lifted a hand to her mouth.

"Oh, my God," she said. Pressure pulsed behind her eyes in a mix of anger and sadness. When he didn't respond, she said, "I thought we might work things out. I guess I was wrong."

He had tried to speak, but she ended the call. His reasons didn't matter. Not anymore. No amount of talking about his affair could ever fix it. He'd ruined thirty years of history in one weak moment.

It just happened.

She needed a lawyer. They had assets to split up. She didn't want some other woman in her house. Meg swore she would die before ever allowing that.

LILY

Before her high school play

47

"Purr like your kitty, Lil."

"Bootsie does this when she purrs, Dad," Lily said. The soft thudding of air jiggled her lips when she imitated Bootsie. Then she giggled and raised her hand over her mouth. She blushed. It was such a teenage girl thing. Meg shook her head. She used to do the same when she was in her teens—the apples of her cheeks flashing pink, spreading over her forehead, and down her neck. Lily was the prettier version of Meg when she was the same age. The genes of Jay's nose helped, sitting smaller on Lily's face, straight and tipping up at the end. With her eyes sitting farther apart than either one of her parents.

"How did you get those eyes?" Meg asked.

Lily raised her slim shoulders, keeping focused on Jay's digital camera. She shifted her weight, making her wire-formed cat tail bounce behind her. Meg had covered the wire with fake fur that matched her leotard and tights. Lily was one of the singing black cats and had a short dance number with one of the Tom Cats.

"You're the most beautiful cat I've ever seen, sweetie." Jay's compliment got another blush from Lily and a hug, too. Meg wondered when the hugging stopped between them.

"Come on. You'll be late for the opening." Meg tried to hug her, but Lily turned away.

"Your seats are in the second row behind Dorico," she called over her shoulder as she walked to the backstage entrance—a ramp dipping down between the auditorium wall and another half-wall which enclosed the backstage door. Lily stopped, turned back to them, and looked like she wanted to say something.

"What is it, honey?" Meg asked.

But Lily didn't answer. Instead, she leaned hard away from the door and pulled its heavy metal open. The rubber weather stripping at the base shooshed closed behind her.

Meg sighed. "She's growing up too fast."

"Stop," Jay said.

"I can't. I'm her mother. It was nice Mr. Dorico let her sing that solo. Right?"

"She earned it."

Meg bit at her thumbnail. There was a smattering of hanging clouds so close to the earth she believed she could touch them by raising up on her toes. Hemlocks lined the street in front of the high school and shivered in a fraught wind that was not intending to settle anytime soon. For a few moments, the sun split the clouds, flaring out in an array of brilliant shrapnel, spraying in all directions.

The trees diminished the size of the auditorium and its parking lot, one filled to overflowing that night, mostly from proud parents. Many cars lined the street, parked against a sidewalk trimmed by a long stretch of hemlocks.

But right then the sun was doing its thing. It was setting and refracting over and through limbs as it peeked under the clouds, as if to wish the world a big so long.

Meg breathed deeply.

"Can you believe that sky?"

He checked his watch. "We're going to be late." Jay took a few steps toward the auditorium entrance but paused, "You coming?"

Meg wanted to pause time. Following Jay meant time would progress forward and take her small family along with it. Meg reached her arms over her. "Please God. Stop," she whispered, refusing to cry. She brought her arms down and wrapped them around her chest.

"Jay? How many mothers do you think ask God to stop time?"

"Come on," Jay said. His voice quivered. "Let's cry inside."

She walked up the steps and grabbed Jay around the neck.

"Tell me I'm being silly."

"You're being human."

"You, too?"

"Can we not talk about it?" Jay placed an arm around her waist and tried to lead her up the steps, but she stayed put. He tipped his head. "Babe," he said.

She gazed down at her feet.

"Just walk, right?" she asked.

A tear escaped from the corner of her eye. On the cement step, a dark, gray star exploded where it landed. Tonight, there was no turning back. Meg recoiled when Jay grabbed her hand.

"You go. I'll be in."

He paused so she urged him on.

"Go. Hold my spot."

When he slipped through the auditorium entrance, she sat down. It would piss Lily off to see her mother crying. To see her weak like this.

"Dammit," she whispered.

Meg stood and walked to the door, halting once before entering the building, and wishing on the setting sun.

After Lily's high school play

48

Meg felt an edginess growing in Lily. By now, she could tell when a fight was about to erupt. Maybe it was the musty tinge emanating from the carpet and the heat radiating off the stage lights making them irritable.

Lily shifted back and forth on the slant of the auditorium's floor. She was fidgeting.

"You're so stupid."

Meg couldn't believe what was coming out of her daughter's mouth.

"I just asked if Mr. Dorico liked your performance. Don't tell me I'm stupid, young lady."

"Okay, you two. Turn the volume down," Jay said, as Mr. Dorico stepped up behind them. Lily jerked when he appeared.

"She was great," he said, and set a hand on her shoulder. "Just great."

Lily rolled her eyes and spun toward Jay, away from Dorico's touch.

"Lily!" Meg called to her. She tried to discipline Lily with her eyes. Lily burst into tears and tore off out toward the parking lot, but not before screaming, "I sucked it!"

Jay shook Ewan Dorico's hand. "What is she talking about? I thought she was spectacular."

Meg's nerves frayed, cut to ribbons but she tried to hold it together. "That's because she was spectacular. A little terror, but spectacular."

The parents of Lily's girlfriends approached the three of them. The father spoke first. "Lily did great, didn't she?"

"That one note is hard," the mother said. "Bob and Sandy Gladstone," she said, and extended her hand again.

"The Gladstone's," Meg responded. "Meg and Jay. I'd forgotten your first names."

"Dolly is ours. Lil and Dolly have become quite close."

Dorico backed away and walked off. "Need to go backstage. Actors, you know."

Meg and Jay laughed, but the Gladstone's turned to each other. Bob shook his head at Sandy.

"Why didn't Dolly do the show?" Jay asked.

"She's interested in sports more," Sandy said.

Jay nodded his head. "Oh. That's good."

Then Meg chimed in. "She's athletic."

"Yes."

The air fell still. Lily yelled for her parents. She was standing with her head between the front doors when Dolly ran up.

"Let's go, Ma."

"Well, nice to see you again."

Jay grabbed Meg's hand.

"Gotta get that makeup off Lily's face," Meg said.

Lily yelled again but there was an edge in her voice that prompted Meg to drop Jay's hand and walk off. Her voice sounded different—between that of woman and child.

"Jay," Meg called without pausing for him.

He shook Bob's hand again and walked off to catch up with Meg.

*

The house smelled like fried eggs. Butter-laced potatoes lingered with hints of recently-cut watermelon, offering a fresher note to the air which was as warm as the biscuits Lily refused to eat. She hadn't eaten since her show the night before.

The grain in the wood of the door formed in a pattern that modeled something Klimt might create, with whorls the shape of a warped face—its mouth a gaping hole, eyes elongated, opened wide.

"Nothing happened. Quit asking!" Lily yelled from behind the door, her muffled voice not hiding the lie she'd told her mother.

"Stop fighting!" Jay called. He was in the den watching breaking news about Donald Trump, who had just fired the director of the FBI. Everything from politics to family life was on fire. The world was in turmoil.

"Then why are you crying? Your performance was great," Meg said. Persistence was key with Lily.

"Please, Mom."

Meg knew when to stop.

"Well, baby. I'm here, okay? Please remember that."

Meg's throat tightened, hearing her daughter's delicate sobs. She pressed her forehead against the door that separated them. The last time Meg stood there this way was when Jimmy, a school boy Lily had liked, pushed her to the ground. She was eight. Meg told her that, sometimes, boys like girls but show the way they like them in strange ways. That sometimes, when they're acting mean, they really admire you. She never considered telling Lily that some boys might simply try to hurt you just to hurt you. Something Meg hadn't learned until much later in life, which happened right before Jay, when Meg was testing life's "opportunities." Lily's father was a shining example of how to be a decent man. She loved Jay for all the right reasons, but maybe more because she knew he would be a good father to their children.

Before Meg stepped away, she asked, "Is this about a boy?"

"Mother," she pleaded. Between tears, she whispered, "I can't talk about it."

LILY

OVERTURE OCHO – July 15, 2017

49

After I vomited, I couldn't feel a heartbeat in my wrist. I think I asked for help. Someone must have called 911 because I awoke in the ER.

They split, the others. They didn't want to get arrested.

I was so sick. It felt like the worst case of stomach flu, ever—shakes, chills, nausea. I kept throwing up in the ER. And they kept giving me intravenous fluids to help with dehydration and nausea. They also gave me liquid Lorazepam. A lovely thing if you ever have cause to try it. I could have taken a liter-full. Yummy stuff. No prob. I'm fine. More please.

Overdosing is worth the Lorazepam. If you ever think you might overdose, ask for some Loraz, as the nurses called it. Sounds like a Dr. Seuss character.

"Hey, Loraz. My little friend. You're the best until the end. Tell a story, calm me down. Make me happy, be a clown." I think Dr. Seuss would be proud. I can, I am, Lorazepam!

This is the thing, dying isn't so scary once you realize you're dying. Who knows why. All I can say is that I felt this overwhelming sense of peace in the leaving. This world sucks. I was happy to meet the next one. I wasn't scared. I felt equipped. Ready. I said to myself, "Okay, then. Let it be, Jesus." I wanted it. Almost. Because you do think about other people— Mom, Dad. Dorico. The pig. Even Dolly.

In dying, forgiveness blossoms. I forgave them all. Mom. Dad. Dorico, the pig. That's where peace lives. In forgiveness.

But when I woke up? It was like I was angry all over again.

WESLEY

Late Summer 2017

50

Wesley and the others had seen Lily's father lurking around. They'd seen him drive by.

What did he think he was? A detective? The jerk-wad.

Wesley took a drag from his coke-laced cigarette, spun the steering wheel down, and headed down Tucker Road. His mind raged in all directions. He was organizing a plan for their new problem. El Mayo had told him to "handle" it. Mayo Zambada didn't often communicate with Wesley directly so when he got the call, when Wesley heard Mayo's voice—that low whisper and Mexican accent—he stopped everything else to handle it, as Mayo had said.

Wesley understood what Mayo wanted. Handle meant kill.

He knew his yellow and black El Camino looked like a weasel on wheels, but he didn't care. Wesley loved his vintage 1962 car. He liked the low-level rumble of the remanufactured engine. How it vibrated in his temples. He could see, through the rearview mirror, Lee's arm flung softly out the backseat passenger window. His skin was pink, puffy, and hairless. Lee had started shaving his body, said it would help curb DNA evidence to shave. Wesley figured it was one more of Lee's weird habits—along with tweezing his eyebrows and painting the nails on his fingers and toes.

"Shaving your arms, too?"

Lee pulled his arm back inside the car.

"What about it?"

"It's weird, is all."

"DNA, my friend. DNA."

Then Wesley spotted Jay's car. He had parked out near the back of the building off Tucker. Near his apartment. It was all Lily's fault. What a mistake to get involved with her. Now, Mayo was up his butt.

"He's home," Randy said, having seen the car also. He had been coiling a wrapper around and around his finger, smacking on his gum until Wesley wanted to scream.

"Giving it hell," Wesley said.

"Huh?"

"The gum. Good God. Spit."

Randy rolled the passenger window completely open and hacked out a wad of gum as though hacking out a loogy.

Wesley didn't mention the wrapper. He understood nerves better than ever now, especially given what they'd been ordered to do. To *handle* it.

Maybe Lee was right about the DNA. He slowed in front of Jay's apartment complex but saw another car coming up on him in his rearview. He edged up to the next street north of the building and turned down that road, so he would have room enough to turn the car around.

"The dumpsters," Randy said, then added, "We can unload there. After."

Lee made a mewling noise, a sound between a puppy crying and a grown man whining.

"You scared?" Wesley asked. He wanted Lee to hear the sharp judgment in his voice.

"All 'cause of a girl," Lee said.

"Yeah. Well. You didn't know her like us," Wesley said. He laughed and nudged Randy with his bare elbow. "Right, Ran?" he said. He forced down the lump in his throat. Randy's arm felt clammy and cool. The smile snuck from Wesley's mouth when he turned onto Tucker and again into the apartments.

JAY

51

They had duct-taped Jay in the recliner.

No one held a gun to his head—not yet.

Looking merely to gather more information about the drug dealers on the island, Jay hadn't suspected they were on to him. Not until the three men—they were only boys—showed up at his apartment.

The smell of cigarette skulked invisibly around one of the boys—saturated his clothing, his hair. He'd tossed the smoke onto the cement walkway in front of Jay's apartment. The butt flew from the young man's pinched fingers with a flick, landing somewhere off to the side of Jay's door. Near the stairs.

Three young men pushed into his apartment the second Jay unlatched the lock from inside. The door cracked him in the head and sent him falling to the floor. Once inside, they re-locked the door and whipped closed the drapes, black-out drapes the landlord set up in all the apartments. Wesley had a gun and directed Jay with it to get up from the floor and to sit in his fake leather recliner. He suspected that he looked as if he were simply relaxing in his undershirt and sweats, there on the floor. Like nothing unusual. Albeit a bruising cherry swelling on his forehead.

The recliner sat in front of the TV, an end table next to it holding a book, a fantasy called *The Deer Effect*. The book lay half-open, spine up. He had an open Heineken sitting next to the book. The TV's remote control sat next to the can of beer, and next to the beer sat Jay's gun. The Luger—the one his grandfather had left him.

With the curtains drawn, the apartment was as dark as a crypt. The fluorescent light on the ceiling in the kitchen was standard throughout this apartment complex and wasn't on until Wesley ordered Lee to turn it on. The glow left a pallor in the room, washing color from blues and turning them gray, and turning reds, brown.

"Make a noise and you're dead," Wesley said. Then to Randy, he said, "Find something to write on."

Randy hurried into the kitchen and rifled through the drawers until he located one drawer that held within it a yellow pad of lined paper and a pen. He returned with the writing implement and tossed them onto Jay's lap.

Randy was Wesley's right-hand man and did whatever Wesley asked. No questions.

Wesley was the one Lily had fallen in love with. The leader. Wesley Cogman was his full name. Jay had watched them enough now and knew him to be the main distributor for the island's heroin influx. None of the illicit contraband came through unless this guy had his fingers in it. The other two were Wesley's minions—Lee Stevenson and Randy Toker. From what Jay had learned, Toker had a degree in chemistry from UW, and Stevenson had rich parents as well as a propensity for being a pig with a filthy mouth. He used coke when he needed a lift from his heroin low, alternating between the drugs as though they were coffee and warm milk. Lee Stevenson's hands shook as he slipped on a pair of purple nitrile gloves. His habit was showing.

After learning about each man, Jay figured they had reciprocated the favor about him and got nervous when they saw him at the airport. Jay had tried to be so careful. He was about to ask how they had spotted him but remained silent. With fear locked around his throat, he found it ridiculously difficult to form a word.

Something was off with Lee. He was nervous and frightening. He had a dangerous look. His walk was jumpy. His eyes twitched, were bloodshot. This guy was radioactive and seemed he could melt down at any moment. And it was Lee now holding the gun on Jay. Wesley had passed it off to him.

"Don't move or he'll shoot," Wesley said about Lee. He then turned to Randy and said, "Do it." An order to bring out a folded leather pouch. Randy rolled open the pouch, uncoiled a rubber hose, and tied it around Jay's left arm.

Jay tried to shrink away, but Wesley snatched the gun from Lee and pushed it hard to the middle of Jay's forehead.

"Turn on the tube," he ordered Lee.

"Game's on," Lee said. Then he laughed. "Gotta love the Hawks."

The rig had been previously set in the pouch. Randy withdrew a vial, a spoon, and a cigarette torch.

"You might feel a slight prick," he said. His eyes locked on Jay's, then added, "Lily loved this stuff. Cinnamon was her fave. Turns out she loved it too much." Toker chuckled and burned the sienna-colored heroin in the spoon, melting it into liquid form. He placed the needle against the metal of the spoon and withdrew the full length of the thin syringe.

"How much is that?" Jay asked. Suddenly he felt the urge to cry. But he swallowed so that they wouldn't know.

"Just like morphine, which is used for its analgesic properties. They give it to dying patients at one mil per day. This here," he held up the syringe, "is your daily dose. Don't be scared. It's one cc syringe. Lily was never scared."

But Wesley was irritated. "Shut up. Just do it."

Randy pulled Jay's arm straight, flicked at his vein. But Jay fought against him, trying to snatch back his arm. Wesley jammed Jay's head back against the recliner. "Move, you die."

A weak laugh escaped Jay's lips. "Looks like that's what's gonna happen anyway."

The rubber tourniquet pinched against the skin of his left bicep. Randy slipped the needle into his vein while Jay's attention was on Wesley. He groaned. With the needle in his vein, Jay was gearing up for Randy to depress the plunger. If he fought, he was dead. If he didn't, he was certainly dead. Jay's breathing was rapid-fire. The day had certainly not turned out the way he'd hoped.

"Write!" Wesley demanded.

The needle in his arm made it difficult for Jay to think, let alone write.

"What am I…" When he first started to speak, he choked. His throat was cotton. He tried to swallow. It took two times to bring enough saliva into his mouth. He cleared his voice then spoke again, "What am I writing?" His words trembled.

"Your suicide note," Wesley said. He squinted his eyes.

Jay dropped the pad of paper onto the floor between his legs.

"No."

"Do it or you get the smack."

When Wesley waved him on, Lee bent to pick up the pad of paper. He wanted to kick him in the face but what was the point? On and off for six months, Jay had wanted to end his own life. A flood of emotions rose within him. Why was he fighting it now when they were making the decision for him? He wanted to fix things with Meg. Leanne was a fluke. He wanted revenge for Lily.

Lee had slipped in and put the pad on Jay's lap again.

This might be the last time to make it right with his wife. The last time to tell her he was sorry. He used his free hand to write. The first word looked as though a grade-schooler was writing.

"Hurry up," Wesley said, urging him to finish so they could kill him.

The words poured out. Jay was becoming emotional. Silent tears streamed from his eyes.

"Come on," Wesley said, obviously disgusted by Jay's outpouring.

Jay glanced up at him and said, "You want this to read authentic, don't you?"

Wesley rolled his eyes away from his victim.

"So, then let me write," Jay said.

PART FOUR

TODAY

52

He scrolled through the document on his computer and chuckled, apparently at Meg's analogy because he asked, "A werewolf, huh?"

She scratched her neck and pulled a strand of hair behind her ears. Then she said, "You know. They hunt during full moons then lose their memory about what happened the previous night?"

"Ah. Yes. Of course. The amnesia defense."

"You asked."

Meg was past caring now what this guy thought of her and turned away. The assistant was standing at the sink filling up the coffee maker's reservoir. The smell of freshly-ground, roasted beans drifted to where Meg and the man were sitting. The back of the assistant's hair was carved into sharp squares. His neck was clean shaven but appeared irritated and inflamed.

"Zinc'll help your neck."

He turned to her, rubbed a hand across the nape of his neck, then turned back to his job of preparing coffee. "Doesn't hurt," he said.

"Who was first?"

Meg closed her eyes. No one should know any of this story. "I need to pee. Am I allowed to pee?" She realized that she hadn't relieved herself in nearly twenty hours. She gave a big high-five to her bladder and glanced at the handgun in his shoulder holster. He sat back, pushed the laptop away, then pressed it closed.

"It's right after the first bedroom."

When he didn't get up to walk with her, Meg felt a brief sense of relief and proceeded alone down the hall and into a small room. A metal grill on the inside and outside, barred her from escaping the bathroom window. She pressed the door closed and clicked the button, locking the bolt. A full bathtub-shower combo sat at the end of the room under the window. A white pedestal sink sat nearest the door. And a standard toilet with a plastic seat, one that had been left up, sat between the tub and sink. A thinning roll of tissue sat on the back of the commode. The toilet paper holder held an empty tube on its bar. Meg stretched out her back but felt pressure taut in her gut to the point of explosion. How had she not noticed the urge to go? She hurried off her jeans, letting them drop around her feet.

Afterward, she rinsed her face. The hot water on her hands felt more like a warmer temperature of cool but still refreshed her when she splashed her face. She needed a break in action. No one could help her now. Except for God, perhaps. She looked up at the ceiling. "You there?" She closed her eyes. "'Course not."

She wanted to pray but wouldn't ask for help. She couldn't ask for atonement. She was past all of that.

Asking seemed hypocritical, like a last-ditch effort. She sat down on the lid of the toilet seat to add a few more minutes to the much-needed respite. But one of the men rapped on the door and asked, "You okay in there?" It was the main guy.

There was no way out. Certainly, not through the windows.

She flushed the toilet. "Fine. I'm not done."

"Hurry up."

"I said, I'm not finished."

When he didn't answer, she figured he'd walked off. She ground her fingertips into each eye socket and whispered, "I'm sorry." But, again, who was she talking to? More than that, was anyone listening?

As she sat there on the lid, she depressed the handle, letting the toilet flush again. After flipping off the light, she slipped through the door, but the man was standing there, looming over her in the narrow hallway.

"That was too long."

"Can't squeeze through the bars."

"Make it shorter next time. If there is a next time."

"If my peeing takes five minutes or fifty then that's how long I'll take. I needed a break. Give me a break."

"You think you deserve one?"

"Jesus Christ! I don't know."

"Don't curse," he said.

Great. Another believer. They were everywhere.

At the table, the assistant had already filled up her mug. "You going to drug me?" She said lifting the mug before taking a sip.

"That's not how we roll."

"No. Of course not. You just steal people out of their homes with a sack over their heads. And then drag them to some abandoned house. How could anyone ever think you might drug them?"

"Want to make this harder? 'Cause, we can go harder. If you want."

Meg held up one hand for him to stop. And she said, "Let's just finish."

WESLEY

Late Summer 2017

53

They had given Jay only a little of the drug. He vomited like all newbies to heroin. Wesley instructed Randy, the Rat, to take off the tourniquet. Wesley wasn't sure if that was cruel or kind. Taking it off gave Jay a sense that he might get out of this alive. Which he wouldn't. But at least he didn't have a needle propped in his vein or a noose around his arm. He didn't know why he cared, but perhaps offering this small kindness might buy Wesley some sort of chance out of hell.

Wesley reached around his back and, from his pocket, pulled out a silver-cased tube resembling a small telescope. He pieced the tube, a silencer, onto the end of the gun. The end of the gun appeared like the eye of a cadaver—black and dead.

He liked his .357. Not only was it deadly but it looked deadly. It was a man's gun. Not like a .38—a gun used by rookies and gang-bangers.

Each man wore a plain blue workman's jumpsuit—the kind utility employees wore. Each had hairnet, a protective facemask covering his mouth and nose, and a pair of swim goggles. Lee stood closer to the door. He was holding an attaché in one hand. He switched the case into the other hand, wiping a palm on his pantleg. Then he repeated, switching the attaché back to the original hand.

Randy Toker was in the kitchen, searching a cupboard under the sink. He rose suddenly.

"Hey, Wes," Toker said. His voice was smooth and steady. "Looks like the guy wants to off himself anyway. Let 'im." Wesley lowered the gun. Randy had stopped him from putting a bullet in Jay right then and there.

"Give him the tools, is what you're sayin'?" Wesley asked.

Toker nodded. He said, "I mean, why have it on our hands?"

Randy's wisdom seemed to resonate with Wesley. "You're probably right," Wesley said.

Toker stooped down at a lower cupboard. He reached in and pulled out a bottle of glass cleaner. He pulled a pair of sterile gloves from his pocket and slipped them on. He tore off several sheets of paper towels and sprayed the counter with a mist of blue liquid. Immediately, the scent of alcohol and ammonia wafted through the small confines of the apartment.

"Thanks, Rat," Wesley said, musing at how Randy got his nickname. Rat was short for Lab Rat.

Randy began cleaning. He wiped down places the three might have touched before putting on gloves. The doorknob, the countertop, the drawer handles, buttons on the TV. And around where Jay sat—his end table and the arms of the fake leather recliner where they had him duct-taped. Randy gave some gloves to Wesley. The way they hung in his hand reminded him of a deflated condom.

Wesley slipped on the gloves. Lee was the only one not wearing protection. Maybe it was unavoidable for him, maybe not, but that he refused to wear gloves always irked Wesley. Randy tried to give him a pair anyway, but Lee refused. That's when Lee must have noticed Wesley's face go sour because he said, "Latex. I'm allergic, Wes." He lifted his shoulders with the excuse.

Wesley wasn't going to get into an argument. Not in front of Jay. Not that revealing something like that or even something as private as a social security number to Jay would matter in the coming minutes. Jay would be dead soon. Still, Wesley figured it was sort of a killer's code not to discuss certain topics in front of victims. A kindness of sorts that might make it seem they weren't going to be dead in a matter of moments. Anyway, what was the point? He'd deal with Lee later. Not in front of anyone—not the vic or Rat.

Jay glanced down at the letter lying on his lap. Everything he'd been allowed to say filled a single page. His lips moved over the words as he re-read each line with the slightest murmur exiting from his mouth.

Then Jay spoke—not to anyone in particular—not to Wesley or the others. Wesley had seen this same behavior before. The words of a dying person, words meant to be etched in the listener's memory. These were Jay's last words.

"Leave. Meg. Alone," he said. The pauses—those ever-telling halts were meant, Wesley supposed, to be their legacies spoken to the killer. This was the deal: Wesley remembered each dying statement. "You. Bastards. Leave her out of this." Some words spoken in anger. "She's too good. Better than me." Most said with an overlaying of regret and longing, in hopes the killer would remember. And, yes, Wesley remembered them all. He glanced down and took a breath. He watched Jay waiting for the "ever-telling" pause. When it came, Lee began the process. He snatched the pen and note away.

"No," Jay pleaded.

Wesley slipped behind Jay's chair, lowered his arm to the approximate same level of Jay's then dropped the pen on the floor next to the recliner. It bounced once off the carpet and settled a few inches from where it originally landed.

Next, Wesley took Jay's note and dropped it. The paper floated naturally like a leaf to the floor next to Jay's chair, landing not even a foot away from the pen. Not too far away for a good dose of blood spatter.

Toker unrolled a plastic pouch. Inside the pouch were several needles held in small holsters, and three vials of liquid. He pulled out a syringe and a vial and uncapped the needle. Pulling back the plunger he drew the clear liquid into a syringe, flicked the syringe, and depressed enough to get air out of the line. He knelt near Jay's left knee, lifted Jay's sleeve to his shoulder, and secured rubber tubing around his bicep. He tapped

Jay's left median cubital vein at his elbow. The vein bulged blue, ripening for the needle which Toker slipped in with expedience. He stopped before pushing in the plunger.

He nodded to Wesley, who flipped his hand out at Lee. Immediately, Lee withdrew a pair of kneepads. After slipping them up around his pantlegs, Wesley slid Jay's Luger across the end table closer to his right arm.

After "prepping the set," as they called it, everything went fast.

Wesley nodded to Toker and then to Lee.

Toker pushed the plunger on the syringe.

Lee turned up the TV.

Jay's head fell forward.

Wesley pulled off the duct-tape, picked up the gun, slipped it into Jay's right hand, secured one finger around the trigger, and placed the muzzle of the gun to Jay's temple.

"Turn," he said.

The two men obeyed. They both turned their heads to avoid blood spatter spraying their faces.

Wesley pulled Jay's finger in.

The blast sent Jay's head whipping to the left.

Wesley placed Jay's arm on the recliner and let the gun drop.

After checking for a pulse, Wesley said, "Complete," and the men exited the scene.

DETECTIVE LACH BUCHANAN

54

"Unflippin' believable," Detective Lach Buchanan said more to himself than to Zanie Walker or the crime scene unit who were hurrying to gather evidence.

Lach Buchanan wore plain-clothes today and looked a lot like a model paid by GQ, in his slim jeans and untucked shirt—like a regular guy. His blue eyes strained through the depths of Jay's apartment, noting items that appeared out of place—knocked over, dropped—and past the blood that shone sticky and congealing in places like the Naugahyde recliner where blood had already begun to flake. He didn't know what to expect other than what the apartment manager had told him—the noise, "that there was a smell coming from one of the units," and that he'd "found the tenant's body inside." But it was the TV at first, he'd said to the dispatcher. "The guy wouldn't lower the volume on his TV." People were beginning to complain. When the manager entered the unit to check, he noticed the smell. "Rancid," he'd said, "like a rat's nest."

Buchanan reviewed the dispatcher's notes he'd attached to his clipboard. Jenkins had written Buchanan's name in blue marker on a piece of masking tape and stuck it onto the hinged metal clip.

"Get that," he said to Zanie, his CSU with the digital camera. Buchanan was pointing at trace evidence next to the recliner. The evidence was a negligible impression from the tread of a shoe on the gray carpet. A darker shade of gray, dirt possibly from a wet tennis shoe sole, or a hiking boot.

"Good eye, Lach," Zanie said.

"You do it long enough," Lach didn't finish the sentence.

Zanie snapped some close-ups of the floor then she moved up the recliner, taking photos of the chair itself, and portions of Jay's body with each photo. She moved from his feet to his knees, to his lap, stomach, chest, and up to his head where the left half of his skull had been blown out by the gunshot. She snapped pictures of the needle in his collapsed blue vein. It hung like a cigarette resting between a smoker's lazy inhales. She didn't pause. She'd seen worse, Lach knew. Her duty in Afghanistan had been far worse, with children and mothers blown to bits she'd told him once. Lach admired her steel. The way she managed was by running, working out, and taking care of her deer. She fed them every morning. They brought her peace. He enjoyed when she returned to bed, her hair fresh with morning mist, her hands ripe with grain. She returned to him changed, in almost undetectable ways if only for a short while. Tending the deer melted something hard inside her and wore off throughout the day until the need presented itself again with the next morning out feeding deer.

"Dust the desk. The arms of the chair," Lach said, redirecting his mind to the task at hand, instructing Gregory, the other CSU.

"Now?" Gregory asked.

"No. After the coroner. But do everything. The bedroom, the bathroom, the kitchen. Windows, walls. Even the floor. Power through here. I know him." He paused. "Knew him. And call Peters. He needs to see this," he ordered. "Zane? You call."

"Right," she said. She whirled her camera to the back and let it hang while she punched Peters' number into her cell. "Hey. We're at Jay Storm's apartment." She paused while Peters talked. "An apparent suicide." She put her hand on her head and spun around to look at Buchanan. Her eyes held pain in them, worry. "Okay," she said and ended the call. "Not good," was all she said. Then she stowed her cell, slid the camera back around, and continued to snap photos of Jay's apartment.

"What'd he say?"

Zanie hid her eyes behind the lens. Her chin seemed to implode at the question. She shook her head but didn't speak. She spun toward the door and snapped some images of the floor, wall, and entry. She lowered the camera and was walking out when she said, "He crumbled." Then "I'll be back." It took a lot to upset her but hearing Peters cry had hobbled her. "Want some water?" she called out, tears rippling her voice.

Buchanan said, "Sure." But he wondered if she had heard.

LILY

OVERTURE NUEVE – August 12, 2017

55

Mom went nut-cake bonkers when she found my kit and flipped out. I'd never seen her so amped before. What a drama queen. It's like, you can't see something's wrong? Then when you do find my kit, you decide to take measures? Come on. Get a life, Ma.

She asked a whole bunch of questions—about drugs and sex. I told her I've been having sex since high school. Like she didn't know that either. You can see the change in a girl's face when she's having sex. I didn't really want to, but it happened. It didn't stop. I picked guys like choosing gumballs. Pink, sure. Blue, purple. Yellow. Yep. Yep, and yep. All the colors. All the flavors. All the time. I wasn't afraid of getting pregnant. I don't know why but I just wasn't. Still, I got on BPs just in case. Never worried about it and it never happened. So, I was right. Denial, you know, is strong medicine.

Anyway, Mom lost her ass. She slapped me and then apologized. Like it mattered, the slap or the apology. I hated her for both. She's a denier, too. Stupid bitch. I hate her so much. She's the one who pushed me into taking drama class in the first place. I was timid, and she has this the bright idea that maybe throwing me onto stage will help with my shyness. What a loser.

Maybe just let me be shy, you know? What's wrong with shy?

Anything to relieve your shyness you'll find backstage in the costume room with the perv and his groping hands and hard-on. I should've bit off his dick. You think of these things after, though. You panic when it's happening because you wonder if it's your fault. He threatened to kick me out of the show, to take away my solo. It wasn't that I cared about either of those, but what would I tell Mom? They were so proud. Dad was telling everyone.

So, I let him touch me, and then everything else happened.

Leanne knew. How couldn't Mom? Dad's oblivious to anything girl. It wasn't his fault he didn't know, but Mom? Yeah. She knew. She just didn't want to admit it.

So, thanks bunches, Mom, for being such a great parent. Way to go. You win *Mother of the Year* Award.

MEG

56

This marked the second time in six months they had called Meg in to view a dead body. First, Lily's. Now, her husband's. It was the second time in six months that she would make the trip off the island to Mt. Vernon on a visit to the Skagit County Medical Examiner's office. The second time with Brand Jensen, the undersheriff for the county.

But this was the first time her body didn't quake to the point of her feet melting out from under her. This time felt more like peace than suffering when she looked at Jay. Even with the hole in the right side of his head they tried to cover from her sight. Even with the bandaging around his head, the wound was obvious. There was a concavity to the area—an emptiness beneath the gauze, lacking the presence of bone and brain matter—that compiled what used to be his nose, eye socket, and temple. The gauze, by its nature alone, and the size of the spot taped against his skin trying to pass for cover, told Meg he'd lost half his skull upon the bullet's exit. His death had been immediate.

A tinge of orange tinted his skin where the ME had cleaned the area with antimicrobial, probably from syrupy red iodine. She couldn't help but stare. At this point, why not?

"Yes," Meg said. "It's Jay." She identified him by the left side of his face.

An assistant ME stood next to her outside the room where Jay's body lay. He flipped the viewing window blinds closed using a mechanical lever that was screwed into the wall.

"Do you want to sit?" Brand asked.

She didn't answer him, so he repeated, "Mrs. Storm? Do you need a chair?"

"Oh." She had gone numb. "No. Let's go."

No one had mentioned if there was another dead body there—a woman's, and she didn't ask about it. And as hard as she tried, she felt no anger toward her husband now. He looked so vulnerable lying there. Like any other occasion when her eyes lingered during the night of him lying in bed. He looked like he was sleeping. That is, aside from the bulk of woven dressing affixed to his head.

The drive to and from Mt. Vernon to the ME's office and back to the ferry terminal in Anacortes took on a strange quality. A fog had fallen over Harbor Strait, which added a floating sensation to the ferry ride. It felt like driving through whipping cream. She took the time to rest within the sullen environs of the car. A flurry of activity about matters of death would follow soon enough. For now, she'd rest.

"Coffee?" Brand asked. Meg nodded but didn't speak until he pressed her further about the damned coffee. "Anything in it?"

"Cream." The word rang more like a demand. Well, he'd would have to understand her slight in manners.

The gray sky reflected her mood, painting a pallor on the surface of the marina's water where the ferry was pulling away. Meg was sitting in the back and watched through a window where black cormorants were fighting with gulls for territory. They lifted off and back on pylons covered in pine tar and bird feces.

She wanted to hold Jay's funeral sooner than later. Meg and Jay had purchased two additional plots next to Lily's while they were planning her funeral arrangements. Meg's was on the north side and Jay's the south.

"Here," Brand said, startling Meg out of her thoughts, "Sorry, ma'am." His hand was in front of her face when she turned away from the birds.

"Ma'am?" she asked. "Brand, when did I become ma'am to you?"

"Formality."

Meg lifted her eyebrows and nodded, then took the coffee with both hands. She sipped it, testing its heat. It was only lukewarm.

"Okay?" he asked about the coffee.

"Wonderful," she said, forcing a smile. "How long have you lived here, Brand?"

"Long enough to want to move."

She chuckled. "I don't think I could ever leave. Not now."

Brand cocked his head at her. She'd lost her entire family and still wanted to stay. "Not that I want to stay, given the circumstances, but sometimes circumstances root you to a place. How could I ever leave them here alone?"

The car rocked when he shifted his weight back into his seat. He had angled himself so that he could talk with her in a more comfortable position. Now, he took a deep breath and strapped the safety belt around his hips. He grunted low and moved his large frame with effort.

"How often do you do this?" she asked Brand

"You mean, go to the ME?"

"Yeah."

Meg took a sip and waited for him to reply.

"Oh, well, let's see. This makes twice this year," he said. He realized that the first time was for Lily. He flashed an embarrassed glance into the rearview mirror, but just as fast he looked away. He sucked the coffee loudly.

"Lily and Jay?"

"Yep. Man, I'm sorry, Meg," he said. He stared at her in the mirror. "It's not right. You goin' through this." He paused, then said, "Twice."

Meg gazed out the window over her left shoulder where lanes were filling up with ferry traffic to the other islands—Lopez and Orcas, to Shaw.

"Wonder where they're all going."

"Ma'am?"

"Oh, nothing, Brand. Nothing."

His eyes connected with hers in the mirror again. He looked tired. Older. She crumpled back in the seat when the ferry blew its horn. The bellowing reminded her of some great whale. She glanced back into the mirror, but Brand had relaxed into his seat. He pulled his uniform cap down lower over his eyes to keep light out. He wanted to nap, like so many others in their vehicles within the lower yawning maw of the car deck. Meg hadn't wanted to sit upstairs in the passenger area for fear of seeing people she knew.

Meg drew her eyes off the mirror and couldn't imagine how old *she* looked. Like a childless widow. She pictured herself as a woman in some shapeless black dress, nondescript walking shoes, wearing a black scarf around her head, perhaps walking in some obscure back country of Bulgaria on a gravel path, pulling a cart holding all her worldly belongings— which might amount to enough canned food for the road, water, and a photo album of her dead family members.

She closed her eyes. Six months had wiped out her family. Meg wasn't looking forward to the next six.

57

The ferry slowed as it made the turn near the north side of Brown Island, a quarter-mile or so outside Friday Harbor's marina. The water's surface sat glassy in the harbor except for churning water grinding up from the bow thrusters underneath the vessel as it slowed. A blossoming of seaweed and rotting fish overflowed into the car deck.

After leaving the Anacortes terminal, a moment of sunshine came and went when a surprise shower broke out. The surprise shower also came and went. Since, the air had remained still. Meg checked for a bend in the trees and for chop in the water. The marina was a pool of melted silver. The bulge of low-hanging clouds guaranteed the metal color reflecting in the water for hours to come.

"Tell me about it," Meg said. Her words broke Brand's concentration. He was straining to see the ferry slip through the back window of the car in front of them. The sound of a phone buzzing took his attention from the slip. She watched Brand in the rearview mirror as he checked the front passenger seat. He picked up the phone, checked the call, then silenced it. Brand lifted his head again but wouldn't allow his eyes to connect with Meg's. He breathed out slowly and shook his head.

"You don't want to know," he said, understanding she wanted him to tell her about the crime scene. Finally, his eyes met hers in the mirror. They were sad but kind. He took a sip of his coffee and shifted his back against the door. "Why remember him that way?"

"Call it closure."

Brand breathed out. He was quiet for a while before speaking.

"He was in a recliner."

"Sitting up?" She expected him sprawled out on the floor somewhere in his apartment or on his bed, not sitting.

Brand nodded and glanced over to her and continued.

"The gun fell off to the right next to the chair. The note was on the floor in front of his feet."

Her eyes shifted back and forth, imagining the placement of each item in the room.

"At his feet?"

"Yep," Brand answered.

"Why his feet? Why not lying on a table, or his desk, or on the kitchen counter?"

Brand shook his head.

"The note had blood on it," she said.

"I'm sorry."

"No."

She sipped her coffee and stretched her legs to release a tension that had grown in them during the ride. All the cars rocked in rhythm with the ferry as it glided over the water. She remembered the words to an old lullaby she used to sing to Lily as an infant in her cradle, Rock-a-bye Baby, and how, in that tune, the bough had broken.

The smell of engine oil squirreled amid the deck when they kicked on the front thrusters. Brand flipped on auxiliary power to the car and rolled up the windows.

"Is that normal?" she asked him.

"Normal? Nothing's normal about suicide. For anyone."

"It was a big hole," she said.

"Meg. Please. Don't."

"Why not? Does it make you uncomfortable, Brand? Does it bother you that I've not only lost my only daughter but now my husband, too?" There was a tone of unwarranted accusation. She shifted forward as she spoke. Her face felt hot. Her lips tightened with anger.

"Yes. It does."

Meg sat back, surrendering. She hadn't considered how Lily's or Jay's deaths affected others. Why should she? But she let up anyway and stopped attacking him with questions.

For the rest of the short ride to the Friday Harbor ferry slip, they sat silently. She promised herself she wouldn't ask Brand anymore questions about Jay's death.

The ferry's loudspeaker crackled open and the purser's voice blared a message: "We're now approaching your destination, Friday Harbor. All walk-on passengers—people with bicycles—disembark from the car deck below. All drive-on passengers return to your cars. Friday Harbor!"

Brand faced the steering wheel and re-buckled his seatbelt. Meg straightened in her seat, buckled her belt too, and wiped her nose. They were pulling up to the island. After they unloaded, Brand had been instructed to drive Meg back home, where an empty void would greet her.

58

The digital alarm proved her restlessness. It was 2:07 in the morning. Last checked, it was 1:13.

Damp sheets and blankets wrinkled under her. This made the fifth, maybe sixth time she'd awoken during the night. Sleep was as elusive as holding onto time and was also turning out to be an effort in futility—one of torment versus rest. Visions complete with horrifying depictions of Jay and Lily together in an otherworldly realm, of Jay's bandaged head, of bloody needles pressed into each of their veins. Lily in her cat mask.

Each time Meg stirred it was as if she were coming up for air—that she was drowning and would live solely by breaking the barrier between sleep and consciousness. The room was dim, lit only by a nightlight—a present Lily had given her one year for Christmas. The design would fit the décor of a beach house. The glassblower centered an abstract orange seahorse as the light's focal point. The small light dissipated in moody colors, tarnishing around the glow, and fading into somber tones of nighttime.

Articles of Jay's clothing spotted the bed—a white tee-shirt, a pair of beige cargo pants, a long-sleeved dress shirt. Jay's smell lingered in his clothes and intoxicated Meg. Her mood was a constant loop, flipping from angry to morose and back again. She missed him but wanted to scream at him for leaving, for the whole Leanne thing. But somehow, Meg forgave Jay his one sin—a betrayal the strongest of marriages might never survive. Who was she? Showing up like that not only in Meg's life but Jay's as well? How deep the betrayal. She clawed at the tie around her neck, tightening it at first then loosening it after she lost her nerve. She screamed and fell back onto the bed.

She bundled up his blue high school letter sweater and used it for a pillow. She pulled one of his denim shirts over her torso, as a blanket. His socks hung loose around her ankles, her toes barely reaching the tips.

By killing Lily, they had killed Jay, too. Just not at the same time. His death was slower. Painful and drawn out like someone using a rusty saw against your neck instead of the fine blade of a guillotine. Anger flared and crimped Meg's wet face.

At what point would justice be served? On closing the investigation of Lily's death, they deemed her death a suicide because of one blog posting they said acted as a suicide note. It was the lousiest excuse of a suicide note Meg had ever seen, but they closed the investigation a few weeks after. Then they killed Jay. Another suicide note, this time Jay's. How could they honestly believe Jay's death was a coincidence? No matter how much his note gave the appearance of suicide? Those bastards were as responsible for his death as they were for Lily's—as if they'd pulled the trigger for him. Stuck the needle in his arm.

Meg wiped slime from her face with a sheet. She rolled over onto her stomach and scooted to the center of the bed. Again, she clutched Jay's high school sweater and pulled it under her. It was tattered and old, from his East High School days when he lived in Phoenix. The colors, blue and gold, had faded over the years. A seamstress somewhere sometime back in the 70's had embroidered STORM in big box letters on a label on the right side, high on the chest of the sweater. An E depicting the school name was on the left pocket, and a V for varsity league football on the right one. He had quarterbacked a winning season his senior year. He was homecoming king the year he graduated, in 1976.

The past was all she had. All she could hold in her arms was a mist of memories. Her mother had been long dead, and her father? Was as good as dead to her.

Now, Meg had nothing. The two most important people in her life had been snatched from her. How was she supposed to move forward? What did tomorrow hold?

She slipped one arm through the sweater's sleeve, then the other. The warm knitting encased her—emboldening her, strengthening her.

She kicked the linens down to the foot of the bed and began dressing. She hunted for his pants first and slipped them on. Lying flat on her back, she zipped the fly, and buttoned the waistband. Jay's clothing cloaked her in new power—a power she drew from.

Sitting tall on the edge of the bed, she wrenched off the sweater and slipped on one of Jay's tee-shirts. She dragged a pair of his socks onto her feet, their sloppiness filling the emptiness from her toes to the tip of his hiking boots. Tying the laces was all she needed to ensure the boots stay on her feet.

On the dresser, sat a wooden box the size of an apple crate bearing his grandfather's engraved initials. The box had housed Jay's Luger his grandfather left him when he died. The police had sealed the box with a strip of evidence tape and returned it to her that way. It appeared festive, almost like a birthday present with the red tape around it. The dresser's mirror gave the gun box a double-vision, appearing as two.

Two guns—one for each hand.

When she rose, Jay's pants hung from her hips and threatened to slip off. Meg slid out the top drawer. Several coiled belts bunched together looking like a den of snakes ready to strike. She chose a thin, black leather belt, snugged the buckle tight, rolled up her pantlegs, picked up the gun box, and headed to the kitchen.

59

The cold steel of the knife sliced like a razor through the evidence tape. She peeled the tape back, opened the box, and there it sat. Meg wasn't sure how she would feel once she finally laid her eyes on the weapon that had killed her husband. But there it was. If there had been any of Jay's blood at all, the police had scoured it clean.

The gun's eagle-stamped, leather holster had a cut-out for it within the lid of the box. Gray foam encased the gun and holster, like quail eggs.

The gray foam packaging shifted softly away from her fingertips when she lifted the gun. She took a quick breath. She hadn't expected the bulk, the heaviness, the handle in her palm. Such a small form given its weight. The thing had to weigh three pounds, maybe four. As heavy as one of the hand weights at the gym. But soon, the gun felt natural lying there, becoming one with her hand. Her bicep bulged under the new, added weight.

Thinking how Jay must have done it—sitting there. How his depression had taken hold. The depths his soul must have sunk to commit this kind of sin. She understood.

Meg pulled a chair to the center of the tile floor and sat. Then she raised the gun to her temple and closed her eyes.

60

The gun's box gaped open. It sat on the counter under a bank of kitchen cupboards in the unlit room. It was minutes before three in the morning.

What more could the rest of the day bring?

Meg pressed her hands down within the box, one on top of the gun, the other on the black holster. She had stowed both pieces into the foam encasement.

What did I almost do?

She lowered the lid, latched it, impeaching herself that she was either too cowardly to pull the trigger or not despondent enough to brave killing herself. She wasn't sure about either.

The blue morning horizon appeared like a strand of Christmas lights glistening off to the east. Soon, the sky would go from charcoal to linty gray, from gray to golden. Probably coral with weather forecasts promising showers.

A monolithic shadow from the old Douglas fir out back reminded her how some things remain steady, certain, predictable even. The ghostly shadow seemed to cast its darkness within Meg, a gloom that grew in her heart.

It was true what they said, that life wasn't fair. This wasn't what she expected. She didn't want to die but, more than that, she didn't want to go on living without Lily or Jay.

So, now what? Molder in self-pity? And if so, for how long? Tears glistened on the backs of her hands. She pulled out a canister of coffee beans, the grinder,

273

and set up the coffee maker with fresh water. Within a matter of seconds, the burping coffee machine sent off the aroma of roasting beans. The chair on which she'd set out to kill herself, she'd pushed back under the table. A small mountain of Jay's memorabilia sat inside a box she'd placed in the center of the table. She'd peeled back the box's red evidence tape. It hung off in straps from about halfway down the box. The cover sat upside-down and off to one side.

Lach Buchanan had delivered the box himself. Out of respect, he'd said.

Jay had called Meg about Lily, on-and-off throughout their separation. He rarely talked about their marriage or getting back together. Instead, he spoke to her about specifics regarding how Lily had gotten involved in drugs. Like—

When was Lily's first time using?
Did she start with heroin?
Who got her hooked?

Meg knew some of the answers to his questions, but most of Lily's drug use had been a mystery. Meg assumed Jay was trying to make sense of her death. But after seeing the tomes of paperwork he'd gathered—newspaper articles, police reports, print-outs from online sources, such as Alanon, WebMD— she realized that Jay's grief had consumed him in a different way. He was *intellectualizing*, gathering evidence to feed a need—an emptiness—that he could never fill.

The coffee finished brewing and Meg filled her cup, pulled the chair out, and sat in front of the box. Somehow, going through this information honored him. She wanted to go to Jay's funeral with the same knowledge held in the box. Everyone grieves their own way—with their own eccentricities, their own ennui. The tears. The raging. Grief is a lonely job—one, over time, will rectify when the griever believes appropriate. Who was she to judge Jay's process? She wanted to honor this obsession before his funeral. In doing so, she was fulfilling a portion of her own grief. Reading through documents he had read would help honor him. Touching the papers, reading what he had read, walking his last steps with him might help Meg understand Jay's sadness. As if she needed more sadness.

Meg slipped on a pair of reading glasses, wetted the tips of her fingers with her tongue, and drew the first sheet of paper from the top of the pile. The first sheet was a listing of the street names of heroin. She'd seen the same listing before in Lily's first blog posting—the edited post they used as her intention to commit suicide. The slang terms sounded dirty when she whispered them.

The next sheet was an online article from *The Guardian* about how heroin suppliers traffic the drug into the U.S. Next, was an article from InsightCrime.org naming the cartel responsible for supplying heroin to the western U.S. and Canada. The supplier operated out of Sinaloa, Mexico. The cartel, aptly called the Sinaloa Cartel—had been previously run by drug lord Joaquin Guzman Loera, alias El Chapo—the vulgar Mexican lingo for Captain. El Chapo now spent his days and nights incarcerated in a maximum-security prison called the Metropolitan Detention Center in Brooklyn.

Under that was an article showing another man who went by the alias El Molca. His last name was Pozos. This guy was smiling. A true tough guy with, apparently, not much to smile about. A series of chain shackles hog-tied his wrists, waist, and ankles. He held his manacled hands up high and was giving a big "screw you" to the journalists snapping photos. Below the image was a picture of his gold-plated AK47, with images of two submachine gun clips beneath appearing worn and used.

Meg squinted at the images. "Pig," she muttered.

How many people like El Pozos continued to conduct criminal activities from behind bars? This human equivalent of pig feces was no different. Residents probably revered and feared him on the inside.

She tossed the paper, trying to land it back onto the top of the pile, and looked away. But the sheets skidded off the table, floating pendulously to the floor. She held her mug in both hands and took a deep sip. The hot coffee didn't come close to the heat of fury billowing within her.

Jay had been busy. Why hadn't he told her what he was up to? She covered her mouth. Tears slid down her cheeks. These people were responsible for killing her entire family.

Meg wiped her face with a sleeve. Her heart pounded. She slugged down another gulp of coffee and lifted the next sheet from the pile.

It was as if each question lined up with each sheet in the pile. The next paper named the drug lord out of Filo Mayor, Guerrero—the supply-line city in Mexico to the States and Canada. This was Ismael "El Mayo" Zambada. She guessed El Mayo was colloquial for mayor. El Mayo succeeded El Chapo after his arrest in 1993.

Jay had gathered pipeline information plus names of U.S. citizens involved in the drug trade. Many names were Hispanic but there were a few Anglo names, like Anderson and Weber. Touted as top sellers inside the States and working distribution channels for the cartel.

Documents about how Mexican cartels were hiring Colombian "cooks" to make the Mexican black heroin look cleaner—whiter like Asian heroin. But these cooks, called cocineros, could only clean the drug to a lighter color, a lighter brown, so marketed it as "cinnamon." Cinnamon was one of the slang terms Lily had listed.

By five that morning, Meg had only inched her way deeper into the information Jay had compiled. But she felt a buzzing sensation growing inside her. The sensation emanated from her heart and shook her fingertips when she lifted the next sheet of paper. It was from Jay. It was a note scribbled in his succinct handwriting. To her.

Meg,

Hey, babe. I'm sorry for not understanding how sad you were. I'm sorry I didn't stay with you. All I know is back then I couldn't watch you wither away or pull away from you when all I needed was to hang on to you. I'm sorry I didn't tell you that. I should have said those very words.

If you're reading this, then you found the information I've been accumulating over these months of our separation. I decided to put myself to some use. Do a little investigating, you know? And guess what? It's given me my life back. I guess it has also taken it away. But I don't want to die. I want to live. I want you. I want us back. Because I'm not telling you this in person you have to know something went wrong. Either I'm dead or you've become a big sneak and are with me now, rifling through my personal things. Ha ha. I hope that made you laugh. I want you to laugh again. I miss the sound of your laughter, your voice, so much.

Most likely, I'm dead. Please know that if I am dead, you couldn't have done anything to stop it. I think I've stepped into some pretty smelly crap and will die because of it.

The information I've uncovered spans from China to Mexico to here, Meg. Our own little town on our own little island. They look like any one of us, too. But they're bad men. Bad. Meg, be careful. Watch your back, Meg. Your beautiful back.

And Leanne. Oh, Meg. I was going to tell her that I couldn't see her anymore. I'm sorry I hurt you. The thought of hurting you killed me. That's when I realized that I will love you until time ends and then some. Please forgive me. I'm so sorry. I had no choice but to kill myself.

Forever, Jay.

Meg's hands shook. It was the last sentence—the one that he'd obviously erased and rewritten—that made detectives rule Jay's death a suicide.

Were they stupid? Didn't they read the letter in its entirety? Take in the wholeness of his statement?

She pressed the letter to her heart. Never did she experience a time when she wanted to cry and laugh all at once. She loved Jay for all of her adult life. Now she would miss him for the rest.

She picked up her cell and dialed Jay's number just to hear his voice.

"It's about time you called!" the message said. "Please leave your name and number and I'll get back to you right away." Which wasn't true.

His message was the same. It had been the same message he'd had for years and it broke her heart to think that now she'd only be able to hear a recording of his voice—never to hold him again or kiss his lips.

"If I hadn't pushed him away, he would still be alive." The words bled through her tears and the note fell to the floor when she clutched her stomach.

When will the pain end? God? What do I have to do to make the pain stop?

Meg tripped against the leg of the chair but steadied herself and ran to the cupboard. The bottle sat in the front. She grabbed the vodka, opened it, and let the fluid drain straight from the bottle. The alcohol shocked the back of her throat and she coughed. Still, she took another swig right after, then one more. She walked to the table and poured some into her coffee.

Isn't this what they call Russian coffee? The president would be proud.

A quick chuckle escaped her lips. She prepped her drink by pouring in more coffee and topping it off with more vodka. By the time she returned to the table, the liquor had hit her bloodstream. Lily's heroin was like Meg's vodka. Meg's heart cramped to think that only now did she understand the kind of pain that must have fed her daughter's addiction. Lily's need was trying to quell a terrible pain. Every stick of the needle into her arm was simply Lily hoping the pain would end before the effect of the drug wore off. At least the suffering subsided while under the influence.

And Meg knew she needed to re-read all of Lily's blog postings, from beginning to end.

61

Her voice quaked and sounded distant. "Meg?" she said.

"Yes? Who's this?" Meg didn't recognize the voice at first.

"Aunt Emma, dear."

"Auntie! How are you?"

"Well, not so good, honey," she said, then, "I have some," her voice warbled into Meg's cell phone.

"Auntie, I can't hear you very well. You're breaking up."

"These damn cell phones are worth about the time it takes to throw them into the Columbia River."

"Now, I can hear you. What were you saying?"

"Dear, I have some bad news."

Silence fluttered between the miles separating them.

"Oh no. Dad?" Meg asked.

"Yes, dear. He passed early this morning."

"Oh no." One hand lifted to Meg's mouth. She repeated, "Oh no." Her stomach siezed.

"His heart, honey. It was sudden. Just gave out, is all."

"Oh no, Auntie. I'm so sorry. Are you okay?"

"I will be, honey. You know. Just takes time, is all."

"Time…"

Meg stood in the living room looking out the window and listening to Emma speak of things about the estate and her father's remains. But Meg's eyes drifted across the street to Izzy's house. Izzy must be around the same age as her father was. A bicyclist zipped by and distracted her back to Emma's chatter. One yellow leaf tumbled behind the bike as if trying to catch it but giving up and dying only a few feet after the chase.

"So, you see, he wanted you to have the whole banana. It's a bunch of bananas."

"Emma," Meg said, "I won't cut you out of the money—you or Blythe. You know that, right?"

"Honey, keep it. I'm not too far behind your dad and what would I do with it but bequeath it back to you. That's what old maids do. When we kick-off, we give our belongings to other people's children. Anyway, I don't want your dad's money or his things. Wouldn't take them either even if I was destitute. Like to burn them with his body, is what I'd like to do. That man was mean as a missile. 'Course, I can't speak for Blythe. She may want some of it. May want to leave something to your cousin, not that he's in need. Far from it…"

Meg remembered why she had rarely called her dad. She had to get through Emma to talk to him. Emma was aces at bunny-trailing when she talked. One topic always leading to the next, and the next, and…

"Hey Auntie," she said, interrupting Emma's train of thought, "I just can't talk anymore. I wasn't expecting this. Not after, well, everything."

"Oh honey, of course. I'll let you go. And again, I'm so sorry for your loss."

Again?

"Thank you, Em. Love you. I'll call soon," she said, knowing she wouldn't.

62

The ringing of the phone thrust Meg into consciousness. A numb, rosy patch on her cheek blossomed back to life when blood flowed back into the area, where the table had been her pillow after slipping into sleep.

How long was I out?

How many minutes or hours had passed during the skip in time? She sat back in the chair and tried to focus on the phone when it rang again.

Could it be right? Lily Storm's name showed on the caller ID.

Meg checked the number associated with the name. Sure enough, it was Lily's. Had everything been a dream? Was her daughter still alive, and these past months had all been a horrid nightmare?

Meg's chest leapt toward joy. She answered the call and said, "Lily?"

But when a vacant echo filled the line, Meg repeated her daughter's name with the same hopeful tone. However, the funereal hum filled the receiver.

"Hello?" Meg said. She pulled the receiver away once again to check the caller ID. She hadn't been crazy. It read Lily's name. When no one responded, her heart fell. Had it been a weird technological glitch in the cell towers. What were the odds?

And she was about to turn the phone off when someone spoke. The voice was barely audible, holding within it a low sibilance and baritone quality of a man with an accent.

"Ms. Storm?" he said.

"Who's this?"

"Ms. Storm. Your Lily. She was a perfect flower, no?"

His comment was uncomfortably fresh—crude and presumptuous.

"I said, who is this?" she demanded.

"Far from perfect, Ms. Storm." He paused, then said, "Puta. She was a whore."

It was a vile practical joke.

"How dare you."

"Your husband was a philanderer and your daughter a whore, Ms. Storm. What does that make you?"

"Go to hell!" she said.

The phone split into shards when she threw it at the refrigerator.

63

Meg's forearms trembled. She argued with herself that the shaking came from the weight of Jay's gun. But she knew what had caused her hands to shake, to moisten, and caused her resolve to weaken.

The stamped crosshatching of the handle took away any cause to slip in her sweaty palm. And only then did she realize what the crosshatch pattern had been intended for, exactly that, to prevent slipping in a sweaty palm.

The cat mask allowed every part of her face to be hidden except her mouth. Wearing Lily's cat mask somehow helped to vindicate her actions. Felt like justice.

Jay's clothing hung heavy off her shoulders. His shoes looked clownish and awkward.

The three men sat casually in a circle on the floor, playing a game of cards. The jackpot was a vial of heroin lying in the center of their game.

And when Meg stepped out from the shadows behind their bedroom door, each man held up his hands. Just like a thriller movie, they never heard her enter the house, were busy shooting up, drinking, snorting lines of coke all while she craned open a window and snuck in.

Meg's lips spread with pleasure. A surge of adrenaline hit her, making the gun shake even more.

"Holy crap, lady," the younger creep said. "Don't."

"Listen, man," the oldest one said. "You don't need to do this."

He was bartering. Meg sneered. But then she wondered if Lily had done the same.

Meg stepped closer to their little circle and cocked the gun. Each man shriveled, each covering his own head.

She was only six paces from their little circle of hell.

"Move," Meg said, and flicked the gun at each one to separate them. One fled to the left and one to the right—leaving the oldest sitting one alone in the middle.

Her decision was immediate.

She pulled the trigger.

The middle boy fell silent when the bullet split open his throat.

The two remaining screamed.

Again, Meg cocked the gun. There was no controlling the urge.

One of the boys started to cry, "Why," he repeated, mewling the word each time he spoke. Then he started to plead for his life.

The other one, the pretty one Lily had spoken about, went silent. At first, but then he charged her but slipped on some playing cards. Meg jumped to the side and pulled the trigger.

The bullet hit him in the shoulder, but he grabbed his chest and fell open-armed onto his back. He began gasping for air and Meg knew the bullet must've careened off bone, ricocheting into his lung. He convulsed and writhed moments before going still when his arms splayed to each side of his body. The syrup from his blood spread, staining the rug around him and wicking into the cards.

Meg turned to face the last boy who reminded her of a cornered rabbit.

"She didn't overdose, did she?" Meg said. She needed to know what really happened. This was her last chance.

"What?"

"My daughter, you moron. Lily." She raised the mask above her eyebrows.

His face flushed white. He looked around at his friends and began to cry. This boy must be Lee, the ugly one.

To jar him from his trance, Meg yelled, "Hey! Answer me." She wasn't afraid of doing anything at this point, saying anything, to learn exactly what happened to Lily. "Tell me and I'll let you go." She'd even lie.

He wiped his snotty nose on the front of his tank top.

"It was an accident." He cried through the words.

Meg shook her head at his answer and once again cocked the gun.

He flinched, dropped to the ground, and covered his head. He whimpered, "No."

"Shut up!"

Meg felt zero pity. The concept of pity had left her wheelhouse long ago, right after Lily's last stint in rehab.

Lee sniffed back snot and wiped his nose on his shirt again.

"You filthy pig," she said. "Tell me what happened. Now. Or I'll just shoot you and be done with it."

He was huddled on the ground but managed to gaze up, his hands in the air, surrendering. His face was wet. Black eye makeup smeared and ran from under his eyes. His foundation makeup melted off his cheeks leaving his scarred skin visible to her.

"Tell me!"

"Okay. Okay," he said, cowering and pressing his hands in the air at each word.

Meg leaned back on the dresser giving him a cruel moratorium from the torture. She watched, like a prison guard who was allowing a dead man walking a moment to collect himself.

Behind him where he knelt, was a gold crucifix. It hung on a strand of leather off of a thin nail in the wall. Lee must have noticed her staring at the cross.

"Yeah. That's right. We're all God's children. All of us. Even me."

Meg glanced down at Lee and glared.

"What. Happened. To Lily?"

He shook his head like he wasn't going to tell her.

Meg rushed him. She rammed the gun's muzzle against his forehead, shoving his skull with such force he fell back onto the floor. Meg followed his head to the ground making sure to keep the gun pasted against his skin. He lay there staring up at her, with all that makeup, all those tears, begging her for mercy, "No, no. Please."

But Meg had no mercy. "Shut up!" She shoved the gun harder against his head, grinding the back of his skull into the carpet. She anchored her left hand around the right one steadying the gun and double-fisting the handle.

"Now, or you're dead. Now!"

When Lee began to cry again, she stepped back. She was ready. If he wasn't talking, she wasn't playing. She opened her legs to take the gun's thrust.

"It wasn't her fault," he said. His body heaved with tears.

He was going to tell the truth. But she wasn't about to lower her aim.

"Wes was getting it for her. I could see," he paused and looked over at him, "Lots. A paying for it. I saw him falling for her." Lee began crying harder and wriggled over to Wes' body. He laid half-on, half-off his dead friend.

"And," Meg needed more.

"I loved him."

Meg shook her head. "What?" She couldn't believe what she was hearing. "You're gay?"

"I think, I guess so. I don't know but I've loved Wes since high school. When I figured things out. You know, about me," he placed one hand on his chest and then said, "I told him once, but he thought I meant like brotherly love. So, I dropped it."

"What does that have to do with Lily? If Wesley wasn't gay, why did Lily have to die?"

"I thought, if she was gone, out of the picture, I might have a chance." He paused, but added, "She was dead anyway. We were supposed to handle the problem, but Wesley wouldn't do it. He kept putting it off. Kept making excuses for her."

Her eyes flamed at him. Lily died because of a love triangle? "So, you took matters into your own hands. Took away my daughter's chance of any kind of life because you didn't have one?"

"Because we had to! Or it'd be us!"

"Well, now it's you anyway, isn't it?"

His eyes widened but instead of denying her accusation, he confirmed it by nodding his head, confirming her take on what happened, by confessing.

"And Jay?"

Lee went stiff.

"It doesn't matter. I know you are responsible for his death too. That phony suicide note. He'd never shoot up. He'd never take his life. You stupid bastards."

When Meg backed away from him, Lee rolled into a sitting position, then crouched with his hands balancing him on the floor.

"Oh my God," she said. She was putting everything together. Lee killed Lily. Jay started his investigating. These pigs found him out. And they killed him.

Meg walked to the bodies of the other boys and for a moment, didn't know what to do next. Two boys lay dead on the floor. Meg let her arm go limp and dropped next to her thigh. She covered her mouth with her free hand, cast her eyes down, then turned.

When she did, Lee charged.

Meg went down face-forward, onto her hands, forcing the gun loose. It bounced across the rug and landed near the wall.

Lee scrambled on his knees toward the weapon. But Meg rose fast, tackled him, and dropped him onto his stomach. She slipped her right forearm around his throat and hung on with her left. But he got up to his knees enough to reach the gun.

Meg squeezed his neck tighter and bit his ear. He screamed, and blood sputtered into her mouth.

He was struggling for air when a single blast cut through the cabin. It burned past her left ear frizzling her hair from its heat. He was angling the gun toward her.

Still, Meg held on, tightening her right arm in a vice grip by pulling against the arm around his throat with her left hand. He thrashed under the trickle of oxygen but still tried to shake her off. He was gasping. But she clung to his back like a monkey, her legs securing him around his waist.

He tried to shoot her again. She heard the cock pull back from the hammer. He set the gun on his left shoulder. She squirmed to the right just as the gun went off. The bullet hit Meg's ear. Searing pain coursed through the left side of her head. But the bullet zipped by and hit the ceiling. She howled but still she hung on, pulling tighter. Warm red liquid drenched her neck. Her breathing became as exaggerated as his was erratic. He started to gurgle. Her weight, his own, the lack of air caused him to fall in a heap face down. And still, for the third time, he tried to shoot her. His careless grip of the gun appeared more dangerous than before. Again, he shot but only off to the side. The bullet crashed into the glass of a picture on the wall shattering it.

Lee managed to get to one knee. He was a bucking bronco and she was refusing to let go.

He stumbled down then got back up continuing to trip down to his knees from lack of blood to his brain, from being high on heroin, high on coke. But he dropped the gun.

Again, she yanked her right arm in harder, pulling with all the force she could muster.

He gagged, bent closer to the floor, and wheezed.

The gun had fallen under him. His face was pressed against the carpet, with all his strength draining out of him. And with one final tug, she squeezed harder still.

When she heard the tell-tale pop of his hyoid bone, he collapsed.

Meg crumpled to the ground with him, still holding onto his neck, her legs still wrapped around his body.

With the gun wedged underneath his body.

LILY

OVERTURE DIEZ – September 21, 2017

64

As a user, secrecy is of the utmost concern…even among the people who use with you. The point? Wes and the "others" seemed to be distancing themselves from me since I ended up in the ER. When I talked to Wes, he denied it. Of course, he swore up and down that everything was fine but added that I had to be careful with my blog and to keep them more anonymous. Anyone who reads these posts (like all three of you! LOL), knows by now that Wes is my boyfriend. I'll now refer to the others as "the others," in quotations. I went back and deleted their names from previous posts. Wes was adamant, shall we say, about keeping names out of my writing. Whatever.

We had sex. I guess it was his way to show me that nothing was wrong. We got high. Yay! But it was too much for me. I'm not nearly Wes' size. I think he accidentally gave me his dose. I got sick. Puked my brains out, but I wasn't quite as sick as when I ended up in the ER. That time felt like never coming out of the best sleep you'll ever know. Like you just don't want to and can't open your eyes. Like riding in an adult-sized Radio Flyer, you're just pulled along to places on a bumpy ride, in a mesmerized state. Things happen around you, even to you, but nothing matters. Your arms and legs, your head, nothing moves without your wagon and you just want to stay in it and let it pull you along. To where? Does it matter? It never did with me. I love that feeling of never waking up.

Anyway, the sensation wore off after a good day-long nap. I was starving and a little nauseated when I came out. Wes was right there beside me. He must've gotten worried or something because he even had out a stethoscope! The dope. LOL. It was cute. He'd ordered a pizza sometime during the day and gave me the last cold slice. I didn't mind. It's the thought that counts.

I love him so much. We're soulmates. He doesn't tell me he loves me nearly as often as I tell him, but when I ask him if he does he always says, "Yes." I know he does, too. The intensity and frequency of when we make love shows me. Women know these things. Men can't hide their true feelings when they love a woman. I can see it in Wes' eyes and his moves. 😊

65

Meg ducked down a deer trail, through the woods. She had parked her car a good football-field's length from the drug cabin. The morning light was beginning to come on now. The descending vibrato of a thrush echoed from somewhere behind her, a portent mocking her as she ran deeper into the trail.

She could see each fallen limb that lay in front of her, each bramble, each thorn with branches threatening to trip or behead her if she didn't jump or duck in the nick of time.

Musty cedar filled her lungs. The damp air chilled her skin. A sour reminder of vodka coated her tongue.

When she reached the car the sun was cresting, with shards of light gleaming against trees. Traffic was nonexistent at this hour. She slipped into the car and sat for a moment, trying to gather her thoughts.

What had she done?

Three men were dead by her own hand.

How long in hell would she have to remain to cover this mortal sin?

Meg began to cry, but knew she had to get out. She straightened her leg and fished out the car keys. Her hands shook but she somehow found the ignition, and the car growled to life.

She spun the steering wheel hard to the right and was on road.

After a second, her headlights flicked on automatically. Her foot lay flat on the pedal, so she backed it off.

"Oh my God. Oh my God."

After five minutes, Meg was pulling into the circular driveway of her home. She turned the key off at the same time she flipped the gear into park. The car lunged and rocked from shutting off suddenly. She fell out the door and scraped her knee. Meg felt hot blood caking the fabric of her pant leg.

She pushed up off the ground and ran to the door. Behind it, she stood as if hiding from someone—still trying not to breathe but waiting for someone to spot her.

There was no one around, and yet Meg kept her body plastered to the inside of the door until her breathing normalized.

A bead of sweat dripped down her forehead. Her arms relaxed, and when they did her legs followed. She slid to the floor, curled up, and drew her legs into her stomach and covered her head.

How could she take back what had happened? Take back what had happened by her own hand?

PART FIVE

TODAY

66

"Tell me about the woman," the man said to Meg.

"Which woman?" And, remembering, she asked, "Is she dead?"

"What do you think?"

The man leaned back, his queue for Meg to respond. It irked her that she had to answer his question, to sit through hours of grueling silence and intimidation, as was his choice of questioning, questioning she'd witnessed over the previous hours while holding her in the safe house.

It was ten until midnight. They'd been at it for nearly twenty-four hours.

"I need more coffee," Meg said. The assistant pushed out his chair, grabbed her mug, and went to the kitchen to get the pot. When he was filling her cup, Meg asked, "Do you have instant?"

The assistant replaced the coffee pot, set down her mug, and opened a cupboard. He said, "Folgers."

"Will you add two teaspoons. No cream this time. No sugar," then she said, "Make it three."

The man rubbed his eyes. He was tired too. They all were.

"We have two more points. 'Course, as you are aware by now, each point can lead to other issues."

"Get to it already."

"Answer my question."

Meg leaned back, arching her neck behind the top of the kitchen chair. She raised both arms, stretching them, the strain making them jitter from the tension.

"Wait," she said, trying to remember the last question he asked. She rubbed her hands over her face and into each eye. She yawned and said, "Good lord, can the coffee come any slower?"

The assistant walked back with the cup in his hands. "Here you go, ma'am." His movement was as slow and deliberate as his speech. Meg took in a deep breath, smelling the tarry brew then took one sip, and another. She set down the mug. It was so strong, so bitter, that it stung her nose. But she didn't care. She lifted it again and took another gulp.

"I didn't know her. Not really," Meg said about the woman. "I'd only met her a couple times."

LILY

OVERTURE ÓNCÉ – October 25, 2017

67

I thought I could count on my mom to fix things for me. When did I get so naïve? Hey, Ma! If you're reading this, thanks bunches. I needed you and you bailed on me. Sweet. Right? But what should I expect from someone who has spent their entire life being taking care of? You have become selfish with your treasures, Ma. Unbelievable. All I needed was a place to stay. For a night!

I can't believe you hung up on me. Dad never would have done that. Your idea of tough love? Well, screw you. How's that for tough? Do you even care where I slept that night?

In Sunken Park. Under the steps to the ferry landing. I got a little sleep but then woke up from jones-ing for a fix, even a hit. As it turns out, the shakes were from coming off. And the headache? OMG. Felt like an aneurism. I almost walked to Peace Health and admitted myself to emergency. I would've, too, if I could've stopped vomiting. Or having diarrhea. I've never been so sick in my life.

Boyfriend cut me off after kicking me out. Said I was weighing him down. I finally made it home yesterday after thirty-six hours of coming down. He didn't want to at first, Ma, but he fixed me up and we had sex, "For the last time," as he put it after I begged for an hour. The sugar makes you feel so good that all you want is to do it with the one you love.

So, as it turns out, Ma, I didn't need you after all. I'm back with the boys. They said we're going to have a big party, like a reunion. That's how much they missed me there.

Screw you, Ma. Screw you.

Oh, and tell Dad that I love him.

68

Mist blurred the mirror. Droplets fell in a slow, random succession down the glass, one after the other as the bathroom cooled off from Meg's shower. She sat slumped on the bench in a towel. Straggles of hair separated into wet strands around her eyes. Water drained from each strand, falling like tears onto her shoulders.

The lights were off because morning was coming on, because Meg preferred natural light to artificial. The burgeoning of morning would forever be cathartic to her, more so than a solid night's rest because the advent of mornings was the one thing telling Meg that she was still alive.

A shard of sun lit the wall behind her, making the immediate space near her appear darker than the rest of the room, hazier. Meg wiped a round smudge of steam from the mirror and stared at herself.

Three days had passed since she'd been to the cabin. Driving by the place set her nerves on end. Fury motivated her a week before, but guilt and curiosity led her back.

What had she become? She dragged the skin under her eyes down with her fingertips.

No police had shown up at her home. No one from any law enforcement agency had called. No one questioned her. There was not so much as a mention in *The Journal*. A part of her wondered if she'd imagined the whole scene? But it was folly to imagine it was a nightmare, one she'd lived through, one she couldn't wipe from her memory.

A bottle of beige foundation spilled and smeared onto the creamy marble tile of the sink. A dark powder blush speckled the marble like muddy snow. A flat-iron sat cooling and untethered from the electrical outlet. Her brush was inside an open drawer where a tube of lipstick lay uncapped near the flat-iron. She'd thrown clothing and shoes on and off onto the bathroom floor trying to decide what to wear.

Meg had left Jay's gun behind. She only remembered after she'd scrambled out her car, not until after she got home. Not until the next day when she awoke on the floor.

By then she couldn't have gone back to retrieve it. It would've been too risky. She rubbed at a yellowing bruise on her arm. The fight with Lee was a blur. Did she shoot him too, or did the gun go off while they were struggling? Bits of the action escaped her memory.

Squeezing her eyes tight, she tried to un-remember killing the other two men.

But Meg had no time to think about it now. In thirty minutes, the limousine would be there to pick her up and to take her to Jay's graveside funeral service. She lifted an eye pencil to her eyelid. The thought of sitting in church was enough to unhinge her. Meg's hand spasmed when the phone jangled, leaving a black smear of liner under her right eye. She cursed and snatched up the phone.

"Hello?" Her throat felt like gravel.

"Mrs. Storm?"

The smear of eyeliner made her look like a prison inmate.

"Yes?"

"This is Dane from Classic Limos. We're sending a man now. Will you be ready?"

"No. Not yet. Can you give me twenty minutes?"

"Sure. We'll send him in twenty."

Her heart was running at a canter. She needed oxygen—fresh air. The mugginess of the bathroom was closing in on her.

Downstairs she poured herself a cup of coffee. She added her usual cream and sugar and this time, polished off the bottle of vodka into her mug. It wasn't that much. Maybe two shots. Three at the most making the coffee a watery-looking mocha.

She stumbled on one heel when the phone rang again.

Yes. Sure. You can come now.

Dane's voice irritated her. It was as if he were badgering her about the limo ride. And that syrupy tone like, "I'm here at your beck and call because you're paying me."

And, then there she was again, drifting down the dark trail that led toward the cabin. She was running but running backward as though her mind was trying to undo the wrong. If she had only not gone. But she did go. And although she allowed the fantasy, she simply couldn't reverse what she'd done and what she'd done was take the lives of those men.

The doorbell rang. Her hands were shaking when the man in a black cap helped her walk from the door and lead her to a long black Mercedes limo.

She wore a black pantsuit and black flats after stumbling around the house in heels. She wore black sunglasses.

When the gun brigade popped off three shots, Meg didn't budge. The shots irritated her more than anything. It seemed overplayed when others there reacted, acting startled even after a warning from the gun brigade's "Ready and Set." But a pleasant numbness from the liquor allowed her to let them off the hook.

Meg closed her eyes when the uniformed officers began folding the flag, one they had used to cover Jay's coffin. Thirteen folds were meant for each original colony of the United States. She'd heard that somewhere, once upon a time. And then a man was standing in front of her. But she didn't look at his face.

"Mrs. Storm," he said.

Her eyes focused on the ground around his large feet, feet wearing standard formal black shoes. He bent at the waist and handed her the flag. It felt heavier than she would've expected. She took the flag and set it on her lap.

When she glanced up at him, she noticed his eyes weren't kind.

It was Sheriff Peters.

She wondered if he noticed a sense of fear behind her dark glasses. But he was playing a good part. He grabbed Meg's hands and spoke. Her elbows rested gently upon the flag.

"Mrs. Storm," he said again, "Jay was an important part of our country's history and its freedom. This flag represents how honored we are by his service. You might want to open it soon. Folding it is what we do. But to truly honor your husband, you should open his flag."

The sheriff's statement stumped her. Meg's brow pinched. She'd never heard anything like this before at a funeral and Meg had been to several funerals in her lifetime, and never did she remember someone from the gun brigade offering anything but condolences.

He squeezed Meg's hands, and a small sneer split between his lips.

"Okay," he said. And nodding, he stood erect, saluted her, pivoted on one heel, and then marched back to the other uniforms.

69

After the funeral, Meg's church held a reception for Jay. People she hadn't seen in months, some years, had shown up in support. Meg felt dizzy. Lily's funeral seemed like it had happened days ago. She was sitting on a folding chair after braving the initial rush of people through the receiving line.

"Mrs. Storm, I knew your husband from work. He was always so kind when he came in. I'll miss him." A youngish girl wearing a floral dress, tan nylons, and low pumps stood in front of her. The girl seemed not to know what to do with her hands, and so Meg reached for them to hold them in hers. She had worked at the market. She had helped as a bagger during summers. Then Meg remembered her name. This was Lucy. Lucy Irving.

"Thank you, Lucy," Meg said.

Lucy lowered her eyes and shifted away, allowing another person to move in to speak with Meg. It was a man she barely knew. He was speaking, giving his condolences, before he was standing in front of her. Tears brimmed in his eyes. She wondered how Jay knew him. And then the man was gone, too.

Next were two people who stood together, united—Undersheriff Brand Jensen and Sheriff Peters. Brand held out his hand, not for her to hold but to help her up. Peters lifted her by the elbow.

"We need to talk," Peters said.

Brand squinted and glanced behind him. "Over here," he said.

They walked Meg to a place where they would be out of earshot, alone, near a stack of unused folding chairs shoved against a set of large movable partitions. The partitions created a sliding wall that opened or closed depending on attendees within the sanctuary.

Meg began counting to herself people who had shown up and were standing in the reception hall. She stopped when she reached sixty-eight people. Some held plates of food and were sipping coffee. Not enough people were in attendance to open the sliding walls. A sudden sadness for Jay coursed through her.

"Meg, Brand and I need to speak with you," Peters repeated.

She pressed her handkerchief under each eye and then wiped her nose.

"Yes, Sheriff?"

He pulled out a plain white envelope.

"You shouldn't have," Meg began but Peters cut her off.

"No. It's not what you think. You're an asset now. You need to read it and return it to us as soon as possible."

Meg frowned and began to peel back a corner of the letter when Brand stopped her.

"Not here," he said. His eyes shifted to the sheriff's.

Peters grabbed her hand but not in a way to offer comfort. He wanted to stop her from opening the letter. "Call if you have any questions."

Meg could only wonder what was going on and when he released her. By then, she noticed the bag lady had shown up. The same horror she felt before thrummed in her chest.

"Excuse me, Sheriff," Meg said.

The woman was in line at the food table sampling each dish then piling whatever was in front of her onto her plate. Meg walked over to her. The sheriff and Jensen followed her to the end of the table.

"Sorry," she said to the lady, "what's your name again?"

"Maizy," she responded. The lady smiled, held out one hand, and balanced the plate in the other. Meg noticed her bicep flex under the weight.

"Yes, that's it. Maizy," Meg said, and snatched her plate from her. Then she added, "You know, Maizy, I think you show up to these events because you like the food."

Maizy turned to the table. "Yes," she said and offered up a nervous laugh.

The horror she felt came from a knowledge that, had Meg turned left when she turned right, or when she said "yes" instead of "no," she might be standing there in Maizy's shoes.

Or, in Lily's.

It wasn't horror she felt.

If not for the grace of God, there go I.

It was pity.

"I want you to know that I'm appalled," she paused, "that you won't take home a to-go plate. And the church has a food supply closet. Want me to fill up a bag for you?"

Maizy's eyes opened when she smiled. She nodded her head.

"That would be wonderful," she said.

"Here," Meg said, "let's fill this plate. Go ahead and eat. I'll get a bag for you and some things you can freeze at home," she paused, then asked, "You have a ride home?"

Maizy nodded again. "The taxi man."

"Would you mind if I helped you today? I have a car. You're going to need some help getting into your house with all the food you'll have."

Maizy nodded again. Meg took it as an acceptance to her offer.

"Eat," she said to Maizy. "I'll be right back."

Meg walked to the large food closet, larger than a walk-in and stocked with canned, packaged foods, and dried goods. There were toiletries and paper products. Meg opened two paper sacks and filled them both with an assortment of things to eat. She dropped in a few personal hygiene items and household goods, like toilet paper and a package of glass cleaning wipes. She set the bags by the door but when she turned to go back to where Maizy was standing, Pastor Battles charged up behind her.

"The deacons are the ones authorized to get food for people," he said.

"So, why haven't they?"

"She'd be getting bags of food on a weekly basis."

"That's one of the reasons I give to the church, Pastor."

"It's not up to you."

The pastor worked to keep his tone cool and bent down to collect the bags, to return them but Meg stepped in his way. People noticed and milled in closer. Meg leaned in to whisper, and said, "You're a dirty little man, Brian. I didn't say a word either. To anyone. And look, you're paying anyway." She pulled away and smiled.

But her smile faded. She hadn't seen her at the funeral service, but Leanne emerged from somewhere. She hadn't seen her enter the church. She was wearing black slacks, utilitarian shoes, and a jacket with *Federal Bureau of Investigation* embroidered in big gold letters on the back and, on the front, her name: Special Agent Turner. The sheriff, Leanne, Brand, and Lach closed in on Meg and Battles. Lastly, Zanie Walker joined Peters' group.

Peters said to Meg, "Leave it."

But she ignored him. "People are watching, Brian," she said.

He turned around as though startled. He smiled and called to everyone, "It's nothing. Go back to your refreshments."

But, see, timing is everything when people owe a sympathy for someone, and today, they owed a sympathy for Meg. It was her husband she'd put in the ground, her husband they had come to offer their last respects to and to support her.

Leanne began to speak but Meg cut her off. "Don't. You have nothing to say that I will believe."

But Leanne spoke anyway, "Would you believe I've been demoted and exiled to Bellingham?"

"Is that all? Because you deserve much worse. They should fire you." Meg wanted to say more, give Leanne more of her mind but Zanie Walker slipped in between Battles and Meg and Maizy. She faced

Battles and said, "Hey man, let her have the food, I used to be a deacon at the First Presbyterian Church in Phoenix. If no other deacons object," she eyed the crowd in a challenge, "then I will assist this person in-need."

Battles' cheeks scorched red. He clenched his hands by his hips. Then someone else called out to let Maizy have the bags of food. Then another person.

"Come on, Brian," they said, "let Maizy eat."

Then someone else said, "Really Brian? Isn't that what sinners are made of?"

Now, the kids began started in, chanting, "Give Maizy food! Give Maizy food!"

The congregation was in an uproar. Battles turned to Meg.

"Give Maizy the food, Brian." she glared at the pastor with a smirk.

"This is the thanks I get? For giving one of my finest sermons for Jay?"

The crowd began to shrink in around Meg and the pastor but Maizy hung back.

"I don't think you're acting for me or anyone else, here. I think you're thinking of you and you alone. You didn't even know Jay."

And the crowd continued to shout as they spoke to each other, "Give Maizy food! Give Maizy food!" Their voices grew louder and louder until Battles could no longer handle the embarrassment. He stole away to his back office, but the crowd didn't stop. The two little girls who Meg had seen in the bathroom many months before ran up. They grabbed her around the legs, and they hugged her.

70

It was late that night, after Jay's service. Meg sat alone, naked in the middle of her king-sized bed. She held the open envelope between her fingers. The paper felt cool and slick—it smelled like a business office.

When she pulled out the contents, a check and a yellow slip of lined paper fell out from within the folds.

A note within a note. A mystery.

The check was for $2,500 of reward money. The yellow paper was lined, the words handwritten. She opened the larger note first. It was typewritten, filled with words like "herein" and "the undersigned"— words like "investigation" and "entrapment"— legalese standard in an agreement for a confidential informant. This one was for assignments past and future. The peace officer signing the letter was the sheriff. Two other law enforcement officers had witnessed his signature—Lach Buchanan and Leanne Turner. Meg was the stated CI per the agreement, which had been back-dated two months before.

Meg's first reaction was to call Peters back. Make him tell her again—to hear the same words he'd told her earlier that evening before she opened the note. But why? She knew what they wanted from her. She knew she'd been played. So, she set down her cellphone.

Could it be this simple? That the police simply tap a wand and make a crime disappear? That they were letting her off the hook and ending this chapter of her book?

However, upon reading the yellow slip of paper, Meg understood that nothing was simple. Everything had a catch. Including killing a bunch of bad guys that the sheriff's department couldn't stop without her. Damn them to hell. Her face burned with rage, with resentment. The yellow slip explained that if she didn't sign the contract, they would charge her with three murders.

"Son of a…"

She pressed the note against her legs. They had her coming and going. It was either go to jail for the rest of her life, use the gun on herself, or sign the agreement—the same agreement which would obligate her to law enforcement for as long as they wanted. All she needed to do was to sign the stupid document, keep a copy, and return the other copy to the sheriff's department. She examined the reward check. She flipped it over in her hand. The texture was smooth and cool. It looked clean, fresh, simple. Yet, the act of taking it, simply holding it felt dirty. Reward money for the killing made her sick. Meg wadded it up and threw it onto the floor.

What had the sheriff called her? The perfect asset? More like the perfect ass. She covered her face with the contract. How stupid could she have been? How reckless?

He'd told her, "You were so vulnerable. It was easy." That they had faith in her. They. Battles and

Peters working together in some unholy partnership, manipulating her into action. They'd set her up. Placed the dominoes just right to fall when and where they wanted but it was in her falling, her failure, that they arose victorious. Hell, yes, she blamed them. Almost as much as she blamed herself.

71

At one in the morning, a newspaper sat open in front of her on the bed. There was another report of alleged criminal activity by the president. For one year, he had hijacked the country after a rigged election sending the nation into a whirlwind of investigation that uncovered the underworld of big money corruption, campaign buy-offs, and money laundering.

But who really cared? Not Meg. Not anymore.

A rare clear sky shone diamond-like under a sheet of stars tonight. The lunar cycle beamed waxing gibbous with a full moon coming within three short days.

Even with Jay's flag around her shoulders, she shivered. A chilly fall had settled in. Nights came on sooner. Mornings stayed longer. Autumn was the season when the earth edged out days and allowed nights to linger. A wind whipped against the house so hard the glass creaked under its pressure. The shrill call of a great-horned owl bellowed close to the house. Meg imagined it sitting on the crown of the porch. Lore spoke of owls as harbingers of death. Maybe there was something to those tales.

The stench of bitter wine seeped from her pores and she wanted to take a shower. But a logy-ness had consumed every last ounce of her energy.

A candle on the dresser flickered in the dim room. She stared at the flame without much recognition of the candle or its reflection in the mirror. The wine was going down sweet and easy. She took another long draw of cabernet from the fat crystal goblet she was holding.

Adjusting her weight, she snugged her legs under her in a half-kneel and, when she did, the flag slipped down from her shoulders. Her breasts sagged with age, but her hips shone lean and sinewy from working out, from running and running. A juxtaposition was evident between the person in the mirror and the one kneeling on the bed. The crow's feet around her eyes, the flaccid skin of her chest, contrasted with her muscular arms and legs. The oddity would be unsettling if you didn't understand from where she'd traveled to where she was now.

Her life had become a steady fight, one way or the other—with words, actions, with demons—fighting the past and fisting up for the future. Meg pulled the canvas back up to her neck and tied the flag tighter, letting it cape around her. She stood up to examine her body, head to toe.

Thank God, the lights are low.

A sadness floated in on the chuckle that escaped from her lips. In a dare, she let the flag fall open. It hung off her shoulders and fell in long, striped swags over her arms.

When she reached for the gun the open flag further revealed her mature physique. With the gun in her right hand, she placed the business end of it on the same side of her skull as Jay had. An icy prickling coursed over her skin.

Did he feel the same sick sense fill him? Why did she let him leave?

316

All she needed to do was to say, "Stop." But the selfishness of her grief sent him away. The guilt she held onto was like some morbid badge of honor, empty to the touch, but more splendid than skin-on-skin, more consuming than asking him to stay.

Taking a wedding oath to love each other until death set up their end, providing the perfect punishment for her part in Jay's death—allowing him to walk away.

Pulling the trigger fit a punishment to all of her crimes. Meg knew what the Bible instructed regarding suicide, it also instructed that murder was a mortal sin. She was doomed either way.

She slid onto the carpeting and crossed her legs. She didn't want to fall to the floor. Or, off the bed when the bullet struck. Didn't want to mess the mattress. Better to get to the floor, sit against the bed, and pull the trigger there.

With the muzzle level to her temple, everything crystallized. She knew what she had to do.

This pain in her stomach from missing her daughter would never let up. Meg missed Jay too. She adored him and now, with a gun to her head, more than ever. They'd written their love in a picnic table. She wanted that day back, when Lily was four and they all played her favorite game, *Ring-Around-the-Rosie* until Meg could no longer stand without toppling over.

Meg's finger moved from the trigger guard to the trigger. She took two deep breaths and moaned. Could she do it? Put an end to her suffering?

Hell yes.

The Luger twitched in her hand. Her palm went cold. She started to count backward from ten. Then from five. And then, one.

A crash exploded, and the window burst apart. Glass sprayed onto the carpet.

Her body jerked, and she rolled to the right, ducking down when an owl flailed into the room gripping a bat in its claws. Meg scrambled back, still holding onto the gun.

Together the animals had dropped to the floor, stunned only for a moment when they hit the glass. Suddenly, the bat got loose from the owl's talons and limped across the floor trying to get a way. Meg could see its wing bent and busted. But the owl was faster and hopped after the bat. The bird crossed the floor, recaptured the bat which it flattened under the weight of its leathery talons. The bat's jaws gasped open then closed and its beady eyes went dull as it succumbed to death.

A porchlight outside provided backlighting and silhouetted the owl which stood on top of the bat, still with a bug in its teeth. However, in one stroke, the owl ripped into the bat's neck, halving it, and consuming each half with two gulps. A lump from the bat's body moved down the owl's neck and disappeared as it entered its gullet.

Meg still clung to the gun, flattening it against her sternum. The metal felt cold against her bare skin. She knew if the owl came nearer, she would shoot it.

She eased her grip and placed one finger onto the trigger guard.

Suddenly, the porchlight clicked off and the room darkened. As her eyes adjusted, the moon's luster lit and shone on the floor in a rectangle of the window frame. But something moved. Near the head of the bed, she noticed a shadow grow against the wall. Someone appeared at the window outside.

The person extended their arms through the broken glass, past the darkness. And, holding in their hands, Meg spotted the end of a gun and reacted.

She rose to her knees, pointed the Luger, and fired. More glass shattered. The person's arms flew up then they fell backward out of view.

The gunshot frightened the owl. It began clacking its beak as a threat. It fluttered wildly, hopping, waddling as it scurried from one side of the room to the other, sometimes lifting over the floor as it tried to fly to a place where it might get out.

Meg scrambled backward and away.

The owl continued to clack but began to slow its manic activity after the gun blast. Finally, it calmed down and tried to hide in a dark corner of the room and paused, its chest heaving in and out with fear.

Had the owl not stopped her, she would have pulled the trigger as it set against her head. She knew now she could do it, she could off herself. End it all. A chill swept over her brow. The realization that she was capable of anything—of suicide, of murder—caused a physical reaction.

All her bad habits were turning out to be hard to break. But when faced with imminent danger, she fought back, proving she wanted to live more than die.

Her body quaked. She was drowning in the cold waters of self-recrimination, one that told her to sleep. She obeyed by coiling into a fetal position, pulling Jay's flag over her, and blanketing herself under its weight. But instead of closing her eyes, she kept watch on the owl. It had eaten the bat and was settling down, sitting quietly now on the floor. Its piercing eyes blinked open and closed. Then it turned its attention toward the massive hole where once the window had been. Now, the room was open to the night sky and the air it welcomed in, crisp and clean, ripe with fragrances of ocean spray and plump Hawthorne berries. Again, the bird returned its focus to Meg but already seemed to understand its path out. In one motion, it hopped onto the sill unaffected by the shattered glass covering everything from the window ledge to the carpeting. The owl blinked once again turning its head toward Meg then peered onto the ground outside the window. It shuddered making its feathers puff out and settle. Then it spread its wings, leapt into flight, and was gone. She watched mere seconds before she no longer could see the owl. A smear of bat blood in the carpet was the only evidence the owl had ever been there.

A siren whistled along the main road within a mile of her home. One of the neighbors, maybe Mrs. Adaba had called the sheriff's department about the gunfire.

She curled tighter into a ball and thought about how she had preyed on the boys who had preyed on Lily. Were the species on this planet all scavengers at heart?

Still, a sense of certain victory remained in her revenge—being judge, jury, and hangman. Had she done it for Jay and Lily, or simply for her own gratification, of executing the people responsible for their deaths? What kind of monster had she become? Was her soul still intact and, if it was, what would become of it? Her life had been taken hostage by death. She had spiraled headlong, freefalling through time and space, and had morphed into something ugly, something unrecognizable. And she saw no signs of stopping. Like slipping on black ice.

Soon, lights were flashing outside on the street. They blinked between red and white. The tinny sound of people speaking into and from walky-talkies filled the air. Her charge in life had settled to this single moment. If not death, what else was there? The past was lost existing in a dreamy universe with future as elusive as holding air. Life was a bubble—a walk, a talk, a thought, a sensation, a unique bubble each lapping either upon calm waters or onto a sticker patch. The future wasn't a promise but instead a carrot and as untenable as catching wind.

But sometimes the bubble of time stalls and it either stays afloat or pops.

Right now, people were entering the house. They had busted through her front door.

The sheriff was right. She had a purpose. She could stop living. It was an option—a frightening one but, yes, she had given herself the right to take her own life if she wanted. Or, she could wait for her feet to get out of the sticker patch. She could pursue the option he had given her.

Meg crawled to the crumpled check and pressed it into shape. She grabbed the gun, secured the flag tight around her body, and sat at the edge of the bed.

Catching what might be a final look at herself in the mirror, Meg raised the gun in front of her, slipped her finger onto the trigger, pointed it at the mirror, and whispered, "Boom. You're dead."

"Drop the gun!" A woman officer yelled to Meg. But Meg didn't move. She froze with the gun straight out in front of her.

"I said, Drop. The. Gun!" The officer repeated.

The sheep ringtone of an incoming message sounded from her cell. She knew it was one of Lily's overtures. She almost laughed but nothing was funny about it.

"Ma'am. Don't make me shoot you," the officer warned.

Meg raised her left hand off the gun, holding it high. She let the gun swing loose on her right index finger. "Okay. Okay," she said.

Slowly, she bent forward and placed the pistol onto the dresser. The woman officer rushed forward, knocking Meg off the bed and onto the floor, and retrieved the gun.

"Clear!" The officer yelled to others outside Meg's bedroom and stowed Meg's gun into the back of her belt. Two men rushed in and grabbed Meg under the armpits and lifted her into a standing position. The female officer warned them of the glass on the floor.

"She's not wearing any clothes under that, that flag," the woman said. "I'll get her dressed." The woman snagged Meg's pants and sweatshirt off the chair and tossed them to her. "Put those on." She found a pair of running shoes and tossed them on the bed near her bare hip where Meg was dressing.

"My daughter just called. May I take my phone?" Meg asked the woman officer.

"Sure lady. Whatever."

"My daughter is dead but sends me messages on my phone."

As the two deputies led Meg out onto the front porch, she glanced to the ground outside the master suite window. She knew the woman lying there on the ground and could see the woman was dead. She'd only known her a short while. Her wig had fallen off and was upside-down in the grass next to her body. Her purse was still slung around her elbow, but the skirt of her dress had floated up around her hips when she had fallen, revealing beneath the skirt a set of thick, sturdy thighs, and white cotton briefs.

"Mrs. Adaba was my new neighbor," Meg said. Her words dreamy. "She was nice."

The deputies snatched a glance between themselves and one said, "Lady. That ain't no woman," as he led her away, he added, "and she ain't nice."

LILY

OVERTURE DOCE –
November 17, 2017

72

Hey, Mom. I guess, well, I want to forgive you. I hope you can forgive me too. See, I'm sort of scared right now and, well, you're the first person I wanted to talk to. Funny, right?

The party wasn't much of a party. After strapping me down, they made me do too much junk. I got super sick, Ma. So, I made the decision to get off, well, everything—alcohol, drugs—all the stuff. It's just that I love him so much, you know? I'm sure you feel like that with Dad. It's the kind of love that eats at you all day long. He's really all I want. Still, I took a stand. I think it scared him. He told me I didn't have to leave but I need to, if only for a short break.

It's going to be a hard climb out of this deep hole that I'm in. A hole that I dug for myself, although it sure has been fun blaming you. I'm going to need some rehab and we're going to need counseling. Yes, we. I hope you're down with that. Dad, too. Dad needs to be involved in my recovery, our recovery, too. Please talk to him and if you both think we can work this out after all this time, please call me on my new cell, 360/555-0601.

I know I've been a disappointment for the both of you, so I also wanted to say that I'm sorry. I hope you'll forgive me. I'd like to come see you. If you think that's a good idea, I mean.

Maybe I can get clean. If you let me come home, I'll do whatever you want me to. Anyway, I want it to work this time. I want us to work. I miss you so much, ma. You and dad. See you soon!

Yours truly, Lil.

P.S. And, if anything happens to me, mom? Well, I love you. With all my heart.

TODAY

73

None of the lights were on—save for a single, low-watt table lamp on the kitchen counter. The rest of the room fell in dim tones of black and gray.

They had allowed Meg a short nap and were now dragging her back into the main room. They had no choice but to let her rest. She could barely speak by the end of the interview and kept nodding off.

Lights from town cast bright stripes through the windows and the open door. The disparity set the tone for the entire day. It had been a series of glaring truth and underhanded lies.

Sheriff Peters stood in the doorway. He held a set of handcuffs in his right hand. A streetlamp silhouetted his body. Gnats circled the area around him and although she knew they were gnats, she noticed how tiny they appeared next to him, as if swirling dust particles. However, one thing Meg had never noticed was the thickness of Peters' girth, his height, and how the tips of his ears jutted out from his head with him standing there, backlit against the night.

"She okay?" Peters directed his question to the main guy.

"She's tired but willing."

"I'm also standing here listening to every word you're saying," Meg said. She stood with one hand on the chair she'd been slated to use for the past twenty-three hours.

Directing his comment to the Sheriff, the man said, "She has spunk." He paused, then added, "It's all here," he patted the laptop. It was still on the table.

"No tapes, right?"

"As ordered. No."

"How're you doing?" Peters tipped his chin up, the question to Meg.

"Pissed."

The man spoke up, repeating, "Spunk," in testament to his previous assessment.

"Always," the Sheriff replied. Now, he spoke directly to Meg, "I have to process you, like any other perp. You'll be out by noon. Your CI contract is dated for before. Few are privy. Very few. A case of self-defense. No one will be the wiser, assuming you behave and do what we ask, when we ask. And assuming family doesn't press the issue, but we don't think they will. Most have files. Some incarcerated." Peters glanced to the man, then back to Meg. He said, "Got it?"

"Whatever," she said.

"No. Not whatever. You either cooperate or your file changes. You're indicted and sent away for a long time."

"I have nothing to lose but time."

"Meg. You don't want that. I don't want that. So," he repeated, "got it?"

To stonewall meant prison time. To agree meant her life was owned by these people.

"Fine. Yes. Whatever." She said.

"Time?" Peters asked. The man was at the table. The assistant checked his watch and said, "12:07."

The man bent forward, opened the laptop again, and typed something. Meg assumed the timestamp. The assistant yawned.

"Sign this," the man said to her, "use your finger." The laptop was a touch pad-type. "Here," he said, pointing to a line in the document. Meg scribbled her signature and the man scribbled his. Then he stood by the table. The assistant walked to the sink to rinse dishes and began placing them inside the dishwasher.

And that was that. They were releasing her from this God forsaken house.

By the end of the interview, Meg realized she couldn't recall much of what happened over the last two weeks. Many of the details had slipped into the deep chasm of subconsciousness. She understood what had happened, but actual visuals remained in the distance, feral like a bad dream she wanted to stifle. No matter how hard she worked to recall each action, each movement—each of hers, of theirs—the images stalled out, remained unattainable, like trying to force two north poles of magnets together.

Peters approached her. "Sorry but…" He lifted the cuffs.

"You have got to be kidding," Meg said.

He waited for her to acquiesce. His eyes locked on hers. She looked to the right then left. Not only was this ridiculous it was downright embarrassing.

"Good God," she said, lifting her arms in front of her. When she did, he fastened each cuff around her wrists. Then he led her out and down a set of three concrete steps to an unmarked vehicle, where it sat parked at the end of the walkway. He opened the passenger door and placed one hand on her head, pressing her down into the car.

But anger flamed up when she felt his hand. She balked, shifted her weight onto her left foot. She forced her body backward, away from the car. When she did, she leaned to the right and slammed the heel of her boot onto the arch of his left foot. Peters bellowed out in pain. He released her and stumbled to the side.

"Don't touch me!"

The man rushed to the door. He exited the house, his assistant following right behind. "You okay?" The man called.

Peters raised a halting hand. "We're good," he called back. He bent over his injured foot, at the same time trying not to set Meg free.

"Never touch me again." Meg's eyes glared. Fierceness rumbled deep in her throat.

"Jesus, Meg." Peters erected himself, and said, "standard practice."

"I'll go to prison before you touch me again," she paused but anger only seemed to grow. "And, by the freaking way, it seems you owe me. You all," she circled her hand around in the air and back toward the house where the men stood watching. "You all seem to be as complicit in this whole catastrophe as I am. So, please don't attempt to make it sound like you're doing me favors. That I'm the one at risk. When you know as well as I, that I could walk my ass back inside, tell those feds I won't cooperate, and instead go to court to make a public statement. Understand?"

The main guy came outside and stood at the end of the porch, "Need help?"

When Peters didn't respond, Meg repeated her question, "Do. You. Understand me?"

He glared at her, then grumbled over his shoulder back to the guy at the door, "We're fine." He nodded to her and he said, "Get in." And instead of assisting her into the vehicle, he made a grand sweeping gesture for her to get enter the car.

Once inside, Peters placed a portable magnetic emergency beacon on top of his car. Then he slid the window open that separated the front seat from the back. He gestured to her with one small key, she lifted her wrists to him, and he unlocked the handcuffs, and said, "There you go, Meg."

But she pulled herself close to the small open window between them and whispered, "Not so familiar. Here on out? You call me *Mrs*. Storm."

THE ROAD AFTER

He yanked the steering wheel hard left and sent the car careening crossways skidding over the white line. When the tires hit the slope inside the ditch, the car flipped, inverted, and landed on the roof, crushing it, and busting out the driver side windows.

Meg didn't know how long she'd been unconscious when she awoke. She was hanging upside-down, secured by the seatbelt she'd put on after being locked in the backseat of Peter's vehicle. She remembered they were heading south, out of town. He was driving her home, said processing could wait one more day.

Her head was barely glancing off the crumpled roof. But, just in case, she tested the mobility of her neck, twisting her head first to the right, then the left. The emergency light had fallen off the car and landed on the street, ditch-side but was still circling, still flashing, adding a choppiness—the end of an old film flipping off a reel—to the scene outside the car.

A moth fluttered near the window, first making its way into the light, then disappearing inside the dark, and again reappearing in the light, its dusty body changing from colorless to a pink chroma when it entered each swath of light.

Meg turned her attention to inside the car. She whispered, "Sheriff?" When he didn't respond, Meg spoke louder. Still nothing.

Then she saw. His head bent with an irregular contour, one which lacked symmetry. His left ear sat against his shoulder. The right side of his head nearest his temple, appeared angular and flat. Where her height had allowed the crown of her head to merely graze the car ceiling, his height caused his head to be crushed upon impact and to snap his neck. Death must have been instant. But she couldn't bother with him. She required a new game plan—how to exit the vehicle.

She placed one palm onto the ceiling in support of her weight. And, readying herself for gravity's toll, she unbuckled the seatbelt with her free hand. When it released, she slid against the flattened ceiling and was now lying on her back.

The glass had cracked into a mosaic pattern that swung loose like a wet sheet but remained intact because of wire enmeshed in the safety glass. She barely kicked at the window when the mesh shredded, sending half-inch chunks of glass outside, onto the ground.

She wriggled out of the busted-out window and noticed that her left wrist was tender, but she didn't believe it was broken. And although her back felt like someone had taken a baseball to it, she was okay. Even so, Meg took her time standing up.

Then, she remembered. Peters had swerved to miss the deer. There were two—a doe and its fawn. Then, boom! Lights out.

Meg walked out of the ditch leaving Peters inside the car. And there was the doe. It was lying roadside, on the pavement. She was dead. Still, Meg knelt to check for a pulse and feeling nothing, she took in one long drag of breath.

She cupped her eyes. She struggled to see much of anything under the night's moonless sky. But soon she located the fawn. It huddled in the ditch opposite of where the car buried. The little thing still had spots—a rare, autumn fawn that would soon perish without its mother.

The swirling emergency light added a phantasmagoria of red and white, strobing and blinking on and off over the street, over the doe, and over the fawn's tiny body.

Meg took one shy step closer, careful not to prompt the fawn to dart off. As it turned out, the little thing only coiled tighter. It was paralyzed with fear, and fear was a good thing for the fawn right about now. She took two more steps and was upon the baby. When she placed a hand on its shoulder, the thing bleated, sounding much like the call of a crying lamb.

"It's okay," Meg whispered in a voice so quiet she wondered if she'd spoken the words at all. Her feet were set wide inside the ditch and she evened out her balance, all the while holding the fawn in place. Next, she slipped her hand around the tiny creature's shoulder, making sure to hold it still while she slipped her sore arm underneath its body. In one sweep, she lifted the fawn close, into her chest. The baby couldn't have weighed more than ten pounds, fifteen, max.

After turning in a half-circle, Meg realized they were less than one mile from her house. Peters had crashed the car on Cattle Point Road, just before Portland Fair. After climbing up and out of a shallow incline in the ditch, she realized that she knew a shortcut down Portland Fair, through the woods, to shorten the trip back home. The shortcut wound between two neighboring properties, then opened up onto False Bay Drive, just steps from her driveway. Plus, the shortcut made traveling so she wouldn't have to walk the larger artery where someone might spot her.

Peters was dead. No since hanging around for authorities. She needed to secure the fawn first. Stabilize it and get it fed. Then, she would contact the Sheriff's department, assuming someone hadn't already.

She repositioned the fawn higher in her arms and felt its heart racing against her chest. It didn't fight. Didn't even try to fight. But then, the little thing wriggled tighter, its snout into her armpit.

The flashing emergency light spread wider and higher in the air as they walked further from the car as it began to dissipate against the black velvet of night. Still, a watercolor of red and white painted a wall of bramble and a boulder where someone had built a split-rail fence. The fence ambled up and over the boulder's arc then stair-stepped up and back down matching the lift and fall of the road.

By the time she reached Portland Fair, the flashing red and white of light had all but gone out for her and, Meg assumed, for the fawn. On and off, she looked back checking behind her. The glow, sparking in a *blink, blink, blink*, had melted high above the road and into the sky until, once and for all, she could no longer see it. The light was no longer a witness to her crimes—of leaving the scene and absconding with a child of someone other than her own. She bit back tears that threatened her eyes. Yet further still, she continued, abandoning the light behind them and walking headlong, deeper into darkness, her arms heavy with and warmed by a fawn.

And when she cornered the final bend in the road, she paused, and lifted her eyes to a starry sky. When she recognized the outline of the Big Dipper, she said, "Okay then," to a greater thing she had long forgotten, but no one in particular. She spoke no name but a niggling sense in her understood that name to be God.

And, after making one more claim to the heavens, Meg turned toward the path, near the entrance down a gravelly shortcut. There'd be no turning back. Life hurtled forward, falling through time and space with the same gusto, at the same speed, right along with the earth.

So, Meg braced her jaw, steeling herself for whatever lay in store. Then she stepped one steady foot onto the path and headed toward home.

THE END

You have just finished reading STORM SEASON by Susan Wingate. Susan sincerely hopes you will leave an honest review of this story on the site you purchased this novel.

For purchases on Amazon.com, please follow this link to leave a review:
https://www.amazon.com/dp/B07DKR216S/

You can also write a review of STORM SEASON on Goodreads by following this link:

Thank you again for reading STORM SEASON.

To read more books by Susan Wingate or to sign up for her newsletter, visit her website, www.susanwingate.com.

ABOUT THE AUTHOR

Susan Wingate is a #1 Amazon bestseller and an award-winning author of stories that span the genres of of mystery and family drama.

When Susan isn't writing she's either out feeding a herd of black-tailed deer, chatting with raccoons, or exploring the woods of their five-acre property. Susan lives with her husband and a compendium of cats, a dash of dogs, and a bevy of birds. In fact, Susan posts plenty of animal pics on her Facebook, Twitter, and Instagram pages.

Learn more about Susan by checking out her website: SusanWingate.com

MORE INFORMATION ABOUT THE WRITING OF "STORM SEASON"

In April 2015, I saw two turkey vultures devouring what was left of a just-born fawn out in the field behind our house. The sight set my imagination on fire. The first scene was born, the one of a mother considering the death, the murder of her own child.

Once the story had taken over, research led me to Sinaloa, Mexico and the Sinaloan drug cartel—to El Chapo Garcia and, ultimately, to Ismael "El Mayo" Zambada, with Chapo imprisoned at a federal facility in New York State. I decided to infuse a living person as a fictional character into the story, fictional because the events, circumstances, personality traits, family, is all created—fictionalized—from my imagination.

Some of the names are of real people but again dropped into fictionalized circumstances. Thank you to Detective Lach Buchanan who agreed to be named in one of my novels because I love his name so much.

The research led me on a path filled with darkness, sadness, but also with hope, and glimmers of reconciliation and recovery.

I want to thank my first readers. You know who you are. You have made the story fuller with your keen eyes. I also want to thank J Carson Black who read the story and who gave me such a wonderful blurb.

Thank you also to my readers who have supported me for some twenty years! What an honor to have you alongside me on this journey of storytelling.

Mostly, thank you to my family and my husband, Bob. I love you honey.

~Susan Wingate.

SUSAN'S SOCIAL SITES

Facebook,
www.facebook.com/authorsusanwingate

Twitter, www.twitter.com/susanwingate

Instagram,
www.instagram.com/susanwingatephxborn

LinkedIn, www.linkedin.com/in/susanwingate

Pinterest, www.pinterest.com/pins/susanwingate

Tumblr, www.susanwingate.tumblr.com

StumbleUpon,
www.stumbleupon.com/stumbler/SusanWingate

Google,
plus.google.com/112879489272972691353

MORE WOMEN'S FICTION

And if you enjoyed STORM SEASON, you may enjoy another women's fiction selection by Susan Wingate.

So, we're including an excerpt from THE LAST MAHARAJAN in the following pages for your enjoyment.

The Last Maharajan was previously titled "Drowning" which won the 2011 Forward National Literature Award for family drama. Drowning was also a #1 *Amazon* Bestseller.

"For mothers and daughters everywhere, who may not always see eye-to-eye."

THE LAST MAHARAJAN

PROLOGUE – CHILD'S PLAY

I took my last breath on a blistering hot day, but it felt cool. The second my brother pushed me in, when my feet left the deck, I reacted – my body curving and twisting into correct formation and diving with my fingertips first into the sweet welcome contrast of the pool's frigid water. Young bodies are like that – supple and quick to respond.

He didn't get away with it. He didn't win. See, I decided to play a trick on him for pushing me.

Each millimeter, every dry molecule of my skin became drenched as I dove beneath the surface, deep, deeper to the bottom. I stayed down longer than necessary, and the funny thing was? It made me happy down there.

A beating drum pounded my chest with music from the party above and voices sounding like Charlie Brown's cartoon mother saying *wah wah wah*, swallowed up their words and muffled through a filter of water.

After deciding my time spent below had been long enough, I pushed off the scratchy surface of the pool but there were so many people floating, dog- paddling, coursing the length of the pool, re-surfacing, it reminded me of a fantastical dance, maybe one performed only in heaven, hanging over my head. But, I knew I could hold my breath a long time. We had breath-holding-contests in the shallow end of our pool, at home, all the time.

My heart began to race harder from excitement when I noticed the overload of vibrant swim suits, bodies, and legs – the water saturated with color and movement. I felt like I wanted to stay down there forever and the thick thump in my heart continued. Siphoning down, as I sat on the pool's floor, the muffled drumming of music and disguised chatter above me and people, adults and kids alike playing, laughing, living was mesmerizing!

That's when the trick turned on me.

I sort of remember slipping away when that man lifted me up through the water. Then, I saw mother standing beside me, then in front of me as I stood behind her or to the right or left and above her, whichever my new eyes took me. She crumbled. Slumped, over my body that way and cried but it didn't make me sad. It didn't make me feel anything. I just watched. I just watched.

I had been taunting my brother terribly. He was making eyes at a girl there. I jeered and chanted at him, "Two little love birds sittin' in a tree K-I-S-S-I-N-G!"

He yelled for me to stop but I wouldn't and mocked him over and again with my silly song. He turned to me with a raised hand and his face turned beet red. Frozen, waiting for his hand to connect, my eyes got wide--wider than wide. My mouth shut tight waiting for the inevitable slap but then I could see his hand only threatened. He smirked slightly so I said to him, "Why don't you marry her?"

That's when he pushed me. I screamed and giggled and went under. I could see from below that he walked off in the direction of the girl. The water blanketed me. I swam deeper but stopped midway to watch him as he walked to the end of the pool toward the girl. She was sun-bathing on the diving board and he stood over her and placed his hands on his hips then he stuck out one hand for her to shake. When she took it, I spun like a mermaid and dove deeper to the floor. Even down there I smelled the tart burn of chlorine inside my nose.

People jumped in above me. Everything turned into a kaleidoscope of bodies, a ballet. My head began to pound from the pressure. But I stayed just a little longer, five more seconds, I kept saying to myself, just five more seconds.

At home, we used to blow out all our air to make our bodies sink, so we could sit on the bottom of the pool. What little air was left in my lungs (having performed this stunt many times before), I figured it would be fine. I sat on the drain and watched the show above me. I wasn't down all that long, three minutes, maybe four. That's all.

You know? We're allowed few memories from our time spent on earth. My memories are of the moments before I died, those wavy twinkles, when I was exuberant with joy and of my brother and sister, my mother and father.

I felt doze-y and wanted to come up but the effort of merely standing squeezed my chest. I tried to push off the bottom but rose only a few inches. I had no float! With the air depleted from me, I realized the pool was far deeper than any other I had ever swum. I tried to rise but realized I might be in for some trouble. I tried to climb a wall, but gravity's hands kept holding me down. And, my young arms couldn't reach the ladder when I stretched out, and I stretched.

Energy trickled out of me. My neck and arms ached as though I were carrying an elephant. I tried once more to reach the ladder and it was at that point my body took over. It jerked in odd movements as if I owned it no longer. As my body twisted my legs and arms flailed. My lungs surrendered, and I took in my first deep breath. I swallowed too. The water flowed in so easily through my nose, then in past my throat, finally filling my chest. My body convulsed again searching for air and finding none. Once again, I sucked in water, swallowed more, and for a mere second, I felt fear and, then, all my fear was gone.

I watched my body float aimlessly. It coasted for seconds, with my face pointed toward the floor. It floated like this until the man grabbed me and swam up, lifting me out of the pool.

That was the last time they held one of those big parties, those Maharajans, because of me, because I taunted my brother. It's a shame really.

They'll never understand how happy those last few moments for me were. They'll never understand how beautiful it was to hear people's laughter and singing, to see all those bodies and colors above me, dancing, and living! Through my water lens.

"Dying is something we human beings do continuously, not just at the end of our physical lives on this earth." – Elisabeth Kubler-Ross

CHAPTER ONE

Why would she lie? Why now, knowing she was going to die?

Somehow Belle's words felt contrived, forced. Euly Winger had been calling her mother Belle since around the age of fourteen. When Belle showed signs that Euly could treat her as an equal.

Her mother's words rung like an indictment, allowing a wisp of a notion making Euly recoil from something that happened long ago, evoking a lingering emotion in Euly, a dreamy memory, caught somewhere between the dead and the living and equally unattainable to conjure.

What was it her mother said? The exact phrase, the exact placement of words, the first one and then the next, that stirred in her such a strong reaction?

"He's your brother." Was it that simple? No, she had added the word "probably" and, with emphasis. Euly remembered how, when Belle spoke, her breath leached out a rancid, metallic odor grown from all the intravenous drugs pumping into her, drugs keeping her alive. Her veins plumped like earthworms against her pale mottled alabaster skin. Clear plastic tubes with needles stabbed into her arms with white paper tape to keep the needles secured.

No. That's not what she said. Belle's exact phrase was, "He's probably your brother." There it was. And Euly's mind roller-coastered back to a spot, an exact time, location, and age--the way the scent of mown grass takes you back in a specific point in your history, to your childhood.

Belle had said it as if to sentence her father, yet again, for their divorce. A divorce that happened so many years ago, a lifetime really, that Euly wondered how it could still bother her mother. But it did.

She stared into her cup and dunked her teabag as she tried to puzzle the pieces of yesterday's conversation back in order. She doubted if her mother had tasted the hate drooling off her tongue.

Belle's year-old diagnosis felt like a slap across Euly's face--a swift year that blew by like a fleeting Santa Ana. And, what made it worse? The doctors now gave Belle less than a month. If that.

CHAPTER TWO

Under the quiet blanket of early morning, visions of the past reeled up in foggy fragments from some dusty pigeonhole in Euly's mind. On mornings like these she allowed ghosts to float in and summon up distant scenes. This morning's scene, from some forty years before, was one she'd pressed into a scrapbook – a dried-out rose of a vague history she'd long ago ironed and stowed away, banished, for her own sanity--dragged at her. The corpse, resurrected, felt like a cement block with an anchor chain linking them together, attached to her ankle holding her under water, and keeping her from reaching the surface for air.

Euly sat snugged into an arm of the den's fleecy sofa. In both hands, she hugged her first cup of tea, her ritual. She often sat this way, in the dark of the morning, since she'd moved to the small northwest island, when dull hours hid her, and the sun hadn't fully burned through the veil of the waning night.

With a spotlight shining on those living inside the bell jar of her island, Euly existed under the finite walls of a snow globe--that maddening sense of claustrophobia. With waters licking the entire surround of the small lone island and no bridges to connect people who lived there to humanity on the mainland and travel only by boat or plane, Euly felt trapped.

But, why it mattered to her anymore, she wasn't sure since she rarely left. She landed on the tiny islet ten years ago in 1997 when she ran away from the city and her ex-husband. The trade-off had good and bad points. It too came with skeletons.

Like the bungalow outside calling to her. Now, merely a place set aside for houseguests, the cottage stood alone and empty, in stark contrast from when it her mother had filled it with life, art, and music. All tangled together in a gorge of magic, Belle-style. Her home before her exile to the hospice.

Now, only a husk remained--a locust shell--as Belle Masada spent her final days deposited in a place, a terminus, for the sick and dying.

These days the cottage sat dark and barren on their property like stagnant water reminding Euly that time was not in her mother's favor.

With her legs crooked to her chest, Euly kept her feet warm by pulling on the knobby pair of woolen socks she'd left on the ottoman the night before. While she sat in the corner of the sofa next to the red-hot fireplace she remembered, not too long ago the fireplace would've needed a cedar log and stoking but now a simple remote controller kept the gas on and a fire glowing hot.

She gazed into the flame and seemed to melt into the moment with her dog and cat nestled close by.

Outside, birds beckoned to each other in a scurry within the woods. She turned her head from the glow and gazed through the French door's mullioned window to see if she could spot the noisy culprits, but the gunmetal gray morning made silhouettes tarnish into colorless shards when she tried to focus her eyes. She noticed how birds of the northwest, seemed fewer in number than in Phoenix.

Three years after the break-up of her first marriage, she'd remarried Geoff Winger. Euly wondered why she had done it. She wondered about it the day of their wedding and now, five years later, their relationship suffered all on its own.

Fearing the marriage would crumble, Geoff had planned for them a stay in Lebanon the coming spring. A gesture to her background, she supposed.

Considering the vacation caused Euly hope and concern all at the same time. The trip, intended to spark some renewed sense of romance, zigzagged between euphoria and dread for her. She loved to say she was traveling to the land of her family's roots but, in the quiet of the morning like now, a dense numbing that hobbled her.

Thank you for reading the first three chapters of THE LAST MAHARAJAN by Susan Wingate.

Made in the USA
Middletown, DE
16 May 2019